IRON DRAGON

THE DRAGON MISFITS BOOK 2

D.K. HOLMBERG

ASH
PUBLISHING

A flutter of movement caught Jason's attention and he stared into the distance, searching for the gradient of heat that his dragon sight would show, but came across nothing. The longer he stared, the more certain he was that he had seen something.

It was difficult to make anything out against the steadily circling wind. It tossed snow and ice into the air, swirling it around. Gripping his bow, Jason crouched low, gliding along the snow. His bearskin jacket hung open, letting some of the snow in, the bite of the wind not bothering him as it once had.

His stomach rumbled but he ignored it, trying to focus. It did no good to worry about food until he completed this hunt. If he failed, it would result in more than him going hungry.

Clear your mind of everything but the target.

Twisting away, he tracked along the snow, the way his

father had always taught, but the shifting wind made it difficult to follow any footprints. He had to rely upon his ability to find movement and the gradations of heat, though those weren't nearly as common as they once had been.

The path brought him toward a stream. It flowed rapidly, the water moving with swirls of the current, occasionally sending spray that crashed against unseen rocks in its path. Jason had never seen the stream completely frozen, and yet, its temperature was potentially deadly if he were to fall into it.

He cupped his hands together, bringing some of the water up to his lips and drinking it carefully. It was cold, and it practically burned as it rolled down his throat. There was a time when he wouldn't have dared even dip his hands in the water. Warming up again would have been nearly impossible, and yet since finding the ice dragon, something had changed for him. *He* had changed, and his ability to tolerate the cold had altered. What would his father have thought of that?

He remained along the edge of the stream, bent down, one knee buried in the snow, looking for any signs of movement. There were none.

The shifting sky told him that a storm was coming, though in this place a storm was always on the horizon. He needed to move quickly or he could get trapped out here, and experience had told him that getting trapped out in the snow and in these conditions could be dangerous— even deadly.

Always stay alert. An avalanche is as deadly to you as your arrow is to your target.

Jason knew better than to sit around and wait, but he also knew better than to leave his jacket unbuttoned against the cold and the snow, and yet he still did it.

There wasn't going to be any sign of the creature he'd been hunting. Likely a rabbit, though he hadn't seen it clearly enough to know. Maybe it was something larger. He doubted it was a deer. Those rarely came this high up onto the mountain. It was even less likely with the dragon out hunting.

It would be much easier if he could hunt with the dragon, and yet he had rarely even seen the creature since finding it the first time.

Jason glanced along the stream, turning his attention toward the cave that served as the headwaters, though the true headwaters was somewhere much more distant and difficult for anyone to reach.

Getting to his feet, Jason hurried along the snow and found the cave entrance. It arched about four feet high, and a narrow walkway led on either side of the stream into the cave. It was a dangerous path, and it was one he had never taken very frequently, knowing a misstep would lead him into the potential for danger. There was a time when he'd believed falling into the stream would be fatal, and while it still might be, he no longer feared it as he once did.

He paused as he often did when coming here, looking up at the ceiling. A crystalline structure arched overhead.

It glittered, dozens of hard-edged crystals reflecting the light, catching it in a way that made it so that it practically glowed. Gems, he'd been told. Wealth. Not that they had any value here.

No lamp was needed. It didn't take long for Jason's eyes to adjust and for him to be able to look around the inside of the cave. The water bubbled rapidly where it emerged from someplace deep within the mountain, some hidden reserve that likely waterfalled down, cascading until it reached this point where it poured out and found the entrance. He peered into the depths of the water, searching for signs of the dragon. The creature could hide even in the stream, concealing itself from him.

There didn't even seem to be any sign that the dragon was here. How could a creature like that hide so effectively? It seemed impossible. The dragon had to eat, and there should be some remains. Even droppings, though he didn't like to think of the dragon leaving droppings he might step in. How enormous would those be?

And yet, if he found dragon droppings, he could dry them. They would burn just as well as any other dung.

He took a seat, looking up at the cave. Coming here gave him bittersweet memories. This was where his father had brought him, teaching him how to hunt and provide for the family. This was where his father had wanted to show him some of the secrets of this land, and it was a place few others visited. No one would dare risk the treacherous entrance. It was why it was such a good place for the dragon to hide.

Regardless of anything else, the dragon *had* helped him. Because of the dragon, he had survived the Dragon Souls' attack, making it through what Therin had planned, and yet he thought he should have an opportunity to see the dragon more often than he did. In the months following the attack, Jason had only managed to spot the dragon a handful of times, and never quite as closely as the first. While he knew dragons could talk, this one had not spoken to him since. It was almost as if the dragon didn't want him around.

Then again, why would the dragon want him around? Dragons were in danger of being used. This one in particular. From what he'd experienced, Jason understood he had some way of connecting to the dragons, perhaps serving as a Dragon Soul, and yet, because he only had partial dragon sight, it wouldn't be nearly as potent as someone like Therin or the full-born Dragon Souls.

As he sat there, voices caught his attention.

Jason jerked to his feet.

For a moment, he thought the Dragon Souls had returned. They knew of the dragon, and he feared that Therin might eventually come back here, thinking to use the ice dragon, claiming it and then taking it from here. Jason had seen that the dragons were incredibly powerful, and had also felt something unusual when he had been around one. His whole life had been spent fearing dragons, terrified of what those creatures could do, but working with Henry had shown him another side of the dragons and had helped him understand that while they were powerful, they were also intelligent and had been used by the Dragon Souls.

More than that, speaking to Therin had revealed why his father had died.

He listened, but it didn't seem to be Dragon Souls.

The voice was familiar, the tone mocking.

"I told you there was a cave here," Reltash said.

Jason crouched near the edge of the cave entrance. In the time he had been coming here, he hadn't encountered anyone else who'd risk coming into the cave. Reltash would. Reltash was arrogant enough to think nothing could harm him, and he was skilled enough that it would be unlikely he would be harmed.

The only advantage Jason had was that he wasn't nearly as large as Reltash. Reltash was massive, like most of their people, whereas with his smaller frame, Jason found it easier to slide along the path into the cave.

"What's in there?"

"How do I know?" Reltash asked.

A shadow appeared in front of the cave, and Jason tensed. If they headed in here, there wouldn't be any way to hide. He wasn't about to get into an argument with Reltash and his friends.

"Probably a bear."

Someone laughed softly. Jason craned his neck, trying to see who might be out there, but he couldn't make out anything. "I haven't seen any sign of a bear."

"Because it stays in the cave. We've seen plenty of bears in this part of the world."

Jason grabbed his coat, pulling it tight around himself. There *were* bears in this part of the world, though they weren't all that common. It was what made his bearskin coat as valuable as it was, though not nearly as valuable as the dragonskin jackets people like Reltash wore. There was advantage to that type of clothing. It absorbed the heat of the wearer, and through that, they were able to stay far warmer than they otherwise would in this part of the world. Dragonskin had helped his people survive in these lands. With the bearskin, Jason had survived, though barely. Yet since encountering the dragon, the bearskin was no longer quite as necessary as it once had been. Those who didn't have furs—or dragonskin—used some of the tellum mined nearby, though that was incredibly expensive. It was cheaper—and often easier—to find some animal and use its hide.

"Go in there," Reltash said.

"I'm not going in. Look at how narrow that is."

"We've got to see if there's anything in there."

Jason tensed. If they came into the cave, they might find him, but worse would be the possibility of their finding something that indicated the dragon had been here. As far as he knew, there was no sign of the dragon, and yet, if the creature did return and find that someone else was here, it might attack. He didn't want anything to happen to these people, regardless of how much Reltash annoyed him.

He considered shouting to scare them off, but any noise he might make would only entice them to come and investigate. He thought about throwing something at them, but it would have the same effect. It would be better for them to try and fail than to be tormented.

He backed up into the cave, watching. If nothing else, he had to be prepared for the possibility he might need to hide if they did make it in here. There wasn't really any place for him to hide other than to jump in the stream, and though he had survived the ice-cold water once before, Jason didn't think he would be able to do so again. The last time had been because of the dragon.

Shadows along the mouth of the cave caught his attention as a hulking figure started forward. The strip of land was so narrow that anyone who attempted to enter would have a hard time, though that wasn't really his concern. He was more worried about the possibility that they might damage the ground, making it so that he couldn't get back out again.

As he watched, the person trying to enter the cave took a step, then another, sliding their feet along the edge. When they took one more, they slipped.

Jason had been there, and he understood the treacherous footing, and he knew exactly what the person must be feeling, the way their heart lurched into their throat, the terror as they looked down at the water, the knowledge they might soon plunge into icy cold that would potentially be fatal.

Their arms flailed. If they pushed themselves up against the wall, they should be able to hold their footing, but if they'd never come to the cave before, they might not know that.

They continued to flail, and then slipped.

As Jason watched, it seemed almost as if time stopped. The figure spun, arms whipping at air, grasping for something to hold on to—and failing.

They dropped toward the water.

The splash was loud in the cave.

The cry echoed but then was silenced.

"Grab him," Reltash said.

The stream was fast, the current drifting quickly, and even if the others managed to pull the person out, it would take a miracle for them to be able to survive the cold.

"I couldn't get him."

Jason slipped forward.

"Try again!"

"It's moving too fast."

Wet and cold in these mountains don't mix.

Jason looked out at the water. He had fallen into it before, and yet, he didn't think he could survive it again. There was one thing he could do, though. He understood the way the stream curved as it headed down the slope of the mountain.

Racing out of the mouth of the cave, he slid, jumping across the stream, and glided down the mountain. Reltash shouted something after him, but Jason ignored it. He wasn't about to let somebody drown—or freeze—when there was something he might be able to do. He had no idea if he would even be able to accomplish anything. Time in the water was dangerous, and it wouldn't take very long before they would be overwhelmed by the temperature. How long did he have? Only a few minutes, and perhaps not even that long. The longer they spent in the water, the lower their temperature would drop, and even dragonskin wouldn't be enough to keep them alive.

He dropped to his buttocks, sliding along the snow.

He picked up speed as he went and stared into the distance, praying he would be in time to reach the stream as it worked back around. He didn't know if the person who'd fallen in would have passed here yet, and even if he managed to reach it, what did he really think he could do?

Getting here would be challenging, and once he pulled the person out of the water, he didn't have any supplies to warm them up.

Other than a dragon pearl.

He would have to think about that later. He hadn't tried using it much since surviving the Dragon Soul attack. It was possible that even with the dragon pearl, he wouldn't be able to generate enough heat, but he was determined to try.

He glided. In the distance, the sound of the stream bubbling as it raced down the mountain caught his attention and he dug his heels in, trying to slow himself.

And then he was there.

Bracing as he neared the edge of the stream, he caught himself before plunging into the water.

He looked upslope, searching for anyone who might be

floating along in the water. The stream wasn't very wide here, only a few feet across, but with as cold as it was, Jason understood how panic would set in, making it difficult for anybody to escape.

Movement upslope caught his attention.

A figure cloaked in dragonskin floated.

It was only their face and the dark outline of the cloak that was visible, but Jason braced himself, prepared to grab for them.

As they neared, he reached into the water and grabbed.

The current was fast—almost too fast—and he was nearly torn from his feet. He dug in, holding himself as steady as he could, and pulled. Angus came free.

He had pale skin, made even paler because of the cold, leaving his lips a shade of blue. His eyes were frozen closed, and yet he still seemed to breathe.

Jason tossed him on the shore. Grabbing for the dragon pearl, he pressed his hands upon Angus's chest. Drawing energy from the dragon pearl was tricky. It involved him focusing on some part of himself he wasn't fully aware of, and yet he understood there was power within him that he could reach for, if only he could get to it.

It came like a fluttering deep within him. It connected to the warmth inside of him, and he pushed it out, letting it flow through the dragon pearl, and it exploded on Angus.

He held his hands there. There was an advantage of the dragonskin in that it would absorb most of the heat, and if nothing else, it would provide a certain level of protection for him.

Jason held his hands there, not moving, squeezing Angus's cloak tightly. Heat began to emanate and steam billowed off the cloak, burning off the water.

Color began to return to Angus's face, and slowly his breathing increased.

Jason stepped back, slipping the dragon pearl back into his pocket, and took a seat next to him. It didn't take long for Angus to come back around.

Angus rolled his head from side to side, blinking moisture free from his face. Steam still drifted into the air, mixing with the wind, before disappearing completely.

"What happened?"

"You fell into the stream," Jason said.

"How did I get out?"

"I grabbed you."

Angus sat up, grabbing for his dragonskin before jerking his hands free. Given the steam radiating off it, it likely was still incredibly hot. Maybe Jason had pushed too much power into it, but he didn't have any real control over his use of the dragon pearl. It worked for him, which was all that mattered.

"I've never seen dragonskin like that," Jason said.

It was better to call attention to it rather than have Angus be the one to do so.

"It was my father's," Angus said.

"It must have taken all the heat coming out of you," Jason said.

Angus took a deep breath.

"What happened?" Jason asked.

"We were exploring the stream. We came across a cave. Reltash claimed there was some animal in the cave, and so we were trying to explore it."

"And you slipped in?"

Angus nodded. "There wasn't much to work with."

Jason got to his feet. He stretched a hand out, offering it to Angus, and Angus took it. He looked up the slope, his gaze following the contour of the mountain. From here, it would take the better part of half a day to hike back to the village. The slide had only taken him a moment, but it had carried him quite a ways from the village itself.

With the coming storm, returning would be even more difficult.

"Thanks," Angus said.

"We still have to get back."

Angus grunted and started up the slope.

Jason looked around. There wasn't anything here, and even in the time that he'd grabbed Angus from the water, there was no evidence of his passing. The wind and the coming snow had already begun to drift, shifting so that it covered any sign of him. He supposed he should be thankful for that, but with snow being what it was, it was difficult to trudge through it. There were ways to glide above the snow using the dragon pearl, but even if he had the knowledge of how to do that, he wasn't sure that attempting it around Angus was safe. Angus would notice what was happening, and that wasn't the kind of thing

Jason wanted. He already had enough attention in the village and didn't need anyone else paying any mind to him.

"What were you doing out here?" Angus asked.

"Hunting," he said.

"Hunting?" Angus glanced over, and his eyes widened.

Jason glanced down before cursing to himself. His jacket was unbuttoned, and he had barely felt any of the cold.

He should have thought of that before reviving Angus.

"Don't you usually hunt with a bow?"

He checked his shoulder where he normally carried the bow, and realized he must have thrown it down when he had gone running after Angus.

What was he thinking?

Now if anyone would go into the cave, they would find the bow, maybe his quiver, and they would know he'd been there. Then again, reaching the bow would be difficult. Getting inside the cave was challenging enough, and he would have to go back for it.

"I must've dropped it when I went running after you."

Angus's face clouded. "I'm sorry about that."

"You're alive, aren't you?"

Angus trudged through the snow for a few more steps before nodding slowly. "I'm alive."

They worked their way up the side of the mountain, and Jason hurriedly buttoned his coat, staying behind Angus as he did. The wind swirled around them, picking up force, the cold biting. Jason searched for any sign of movement around them, anything that would suggest Reltash had come downstream to look for Angus, but there was no sign of him. By the time they reached the upper section of the stream, he doubted they would find him.

Which meant Reltash had abandoned Angus.

And why not? The stream moved rapidly enough, and if they weren't able to race down the side of the mountain, the likelihood of being able to save Angus was slim. Their people were pragmatic, and Reltash would've understood there would've been nothing he could do to rescue Angus. Still, it troubled Jason that he would have abandoned his friend.

"I think we were near here," Angus said, breaking the silence between them. Neither of them had spoken much in the time that they'd climbed.

Jason didn't mind. He preferred the silence and tried to ignore the way Angus would glance over at him, avoiding the question that lingered in his gaze, the way he would let it hover on the buttons of his coat, a question remaining unasked on his lips.

"You said there was a cave?"

"Somewhere, but I don't think anyone can reach it. Unless they want to swim like I did." He smiled, and Jason smiled back.

"Who else were you with?"

"Other than Reltash and Hames?"

At least that explained who the other person was. In a

village the size of theirs, everyone knew everyone, and yet, Jason didn't know Hames well enough.

"I can't believe they'd leave me," Angus said.

"They probably tried to get you, but you know how fast the stream's current is."

He leaned down, grabbing a chunk of ice and throwing it into the stream. The current carried it quickly, though it melted as it flowed downstream.

"Still," Angus said.

Angus jumped across the stream. There was a part of Jason that worried he would slip, but he cleared it with a single leap. Jason would have to try more carefully. Jumping the stream could be dangerous, and normally he would wander around it, staying on the edge of the stream itself, not wanting to risk it, but that meant a considerable walk out of their way.

"Can you make the jump?"

Jason nodded, staring at the water.

He'd done it before. When he had gone after Angus, he'd needed to jump the water, and so he knew he could do it, but it didn't make it any easier now. When he'd run after Angus, he'd been in a panic, worried about someone else surviving. Now he was less unsettled, and it wasn't quite as easy.

When he'd jumped it earlier today, he had been heading downslope. This was heading upslope. The difference was enough that it would make it difficult, and yet Jason was determined to prove himself.

He took a few steps back, and jumped.

He knew he wasn't going to clear the distance.

Angus grabbed his arm, pulling him. His boot caught the water, splashing, but he was thrown into the snow.

He rolled over onto his back, looking up at the sky. Snowflakes swirled around overhead. The wind twisted them, sending some of them spiraling, while others came down with more force, tearing at his exposed skin.

"Thanks," he said when Angus loomed over him.

Angus stared and Jason sat up, looking around. From here, they still had a few hours to go. He was getting tired and hungry, and yet, he also didn't want to get stranded in the night. It was bad enough to get caught out in the dark like this, to risk the nature of the storm, but it was even worse to do so with someone else whom he didn't know all that well.

Angus helped him to his feet and they started up the slope.

"I'm sorry we didn't find your bow," he said after they'd gone a little while.

"That's not your fault."

"Maybe the wind will reveal it for you."

If Jason didn't know where he'd dropped his bow, he would have been far more concerned. The wind would cover anything, and with the nature of the snow in this part of the world, it would disappear, getting lost to time. Eventually, the snow might swirl and uncover the weapon, though anticipating that and being present when it happened would be unlikely.

"I'm sure I can—"

A strange sound caught his attention and he tipped his head to the side, listening. It had come from his left, toward the cave. It was slightly downslope, and it sounded something like a strangled cry.

Or it could be nothing more than the wind. Jason didn't know if he was hearing anything correctly or not, and if it was just the wind, then anything else could be his imagination adding to it, twisting it so that it made it seem as if he were hearing something else.

Angus didn't seem to notice.

"Why don't you keep going. I'm going to see if I can't find my bow."

"You're going to *what?*"

"I know where I might've left it."

"Dreshen, you're not going to find anything like this at night."

"I have to look before the storm rolls through."

"At least let me come with you."

"There's no point in both of us getting caught out in the night."

Angus regarded him and finally shrugged. "Good luck."

He headed upslope, pulling his cloak around him.

Were the situation any different, Jason might find it strange that Angus would abandon him within the storm, and yet he didn't owe him anything, and more than that, Jason wasn't risking himself by staying out in the storm.

As he stood there, the strange sound came again.

He didn't know if he was imagining it, but against the

night and with the wind being what it was, it was difficult to let it go.

He hurried back down the slope, veering off toward where he thought the cave entrance would be. If nothing else, he wanted to grab his bow and quiver so that when he did return to the village, he would have some way of explaining his absence. It took much less time to make his way downslope. Every so often, he would drop and slide before catching himself and getting back to his feet, scrambling along the snow. He found that he didn't plunge nearly as deeply as he had before, though he wasn't really trying to float along the surface of the snow.

Reaching the cave, he hesitated. The strange cry had not come again, but he couldn't shake the feeling that there had been something. He frowned before heading into the cave. He did so carefully, pushing his back along the wall, gliding his feet on the lip of ground. He slid forward, and then once inside, he staggered free before collapsing on the ground.

His quiver and bow were where he'd left them.

As he grabbed them, he realized there was something else in the cave with him.

Jason reached for the dragon pearl, pushing a hint of power into it, just enough for the pearl to start glowing and illuminate everything within the cave. The light caught the crystal surface of the cave, reflecting it like a lantern, and he came face-to-face with the dragon.

Jason dropped the pearl, and the light in the cave blinked out.

2

He scrambled for the pearl, sweeping his hands along the floor of the cave, trying to find where it had fallen. As he did, the only thing that filled his mind was the memory of the dragon's icy blue eyes and the way the creature had looked at him. It had been weeks since he'd seen the dragon, and in that time, the creature seemed considerably larger than before. Large enough that he worried it would soon outgrow the cave. Then where would it go?

It surprised Jason that he would feel any sense of sadness at the idea of losing the dragon, but there was some part of him that wanted to keep the dragon around, if only so he could better understand the creature and whether he was at all connected to it.

He found the dragon pearl and raised it in his hand, pushing power through it. It began to glow, reflecting light off the top of the cave once again. When it did, it seemed almost as if the dragon were watching him, amusement flashing in the creature's eyes.

This time, Jason held on to the pearl, clutching it tightly, watching the dragon. The creature sat back on its hind legs, resting on its wings. It was easily three times his size, large enough that it filled the inside of the cave, and yet he'd seen it glide through the stream, folding itself up to become small enough to fit within that space.

He swallowed. This close to the dragon, some ancient part of his brain felt fear of facing it and yet, he knew the dragon didn't want to harm him. If it did, it would've done so other times. There had been ample opportunities for the dragon to have killed him or to have simply allowed him to die, yet it had not.

"You're getting big," he said.

It felt like the wrong thing to open with, but he wasn't exactly sure what he should say to the dragon. He hadn't seen it in long enough that he didn't know.

The dragon rumbled, folding its wings in, wrapping them around its body. "And you remain the same size."

Its voice was a strange scream, like ice shearing.

"I think I'm mostly done growing," Jason said.

"And I am not."

The dragon backed away from him.

"Was that your cry I heard?"

He flicked his gaze toward the entrance to the cave, but there was no sign of any other movement. After he'd reached the cave, he hadn't heard anything else, though it was possible he wouldn't.

"I was hunting," the dragon said.

"Hunting what?"

"Hunting."

"Where do you go to hunt?"

"Down."

The hunting would be better down the slope. The trees were thicker, and there were other animals farther down the mountain. Rabbits and squirrels were more plentiful, and even the deer that occasionally wandered this high up the mountainside would be easier to find.

"What did you catch?"

"Food," the dragon said.

Jason smiled to himself. "How do you make sure no one sees you?"

"No one hunts at night but me."

It was an easy way for the dragon to be safe. People in his village stayed inside during the night, or at least within the village itself. Heading out of the village at night and risking one of the usual storms was typically a death sentence.

"Where were you earlier today?"

"Hunting," the dragon said.

"You were hunting during the day then?"

The dragon rumbled. "I was hungry."

He looked around the cave. If the dragon was leaving that often—and he knew it had to be—it would explain why there was little evidence of the creature. It would be gone, and much like anything else that happened outside with the snow and the swirling wind, any remains it might leave would be carried away.

"I could help you," Jason said.

"Help me hunt? You're so little."

"Little, but I have my uses."

He watched the dragon, thinking of the way Henry had ridden the other dragon. If he could do the same with the ice dragon, how much more would he be able to find?

It was possible he'd be able to travel to places he wouldn't otherwise be able to approach.

It was likely to raise questions if he were to do so.

"Where would you go?" the dragon asked.

"Elsewhere," Jason said.

The dragon rumbled. "That is not an answer."

It lowered itself to the ground, curling up, resting its back along the wall. Within the glowing light of the dragon pearl, it seemed as if the dragon itself glistened, catching that reflected light, and it sighed softly. Strangely, there was a warmth within the cave that seemed to radiate off the dragon, though as far as Jason had been able to tell, the dragon was tied to snow and ice, not to heat, as the other dragons were.

"I thought I wanted to be home," Jason said. "I returned to my village because of my mother and my sister." It wasn't the only reason he'd returned, and after uncovering what happened to his father, he had thought he might be able to have answers and bring some sense of peace to his mother, but how could he when she still suffered? She wasn't able to move past what had happened to his father and wasn't able to heal herself, let alone anyone else. She'd been caught up in her own trauma and had not been able to overcome it.

The people of their village had been through enough over the years that most people were far heartier than his mother. That troubled Jason, though he never said anything to her. It was better for him to hunt, to bring the food she needed, and then wander out of the village.

"I don't know who my hatch mates are."

"Hatch mates?"

The dragon breathed out. It seemed as if steam and ice showered out of his nostrils with it. "There are others like me. I can feel them."

Jason scooted forward, wanting to get closer to the dragon. "I could help with that, too."

"How?"

"If you can feel them, we can search for them." It wasn't altogether surprising that Therin would have hidden other dragon eggs, but from what Jason understood, it was rare enough for dragons to lay an egg, so how could there be so many hatch mates?

The dragon likely wouldn't know. The other dragons —if they even survived—would be elsewhere. Jason doubted they would be on the same mountain, and without knowing where Therin had traveled, he wouldn't be able to determine where Therin had left the other eggs.

"I feel they survived, but nothing more than that," the dragon said.

"Can we follow what you can feel?"

Any move he would make would carry him out of the village, and he should know better than to do that, and yet, he thought it would be beneficial to go with the dragon, to search for these other dragons. If he could find them before the Dragon Souls, if they were aware they existed, he wanted to do that.

The dragon rumbled, and Jason didn't know whether that indicated that he could follow or not. He continued watching the dragon, but the dragon seemed to settle into a slumber.

For his part, Jason was tired. He'd been up for most of the day, and having chased after Angus, rescuing him, and then heading back up the mountain, he was exhausted. What would it hurt to rest?

He might be able to make it back to the village tonight, but doing so meant he would brave the wind and the storm. He might not struggle nearly as much as he once had against either of those, but he didn't want to face the weather if he didn't have to.

It was better to stay here.

And if the dragon wanted to be quiet, then there was no point in trying to force the creature to talk.

He settled down, resting his head on his arm, and he drifted. Dreams came to him, though they were little more than stirrings of memories. In them, he caught images, those of his father, of times in the village, but other times as well. In one image, he was riding on a dragon, and rather than the warmth of the dragon Henry traveled with, it was cold, almost painfully so.

When he stirred awake, he looked over, expecting to find himself sitting on the ice dragon, but the dragon was gone.

He sat up and looked toward the entrance of the cave.

There was no sign of the dragon. It was almost as if he'd had a dream, and in that dream, he had experienced the dragon. Light drifted in the entrance of the cave. How long had he slept? It didn't feel as if it was restive, and yet he thought that he been out for quite some time.

He looked down at the stream for a moment before deciding the dragon had disappeared again, leaving him.

He slipped along the edge of the stretch of earth before stepping into the daylight. The sun was bright overhead and a blue sky greeted him. It was rare to have days like this. On a day like this, snow would melt in the village. Streets would become slick with ice, and yet, there would be great celebration. There was something peaceful and relaxing about skies like this.

He searched for any sign of the dragon but found nothing.

Jason checked his bow and quiver and started up the slope. It didn't take long before he reached the outer edge of the village.

He paused, thinking he'd failed his family. He'd come out to hunt and hadn't managed to find anything. That meant returning was a mistake. There was enough food left from the last rabbit he'd caught, but they needed to stay on top of things, otherwise they would run out of meat. He didn't want his family to go hungry. There had been enough days where they'd not had nearly enough food to eat, and he didn't want to go through that again.

He paused first at his home. The room was warm, and he thought that his mother or sister had been burning far too much dung, but found neither of them here.

Why would they waste heat if they weren't even here?

He checked the back room, but his mother wasn't there. There was no sign of anyone, and yet, he thought that they must be somewhere.

Jason left his bow and quiver and headed back out.

On a day like this, there were often more people out in the streets than usual. It didn't surprise him to come across a group of kids racing through the streets, chasing each other, coats flapping behind them as if unmindful of the cold. They probably didn't mind the cold. There wasn't much to it, at least not today.

He meandered, searching for where his mother and sister would've gone, but didn't find any sign of them. He nodded to the few familiar faces, and paused at the local butcher.

Master Erich had been friendlier to Jason since he'd been more successful in hunting, but he still wasn't willing to trade with him openly. Jason wasn't a part of the hunting party that would head out of the village, taking the back slope, and because of that, he was treated differently. He wasn't large enough to go with them, and most felt that he was useless. He'd tried hunting in that direction in the past, but he had to travel farther than the others, and finding a place that wasn't already overhunted was difficult. It was part of the reason he went down the front face of the mountain. At least that way, anything he might find would be his. It made it more difficult to hunt, but it also left him alone, which was the way he liked it.

He reached the central part of the village, the festival grounds, and paused. There wasn't much here for him, either, yet he was left with memories. This was where he had worked with his father, learning how to manage the cannon, a cannon he would never be allowed to fire on his own. That wasn't in his future, though the longer he was around the dragon, the more he wondered what was really going to be in his future.

A familiar face loomed into view. Tessa was lovely. She had dark hair, and she styled it differently than usual today, her black hair tucked underneath a dragonskin hat.

She smiled as he neared, watching him. "Jason. I don't see you nearly as often as I once did."

He smiled at her. There was a time when he and Tessa were much closer. He didn't think his father's death was the reason they had grown apart, and didn't blame her for his father's loss, not the way he once would have. Still, there was a distance now between them.

"I've been hunting."

"Successfully, from what I hear."

He nodded. "Mostly. It takes me away, but for my sister and my mother..."

Tessa's face clouded. "And how is your mother?"

"About the same. She doesn't change much these days."

"I'm sorry. If there's anything I can do..."

Jason nodded. There was a strange awkwardness between them that hadn't been there before, but he didn't blame her for that. He had changed as much as she had after his father's death.

He still hadn't mustered the courage to question her and find out what she knew about his father's death, though he didn't think she had any significant insight. She had been terrified. All she remembered, at least reportedly, was flames.

It had been Therin. Jason knew that now. If not necessarily Therin directly, then Dragon Souls.

"Thank you."

She looked as if she wanted to say more, before glancing past him and smiling. "I really should be going."

Jason nodded, and he moved past her along the street. He heard a familiar voice and headed toward it. He found Kayla talking quickly to two others. When he approached, she cut off, turning toward him.

"What happened to you?"

She grabbed him, checking him over before releasing him. She was almost the same height as him, a typical height for women in the village, and she had deep blue eyes that matched everyone else—other than Jason.

"I got stuck out of the village last night."

She took a step toward him, and her long bearskin jacket, which draped almost to the snow, dragged through it. "Angus said you decided to stay out. You went after your bow, of all things."

"I need my bow to hunt."

"How can you hunt if you lose your life?"

"I didn't lose my life."

"You could have."

Jason shrugged. "I could have many times, but I haven't."

Kayla shook her head, and her tight braid swung beneath her hat. "Why do you make us worry about you like that?"

"I wasn't trying to make you worry about me, I was just—"

"You were just going after your bow."

Jason looked past her, realizing whom she'd been talking to. He nodded to Terrence and Selena, smiling at them. They were a few years older than him, and newly married. Selena came from one of the smaller villages farther down the back face of the mountain, and he didn't know her as well as he knew Terrence. But then, Jason didn't know Terrence all that well, either.

"Like I said. I need my bow to hunt."

"What happens if you freeze? How will we know what happened to you?"

"I wouldn't have gone after it if I thought I was in any danger."

"But the storm last night was one of the worst we've had in weeks!"

The cave had offered a certain protection from the weather, enough that he hadn't feared getting caught out in it, and yet, even finding out that the storm had been bad, he hadn't realized that he was in any danger.

He needed to be careful. He didn't want his sister worrying for him, and he didn't need his mother retreating any more than she already had. Both of them already had gone through enough, and it was his job to protect them now. It was the reason he'd remained rather than going with Henry. As much as he might have wanted to understand what it meant to have some potential to become a Dragon Soul, he had to do so carefully.

"At least tell me you caught something?"

He shook his head. "Not this time."

"We're getting thin with our stores."

They still had quite a bit more than they ever had before. Since Jason had managed to bring down the deer, they had been well supplied. It had given him a buffer, time he could hunt and not have to worry about not bringing anything home. He still went out every day, trying to stay ahead, wanting to make sure that they had enough. It was better to have a full belly than to worry about when the next meal might come. In the time since then, he found himself getting stronger. It made hunts go more easily. He was able to climb faster than he had before. It was one thing he hadn't expected to change so dramatically with a full belly, but he shouldn't have been surprised by that.

"I'll go back out tomorrow," he said before catching himself. "What do you mean we're getting thin?"

Kayla glanced behind her and flashed a smile at Terrence and Selena before turning her attention to him.

She twisted so that her back was to them, lowering her voice. "We have one rabbit left."

"One? When I brought the last one, we still had two squirrels and two rabbits."

"That was several days ago," she whispered.

"With that much, it should last a few more days than that."

She nodded.

"Who's getting into our supplies?"

A flush of color flashed across Kayla's cheeks. "I don't know," she said.

Stealing was rare in the village, though not unheard of. Finding enough food could be difficult, and there were plenty of people who went hungry, the same way that Jason and his family had been going hungry before he had managed to find the deer.

"I can keep a watch."

"You need to be out hunting. Mother and I can watch."

He cocked a brow at her.

"Fine. I can watch."

"Where is Mother?"

"Why?"

"She wasn't there when I stopped by our house."

Kayla frowned, but turned and went racing through the village.

Jason could do nothing other than chase after.

He followed her back to the home, and when he reached it, she had thrown the door open, unmindful of the heat dissipating through the open door. He stepped inside as she was searching through the back room, calling out for their mother.

"She wasn't here," he said.

"Where would she have gone?"

"I thought she was with you."

Kayla shook her head. "When was the last time you remember Mother leaving the house?"

"The last time was before Father…"

He should have been more surprised by his mother's absence. She had been here ever since his father had been killed, and finding her missing was unusual enough that he should have known something was wrong.

He glanced at the rack along the wall to find that her coat and hat were missing. At least she wouldn't be out in the weather without any sort of protection, but where would she have gone? He followed Kayla back outside and closed the door tightly behind him, searching through the village with her.

"I'm going to stop at Keva's place and see if she might know where Mother has gone."

Jason nodded. The two women had once been close, but since his father had died, his mother had retreated, spending no time with anyone else. She'd been no place other than her bed.

Jason followed his sister, and when he reached the door to Keva's home, he paused, listening in, but there were no voices coming from the inside.

His sister knocked, and it took a moment for the door to open and the solid woman on the other side to glance at them. "I haven't seen either of you for quite some time," she said.

"Is Mother here?"

She shook her head. "I haven't seen your mother since your father died."

Kayla nodded, turning back toward Jason. Her eyes were moist, and she dabbed her knuckle at the corner of her left eye, trying to smear away the tears before they dropped.

Where would their mother have gone? She should not have disappeared like this, not gone out into the village without letting them know, but then again, had she not retreated from the world as she had, it wouldn't have been all that strange for her to have explored.

"I can help you look," Keva said.

"That's all right," Kayla said.

They went to the village, pausing at several shops, looking inside, and there was no sign of their mother.

They stopped again near the center part of the village, near the festival square where he had first encountered his sister. He glanced over toward the cannon, wondering if perhaps she might have gone there. At least the cannon might be tied to their father, a way of reminiscing, but there was no sign of her there, either.

"Where else would she have gone?" Kayla asked.

"I don't know."

"Would she have gone to her shop?"

There was an element of hope in her voice. Jason didn't want to squash it, but at the same time, their mother hadn't been to her shop since before their father died.

"We can check," he said.

She started off and he followed, trailing after his sister, and they meandered toward the northern edge of the village. The shop was little more than a hut, a building that had been abandoned for the last year, and he expected to find no sign of anyone near it, but as he approached, he saw footprints in the snow.

That was unusual. Could someone have taken over the shop? The village certainly needed healers, and with his mother disappearing the way she had, there wasn't anyone else, but he didn't think anyone else had the necessary skill. His mother had trained for a long time in order to serve, and she had taken on that role, willingly working with anyone, and because of that, she had become a vital part of the village.

Smoke drifted from the chimney of the shop.

Jason paused, knocking.

When no answer came, he pushed the door open.

On the other side, he found his mother.

He froze, unable to do much of anything other than stare.

Her coat hung over a chair and she was dressed in a tattered dress. Her hair was pulled back, tied behind her head, and her cheeks were rosy. Sweat dripped down her forehead.

She was busy cleaning. She swept the floor, heat radiating from the small stove off to the side and filling the tiny hut. She'd already cleaned off the cot and prepared it for anyone who might need it.

"Oh, good. You're both here. You can help me clean up."

"Mother?" Jason asked.

"What is it? There's quite a bit to do."

"Are you feeling all right?"

Kayla stood near the door, letting the cold air in.

Jason shot her a look. She shuffled off to the side, pushing the door closed behind her.

"I'm feeling wonderful. We need to get everything cleaned up."

"I just haven't seen you out of bed in a while."

His mother paused, glancing up at him. "I think it's about time I change that, don't you?"

Jason paused before nodding. "I guess I do."

He nodded to Kayla, and the two of them began to join their mother, helping, neither of them saying anything.

3

J ason looked around the inside of the hut, marveling at how clean it was. It had taken them the better part of the day to get it back into order, but now that it was, there was a sense of calm hanging over everything. Some of it came from the work they'd done to get everything back into place, but some of it came from the fact that his mother had returned to them.

He still couldn't believe it. He had no idea what had changed for her, or why she would have suddenly stepped out of whatever fugue she'd been in, but he was thankful that she was seemingly back to herself.

More than just back to herself. She had energy she hadn't before. Her face remained gaunt, a reminder of what she'd gone through, and yet there was a spark to her he hadn't seen since before his father died.

Kayla sat in a chair near the door, watching his

mother, saying nothing. Neither of them really knew what to say.

"I'm going out for supplies," their mother said, grabbing her coat off the chair and flipping it on. She nodded to Kayla before turning to Jason. "Will you two finish up?"

He nodded, unable to think of anything else to say.

When she stepped outside, pulling the door closed behind her, Kayla jumped to her feet, looking over at him. "What's going on?"

"I don't know."

"I mean, she's been basically unresponsive for the last year. I had to force-feed her so many times, I can't even keep it straight."

Kayla had borne the brunt of caring for their mother, and Jason had borne the brunt of trying to feed them both, but this was unexpected.

"Have you been giving her any different medicine?"

"Not that I can think of. Besides, she didn't want me to give her any different medicine. She was aware of anything that I might give her."

He thought about everything they had done, and other than feeding her regularly, he couldn't think of what might have caused this shift.

The only other thing that had changed, other than an improvement in food, was the way he'd taken to heating water. Using the dragon pearl, Jason had begun heating it differently, using power rather than wasting dung for something so simple. Most of the time, Kayla wasn't even aware that he had done so. That was the way he wanted it. It was better to keep that ability hidden.

Could it be that?

The dragon pearl had power. He'd seen that himself, and he'd used it often enough, but he wouldn't have expected it to have healed his mother.

And there wasn't really anything to have healed her of. It was a matter of moving past what happened, of finding strength within herself that she otherwise had neglected. The dragon pearl wouldn't have been able to accomplish that, would it?

He and his sister continued to work, cleaning the hut. Neither said anything more, and as he worked, he couldn't help but wonder if perhaps he *might* have been responsible for helping his mother.

When she returned, she nodded, looking around. "I think everything is back in order." She set a stack of jars on the counter, and Jason frowned.

"Where did you get the money to pay for that?"

"I traded services," she said.

"What services did you trade?"

His mother frowned. "Honestly, Jason. You should know there are various ways of bartering."

When it came to his ability to barter, Jason was limited. He didn't have much to offer anyone. He could hunt, but that depended on catching something. Otherwise he had to beg for help.

"When you and Tessa move off on your own—"

"Mother, Tessa and I aren't going to move off on our own."

"You can't stay with us."

"I don't think that I can stay with Tessa, either."

"You aren't interested in her?"

Jason squeezed his eyes closed. There was a time when he would've said that he was, though at the same time, he would've felt as if that was beyond him. After having met Sarah, he'd started to wonder if perhaps…

Jason shook those thoughts out of his mind. "I'm more concerned about taking care of you and Kayla."

"You don't need to worry about us. Now. What are we eating tonight?" she asked him.

"Rabbit," he said.

She nodded and waved for Kayla to get to her feet. "Good. Now why don't you two run along, and I will continue my preparations. I need to get everything ready for us to reopen tomorrow."

Jason nodded. If his mother was going to reopen her shop, then they would have another source of income. It seemed impossible to believe.

As they made their way back toward their home, Kayla didn't say anything.

"You'll stay with Mother tomorrow?" he asked her.

"I think I have to."

"I don't know what's going on, but hopefully this is a permanent change."

Kayla nodded.

When they reached the home, he hurried around back and dug through the snow for the rabbit but didn't find it.

He moved over, trying a different section, but there was no sign of it there, either.

Jason hurried back inside and found Kayla working with a pot over the hearth.

"Where was the rabbit?"

"You had your marker out back," she said.

He nodded. The marker was so that he could find it again, but there was no sign of where he had buried it.

It had to be somewhere, but he didn't know where it had ended up.

"Can you come out and help?"

She cocked her head, frowning at him, and shrugged. After slipping on her coat and gloves, she followed him back around the house, and the two of them dug through the snow, searching for the rabbit, but there was no sign of it.

"Nothing?" Kayla asked, leaning back on her heels.

"I thought you said we still had one remaining?"

"We *should* have one remaining."

Jason breathed out. As far as he knew, there should be more than just one left. There should be many, and yet, there were not.

His stomach rumbled.

He wasn't as accustomed to going hungry as he had been.

"We still have some dried meat inside. I think we can

make do with that until you can catch something tomorrow," she said.

He nodded, following her back into the home. Why couldn't it be easier? If his mother had come around, then there was the hope they would finally find a way out of the trouble they'd known ever since his father had passed, but now they had to figure out who was stealing from them.

Somebody *had* to be stealing. It was not that common for people within the village to steal from others, and so Jason didn't know who might have been responsible. It would've been a simple thing for someone to sit and keep watch for his return, noticing where he buried the meat and taking it.

Without having any way of keeping track, he wouldn't be able to identify who it was.

Unless he set some sort of a trap. It was the kind of thing that could cause trouble in the village, especially as small as it was and with as few people as were here, but he needed to know. If they were going to go hungry, then he wanted to find out who was stealing from them.

The village works best when we care for each other.

If only Jason were able to see that more often in the village.

Kayla returned to her work, boiling the water and pouring it out into three mugs and steeping the spices for tea. She tore off strips of dried meat and set them onto a plate.

They took a seat at the table, neither of them saying anything, looking toward the door.

Minutes passed, and still their mother hadn't returned. It was hard to know when exactly she might return, and now with her feeling better, it was possible she might've stayed at the shop to get everything back in order. They might have cleaned everything up, but there would still be quite a bit for her to do to prepare to help others again.

Kayla was picking at her meat and Jason tore off a chunk, chewing it slowly. It was tough, though she had seasoned it well. It tasted fine, but he would have much preferred something fresher.

Sipping at the tea, he breathed in the spiced aroma, staring through the steam rising off it toward the door.

"I should go check on her," he said.

"We can both go," she said.

"You need to eat."

"So does she."

"Stay here. I'll see if anything happened."

He got to his feet, throwing on his coat, his gloves, and his hat and hurrying out the door and along the outer edge of the city. When he reached the hut, he found the smoke still drifting from the chimney, and he pulled the door open.

The flames had been quenched in the stove, yet heat still filled the inside of the hearth. There was no sign of his mother, and everything that she'd been working on had been neatly stacked away.

Jason frowned.

Where would she have gone?

They should have stayed with her, especially with as strangely as she had been acting. Someone should have remained with her.

He closed the door, sealing it shut, and took a different way back toward their home. When he was nearly back, thinking that he might have to sweep along a different route, he found someone lying on the ground.

Jason went racing toward the fallen form and rolled her over.

"Mother?"

He checked her neck, feeling for the artery there as she'd taught him. She was still alive, but she was cold. It reminded him of what he'd seen with Angus.

He scooped her off the ground and debated. He could carry her back to their home, but any supplies that might be needed to heal her weren't going to be there. Anything she might have acquired today could be useful.

He ran, praying for speed, and reached the hut, threw the door open, and set her down on the recently cleaned cot.

He looked around. He'd never taken the time to learn from his mother. It was never something he'd thought would be beneficial for him. He was a hunter like his father. His sister was going to follow in his mother's footsteps, and she was the one who was going to train to be a healer—or would have, had their mother not let herself go.

He didn't have any idea what to do or what medicines

might be useful.

The only thing he had was the dragon pearl.

Would it even work?

Jason had no idea. He squeezed the pearl, pulling it from his pocket, and rested it on her chest. Focusing on the heat deep within himself, he pushed it out through the dragon pearl and let it roll away from him and into his mother.

At first, he detected nothing.

There seemed to be a strange resistance to that pressure as he tried to push it through her, but the longer he focused, the more he felt it drawing up through him. There was some resistance still, and he forced his connection to the dragon pearl, to the power he knew was within it, and let it roll out through her.

She gasped.

Jason held on to the connection to the dragon pearl, to the heat, and waited. It continued to flow through her, no longer meeting the same resistance.

She took in another breath. Her eyes blinked open and she rolled over toward him. "Jason?"

"It's all right. I'm here."

"What happened?"

"I don't know. We found you outside."

"We? Is Kayla here?"

He sighed, shaking his head. "No. I guess I found you out here."

"Where am I?"

"Back in your shop."

"Shop?"

Her gaze swept around the inside of the room before turning back to him. She held his eyes for a long moment and then fell back into a slumber.

At least she seemed to breathe more easily. He pulled up a chair, watching her.

How had he helped heal her?

He didn't really understand the magic of the dragon pearl, only that there was some within it, and because of that, he was able to connect to it. He was able to use the power of the dragon, borrowing from it.

It was strange that the power from this dragon pearl seemed to be heat, but that was always the way he detected it. The dragon within the cave was an ice dragon, so different than the one Henry rode, and he would've expected the power to be different, too.

The more he focused on that power, the more he felt it was a similar sort of thing.

Kayla needed to know that their mother was resting. He needed to let her know that he'd found her, but he didn't feel comfortable leaving.

Would it be safe to carry her back to their home?

She should rest, but he wasn't about to leave her alone and have her wander again.

He lifted her, and she stirred briefly before falling back into a stupor. When he stepped back outside, he discovered that the wind had picked up, kicking through the village. The bright and sunny day had ended, leaving nothing more than a cold chill in the air.

He let out a heavy sigh and hurried back through the streets, making his way toward their home. As he neared it, a figure behind the home caught his attention.

Jason swore under his breath.

He raced inside, setting his mother down in the chair, motioning to Kayla and ignoring her objection, and then ran outside.

A section of snow had been dug up.

Where was that figure?

He looked around. All he needed was to find movement. With his dragon sight, he should have enough of an advantage, but he didn't see anything.

Someone had been out here.

Who would steal from them? It was such a terrible thing for anyone to do, to take from those who had so little, who had suffered so much, and yet now he had proof that someone was there.

Jason glanced along the street in either direction but found nothing.

Back in his home, he stood in the doorway. "Keep an eye on her. I found her passed out in the street."

"You found her *where?*"

"In the street. And when I was carrying her here, I saw someone digging behind our house."

Kayla's breath caught and she glanced toward the back of the house. "Who would do such a thing?"

"I don't know. But when I find them…"

He grabbed for his bow, strapping on the quiver, and stepped back outside.

Kayla followed. "Jason, you don't need to do this. We can figure it out another time."

"Someone has been stealing from us."

"Does it matter?"

"It matters if we starve."

"Does it matter right *now*?"

He took a deep breath, forcing down the irritation rolling within him. She was right. It didn't matter right now. The thief could have returned to their home, hiding from him.

There was no way to know who it was. The only way he thought he might be able to uncover the culprit would be to watch, and he had no idea what that would take. He certainly couldn't do it tonight. Whoever was responsible for stealing from them now knew he was on to them.

Letting out a frustrated sigh, he returned to their home, taking a seat at the table next to his mother. Kayla sat across from him and chewed slowly at her meat. She sipped at her tea, saying nothing. When she was done, she sighed, carrying her dishes back to the washbasin and setting them inside.

"Will you help me carry her back to the room?"

Jason nodded and, between the two of them, they guided their mother back into her room and onto the bed. She looked no different than she had every day over the last year.

How could she be so vibrant for most of the day, and then crash like this?

"I wish she would have stayed awake a little bit longer,"

Kayla said. She stood at the edge of the bed, looking down at their mother, twisting the fabric of her dress and her fingers.

"At least we know that she can come around," Jason said.

"I've always known she could come around," Kayla said. She didn't look up. "This has always been her choice."

"I think it's been too hard," Jason said.

"Hard for her? How has it been any easier on us? For you? You nearly died—twice."

He didn't look up and meet her eyes. She didn't know what he'd gone through, not yet. He needed to share more, but he didn't know whether there was anything he could say to her. How could she understand the dragons weren't what she believed? How could she understand the dragons weren't responsible for what had happened to their father?

Unless he showed her.

If anyone needed to know, it was Kayla.

If they could find someone to watch their mother, Jason knew he needed to bring Kayla down to the cave, and once there, he needed to introduce her to the dragon.

"At least she woke up for a little while today," he said.

"You think she'll come around tomorrow, like she said?"

He watched his mother as she breathed, each one coming slowly, steadily, and yet a bit raggedly. "I don't know."

Kayla stood there for another moment before heading

out of the back room. She returned a moment later with the chair and rested it against the wall, taking a seat.

"You don't have to stay with her," Jason said.

"We both agreed we need to keep an eye on her. I'll do this."

"You could sleep next to her."

She shot him a darkened look. "Last time I did that, she wet all over me."

He resisted the urge to gag. They'd been through enough with their mother that both of them knew she didn't have the same control over her bodily functions as she once did—or should. It wasn't that she wanted to do the things that she did; it was just that she had changed, had reached a state where she could no longer function. Both of them believed it was intentional, and yet he couldn't help but hope that she might find some way beyond it.

If she didn't, what would become of Kayla?

Without any way of making a living, she would probably have to marry. That meant leaving the village. And perhaps that wasn't the worst thing that could happen for her. Everything in the village would serve as a reminder of what they'd lost, of their mother, their father, and his inability to provide for them.

In another year—if they made it another year—they might not have much of a choice. At least they could look into marrying her off to someone who might be able to provide for her.

If Kayla were married off, that would only leave Jason,

and though he didn't have any intention of marrying at this time, eventually, the village would expect it of him.

What would he do then?

"You should get some sleep."

"So should you."

"I've learned how to sleep in the chair," Kayla said.

She rested her head back, staring at their mother, and Jason remained there for another moment. There wasn't anything he could do. If she was sleeping, then Kayla was right and he needed to take the opportunity to get more rest for himself. He needed to hunt, and he needed to be successful. Not only did his mother need it, but his sister did, too.

He'd thought Kayla was hopeless before, but he hadn't paid as much attention to what she was going through as he should have. In the time since he'd returned from his dragon hunt, he'd thought he understood, but it didn't seem as if he did. They might have been better fed, but even their full bellies didn't change the fact of what they were going through. It was nothing more than continuing the motions of living.

Now that he'd found the dragon, and now that he had a possibility of trying to understand something more, he'd begun to find hope.

His sister didn't share that hope.

More than anything, that troubled him. She deserved more. As her big brother, it was his responsibility to help her find more. Especially if their mother wasn't going to be able to help.

Jason took a seat at the table, lifting his mug of spiced tea and inhaling the steam. He breathed it in, thinking.

Somehow, they would have to do something else.

And perhaps it was time for a more drastic answer.

He'd been to the base of the mountain where there were others. Life wasn't nearly as hard as it was here, and though it would be a long and arduous journey, he couldn't help but think that for his sister and mother, it was a journey that needed to be taken.

It would mean leaving behind everything and everyone they knew, but if they reached it, then they could start a new life. Maybe there would be someone there who could provide help for their mother, a healer who had knowledge that could bring her back permanently.

Or perhaps they would run into someone like Gary. Or Dragon Souls. Either way, danger.

That threat was enough for him to hesitate.

Jason hated that he allowed himself to fear those others, but what choice did he have? If he wanted to protect those he cared about, he needed to choose the right way on their behalf. For the sake of his mother and what she was going through, he thought he had to find some way to help her. And for his sister, if she had lost all hope, then it was up to him to help her find it again.

Jason stared into space, sipping his tea, his mind turning. As tired as he was, and as much as he needed to rest, he wasn't sure he would be able to.

4

He headed down the slope, clutching his bow tightly, his quiver of arrows at his side and his mind turning. He'd left Kayla and his mother behind, though he doubted his sister would leave her alone. At least his mother still seemed to be sleeping peacefully, almost as if she'd exerted herself too much the day before. Perhaps that was all it was. He had to hope she might come around and that she would be able to return to being a healer.

Kayla's haggard features suggested she hadn't slept nearly as well as she claimed. She had nodded to him when he left, saying nothing, and Jason had no idea what he could say to his sister.

Nothing.

All he could do was succeed in his hunt.

He'd spent the last few hours searching for any movement, creeping steadily downslope, wanting nothing more than a rabbit, any creature that would provide them with fresh meat, but he hadn't seen anything.

A growing frustration built within him. If he failed to bring home a successful hunt, what would happen to Kayla? More likely than not, she would continue to fade. It was the same thing he'd seen with his mother, the way she'd gradually retreated, becoming nothing more than a shell of a person.

If that happened to his sister, Jason had no idea how he could help both of them.

Which was why he had to be successful. Only there was no sign of movement.

He had crouched in place for quite some time, staying near a ridgeline on which he'd frequently encountered rabbits before, but this time, there were none.

Move slowly and carefully. Watch for movement around you. Use that as you hunt.

He poked his head up, and when he did, his stomach sank.

Three figures were beyond the line of sight.

Reltash was one of them, but so too was Angus, and another.

Jason got to his feet, still holding on to his bow, but loosened his grip.

There was no way he was going to find anything with these three out here. And why would they be hunting in this direction anyway? There should be no reason for it. Reltash typically went with the others to the back face of the mountain, where the hunting was better, though often more difficult. At least the snow wasn't nearly as deep, and they would occasionally come across entire herds of deer—until their shots missed and they chased them off. Jason had seen that enough times to know that the hunters were generally successful, but they weren't always the most skilled.

Reltash seemed to notice him, as he motioned in Jason's direction. The three started toward him and Jason crouched where he was, not heading toward them.

"What are you doing out here?" Reltash hollered up at him. He was a large man, and his dragonskin coat reflected the sunlight. His dark eyes glared at Jason.

"I was going to ask you the same thing. It seems to me you're scaring off any game that might be here."

"There is no game out here," Reltash said.

"With you out here, there certainly won't be."

Angus watched Jason, his gaze alternating between the bow slung over his shoulder and the buttons on his coat. Jason was now making a point of ensuring he kept his coat buttoned, not wanting anyone to pay any more attention to his distinct lack of discomfort with the weather.

"Aren't you a little far from home?"

"Aren't you?" Jason asked.

He didn't think Reltash would try anything foolish, but this far away from the village, it was difficult to know with any certainty. He'd taunt him back home, but out here, as far as they were, it was possible Reltash would decide he was tired of dealing with Jason.

"Maybe you should head back," Reltash said.

Next to him, Angus watched Jason a bit nervously. Marl, a young man about his age but much larger than him, shared Reltash's sneer.

"I haven't finished my hunting for the day," Jason said.

"I think you have. It's time for you to get moving."

Jason frowned. "Why are you out here? Do you intend to abandon your friend again?"

He watched Angus as he said it, curious how much Angus would have admitted to Reltash. Would he share that Jason had been the one to save him?

It opened him up to questions, but he didn't really care.

"We didn't abandon him. He fell into the stream on his own. We couldn't reach him in time." Reltash looked up at him, smirking. "What were you doing so far downstream?"

"Hunting. And considering that I've now run into you, I understand why I haven't been able to find anything."

There had to be a reason Reltash and the others were out. They'd gone to the cave, which suggested there was something more to what they were looking for. Had there been rumors of something else? It was the kind of thing he wouldn't have known much about. He didn't spend much time in the village these days, preferring to wander and hunt, hoping he might have a chance to speak with the dragon more, but there was the possibility they'd heard something in the village.

He had shifted his feet, gripping his bow, when Reltash lunged toward him.

Jason scrambled back, and his feet slipped.

Swearing under his breath, he tried to roll, but he slid directly toward Reltash. Reltash grabbed for him, and Jason swung the bow around but restrained himself at the last moment. He didn't want to connect to Reltash's body, not wanting to break his only means of hunting. Finding a replacement would be incredibly hard, at least here. It would require that he head downslope, locate the right kind of branch, and then shape and restring it. The only other option would be to head along the back face of the mountain, but he didn't want to do that, either.

"Grab him. He doesn't need to know what we're doing," Reltash said.

Jason rolled off to the side, sliding along the snow. The others raced toward him, their boots thundering, and he leaned back, trying to slide, but someone was there, grabbing him. The bow was jerked free and he scrambled for it, but Reltash had it.

He watched Jason, a dark look on his face.

"You need to get back to the village."

Jason took a step toward him, and though the others were larger than him, he wasn't about to ignore the bow. His hand slipped into his pocket, gripping the dragon pearl. If it came down to it, he had some means of protecting his weapon, though it might involve revealing something about himself.

"Hand it over," he said.

"This?" Reltash turned the bow in his hands, sneering. "It's not even all that well made. You do realize if you were more willing to hunt with the others, you might have a better weapon."

"That was my father's. Hand it over."

Reltash turned toward him.

"Give it back to him," Angus said.

"Stay out of this," Reltash said.

"You can't keep it. He needs it to help feed his sister and mother."

"You mean the same woman who can't function since her husband was killed by a dragon? How many other people have been lost like that?" Reltash swung the bow from side to side and Jason braced himself, watching the weapon. When he had the opportunity, he intended to launch toward it, grabbing it.

He continued to hold on to the dragon pearl, squeezing the smooth surface. All he needed to do was push out power from it, but how could he do so in a way that wouldn't draw attention to what he had done?

The snow.

He focused on the snow beneath Reltash's feet. If he could send a little power through that, maybe unsettle him, trigger a small avalanche, then he could recover his bow. Reltash might end up sliding down the side of the mountain, but if he were careful, he could prevent him from gliding too far.

Only, Jason didn't know that he had enough control to be able to do so effectively. Which meant that he had to be extra cautious.

Triggering an avalanche wasn't going to be the right

strategy. It was a surefire way of having others realize what he was doing.

Reltash swung the bow and Jason lunged.

When he did, he grabbed the bow, twisted, and yanked. He pushed a hint of the dragon pearl power through his hand as he slammed his fist into Reltash's chest.

Reltash went flying backward and Jason kept one hand squeezing the bow.

It cracked.

The sound of it snapping echoed, filling his ears, and he went sliding down the side of the mountain, twisting backward.

Reltash sat up on the slope, anger on his face gradually twisting over to something else. The bow hung uselessly in Jason's hand, one end twisted and cracked.

Marl helped Reltash to his feet, and Reltash stared at Jason, grinning widely.

"I guess now you have to return to the village."

They turned away, Reltash laughing. Angus's gaze lingered on Jason for a moment, and he shook his head.

They disappeared beyond the ridgeline but Jason sat where he was, unmoving.

And here he thought his sister was the one who was beginning to feel hopeless.

His own sense of despair built. Without the bow, there would be no way to effectively hunt. He could return to the village, check to see if there was anyone who might have one he could trade for, but anything he might come across would be not nearly as high quality as what he had.

His father had taken great care of the bow. It was lovingly maintained, the wood frequently oiled, and because of it, Jason had incredible accuracy with it.

No longer.

The bow is your greatest weapon against hunger.

He lost track of how long he sat there, staring at the broken bow. After a while, he got to his feet and started up the slope of the mountain. There was no purpose in staying any longer than he had. From here, he needed to return, to see if he couldn't figure out something else, and perhaps find someone who might pity him.

It was possible his mother had come back around, too. If so, maybe the promise of her healing would inspire others to make trades, though he wasn't terribly optimistic that would happen. It was more likely that she was still unconscious, or sleeping, or anything else.

As he trudged up the side of the mountain, his sense of hope faded. Wind whistled around him, snow trapped within it tearing at his exposed cheeks. He ignored it. He still had the dragon pearl in one hand, and he squeezed on it, the hopelessness rolling through him, through the dragon pearl, and away from him.

Maybe that was a mistake, but then again, all of this was a mistake. He should've ignored Reltash, knowing that their distance from the village would be an invitation for the other man to taunt him. At the same time, he hadn't really expected Reltash to damage his bow.

The stream's burbling drew his attention and Jason

paused, taking a drink from it. The water was cold, though not nearly as blindingly cold as it had been before. Maybe that was only because he'd been holding on to the dragon pearl while climbing, but it didn't burn his throat as he drank.

After a while, he looked up the mountainside, debating returning home. There was still quite a bit of the day left, and even if he did return, he would have to face his sister, admit what happened, and then go hunting for a replacement.

He wasn't in the mood for it.

Instead he wandered along the stream before reaching the entrance to the cave inside. Pausing there for a moment, he listened but didn't hear any sign of the dragon on the other side. Creeping along the narrow ledge, he pressed his back along the wall of the cave and crawled inside. Once inside, he dropped down to the ground, leaving the bow there.

There was no sign of the dragon, though Jason hadn't expected him to be here. The dragon was probably out hunting—and likely much more successfully than Jason had been.

He stared down at the bow. The wood had splintered, separating it into two irregular pieces. Would there be any way to use the dragon pearl that might restore it?

That involved knowing more about the power he could draw through the dragon pearl, but hadn't he attempted to heal his mother the night before? What was this but another attempt at healing?

Slipping the string off one end, he aligned the bow and held the dragon pearl up against the wood.

He focused on the warmth within him. It came slowly, as if the journey up the mountainside, filled with despair, had drained him of all warmth, and he pushed that into the dragon pearl.

The energy he knew should be there didn't respond.

What if there was another way?

Could he borrow the cold?

That was easier. It filled him, and he pulled on the cold all around him, the chill that washed over him, the sense of it in the air, even the cold that he knew flowed through the stream. As he did, he pushed that into the dragon pearl.

Strangely, that seemed to be much more effective.

As he pushed, he focused on the crack and tried to imagine the bow reformed.

In doing so, Jason didn't expect to be successful. How could he be? The dragon pearl did possess magic, but from everything he'd seen, the kind of magic it contained wasn't able to restore broken bows. Then again, Jason didn't really know what the magic of the dragon pearl would be capable of doing. He didn't have enough experience with it to know whether or not twisting it in such a way would do what he needed.

He held on to that cold, continuing to push it out from him, into the bow.

It flowed outward, a torrent of energy, in much the

same way as the warmth had flowed out of him through the dragon pearl.

Ice began to form along the surface of the bow, and he wondered if perhaps that was all he was doing. If he manifested ice on the bow, it would crack if he tried to draw it, making it useless.

Still, he forced more and more power through the dragon pearl, summoning as much magic as he could and letting it drain into the bow.

A splashing drew his attention and he looked up. The dragon poked his head up out of the stream. Icy blue eyes locked with his.

"You called to me," the dragon said.

"I did what?"

"You called to me."

Jason looked down at the dragon pearl. "I didn't mean to. I was just…" How could he explain what he had done? The dragon might not understand. *He* didn't even understand.

"I'm just trying to repair my bow."

The dragon looked down at the bow, and when he did, there came a surge of energy from him, though it was the kind of surge that Jason could only barely feel. He wasn't entirely certain how much of it was real and how much of it was his imagination, and when it came to the dragon, he wasn't sure he would even know. With the kind of power the dragon possessed, the energy that radiated from the creature, it was possible that what he was detecting was the dragon's natural state and nothing more than that.

"This is valuable to you?"

Jason stared down at it. "I need it to hunt."

"There are other ways to hunt."

"Not for me. And yes. It's valuable to me." He wondered how the dragon hunted. He'd seen the dragon using his spikes, shooting ice from them, and had to wonder if there was some other way he would hunt rather than just flying and dropping down toward his prey. "My father gave it to me. Taught me to use it. Without it, my family will be hungry."

Even with it, his family might end up going hungry. If someone was stealing from them, he didn't know if he would have any way of ensuring they had enough. That was what it came down to, after all. He needed to find some way for his sister and mother to have full bellies. It was more than that, though. He needed to ensure his mother and sister had hope.

Doing so was difficult. Mostly because Jason wasn't sure how or whether *he* had hope. Not anymore, not after having lost his bow and having someone steal from them, taking the things he had hunted for.

The dragon pulled itself out of the water and shook itself dry. Jason braced for ice to target him, but it never came. Instead, it seemed almost as if the water disappeared, turning to a faint trace of steam before fading.

"Come."

Jason frowned, but the dragon nudged him with his head and guided him toward the end of the cave. Faster than Jason could even think, the dragon forced his head underneath him, tossing Jason to his back. And then they glided free of the cave.

The dragon soared above the surface of the snow, keeping low, gliding just above it, and it took a moment for Jason to realize it wasn't so much that the dragon was gliding above the surface as he was skiing down it. The dragon moved quickly, using wings and claws in order to stay above the surface, wings arched back from his enormous body. Strangely, it wasn't nearly as frigid as he would've expected, and as he clung to the dragon's back, he felt no sense of danger.

And he wasn't cold.

Truthfully, in the time since uncovering the dragon, Jason had not felt cold at all. There was something protective about the dragon, and since he'd reached the massive creature, since he had made that connection, a bond of sorts had formed between them. It allowed Jason not only to better understand the dragon, but to tolerate the temperature.

He held on tightly. He didn't say anything, but the wind whistled around him, stealing his breath and making it so he wouldn't even be able to say anything if it were necessary. He remembered sitting atop the dragon with Henry, the way the heat radiated from the creature, almost unpleasantly so. With this dragon, there was none of that sense. There was only the wind and the snow and the cold. None of it was unpleasant.

And then the dragon stretched its wings.

Within a moment, they took to the air, gliding above

the ground. Jason braced, wondering where the dragon might take him, but he didn't have an opportunity to think about that for very long. The dragon arched down, massive jaw open, and he snapped.

As they banked, twisting off to the side, Jason realized the dragon had grabbed a deer. There was a herd of them, dozens of deer, and they scattered.

The movement seemed to entice the dragon, and with a shake of his tail, two more fell. The dragon dropped, spreading his enormous legs, and grabbed each of the fallen deer before banking and heading back up the slope.

Within another moment, they were slowing, and then descended once again back to the snow. As they did, they glided up the slope, reaching the stream. The dragon tucked his wings away and then flowed into the cave, dropping once more.

When the dragon lowered his head, Jason climbed off, knowing that was expected of him. The dragon turned, meeting his eyes with an icy stare.

"What was that about?" Jason asked.

"Another way to hunt."

Jason looked down at the deer, understanding what the dragon was getting at. Two of them would feed his family for a long time.

Tears formed in his eyes, and he didn't know what to say.

5

A fter binding the deer, letting them bleed out, the blood dripping into the stream, Jason dragged them off to the side of the cave. It was a precious gift, and it was one that would allow his family to survive. Though they might not thrive, at least it was something more than he currently had. Knowing there was someone who had stolen from them, he would have to find some way of keeping these deer safe.

He turned toward the dragon. He'd been willing to help Jason. It was his turn to do the same.

"You said you could feel the others," he said.

The dragon rumbled softly, moving back toward the water and almost lowering himself before changing his mind. "I can feel the other hatch mates."

"Do you know where they are?"

"It's difficult for me to determine. There is an awareness of them, but anything more than that is difficult."

The dragon curled up along the side of the cave, resting his enormous head on the ground. When he did, he was able to look into Jason's eyes more easily, the icy blue meeting his own, and a surge of energy came off the dragon again, radiating from him like it had done before.

"What happens if they're alone?"

"Dragons can hunt alone," the dragon said.

"I understand the dragons can hunt alone, but will something happen to them?"

He thought about his sister and his mother and the way they were helpless without him searching for food on their behalf. Would they become hopeless as well?

Even if they didn't, he thought there was something he would need to do. This was something he *could* do. The dragon needed him, and more than that, he needed the dragon. If it took little more than a few moments for the dragon to bring down the deer, he wouldn't have to worry. He wouldn't have to scramble for food, and he wouldn't have to worry about where their next meal would come from. He could bring his sister hope.

More than that, he could ensure his family thrived. Maybe his mother would return, her mind reawakening. In time, she could become the same woman she had been before, and perhaps she could resume working in her hut, healing others and not needing him to hunt quite as much.

All of that depended upon his ability to provide what she needed while she was recovering. And all of that required that he find some way of helping his sister. She needed hope almost more than his mother did.

"I can't tell," the dragon said.

Jason got to his feet and faced the dragon. "The Dragon Souls will search for them. If they find them, they will try to use them."

"You have seen this?"

He shook his head. "I don't know enough about the Dragon Souls to be confident of how they will use the dragons. I have very little experience with them. The only thing I know is that I've faced a man who has incredible power, and he would use it to try to control the dragons."

"Dragons are meant to be free."

Jason inhaled deeply. As he looked at the dragon, he couldn't help but feel the same way. It was a strange sensation, especially after having lived for the last year fearing the dragons, thinking he hated them, that he wanted nothing more than to destroy anything that might be tied to the dragons; and yet here he was, wanting to offer his assistance to this dragon, to do whatever he could to help the creature.

And how could he not?

Looking at the dragon, speaking to the dragon, he understood more than he ever had before.

"How are you connected to the hatch mates?"

"They are dragons."

"I understand, but are they family?"

"Family?"

Jason took a seat in front of the dragon, meeting his

eyes. "Family. I have a mother and had a father. They had me. My sister. Eventually I will find a wife and we will have children." Tessa would once have been an option for him, though he wondered if she could be now.

Family, then village. Care for family first, but don't neglect your duty to your people.

"I don't know who bore my egg. I don't know anything other than the fact that there are dragons I share a connection with. Hatch mates."

Maybe they were the same as siblings. And if they were, shouldn't the dragon want to help them the same way that Jason would want to help his sister?

Family, then village.

Would the dragon be part of his village?

"I can help you look for them."

"Why would you do this thing?"

"Because you need my help. I understand these lands, and more than that, if the hatch mates have ended up somewhere only a human could reach, you will need me."

The dragon let out a low rumble, and Jason wasn't sure if he'd angered the creature or not, but then the dragon sat up and started toward the entrance to the cave. "We will go."

Jason shook his head. "I can't go just yet."

"I thought you said you would do this."

"I will, but first I need to bring some food to my family."

The dragon crawled toward the stream, dropping into it, saying nothing else.

Jason had a sense that the creature was annoyed, perhaps disappointed. Why would that be? He had offered to help, so there should be no reason for the dragon to be upset with him.

But then, he was leaving.

He looked at the deer, studying it for a moment. If he brought an entire deer back home, there was a danger that someone would steal from them again.

If he was going to go away for a little while, he didn't want to risk that.

Which meant he couldn't bring the deer.

After cutting off a large section of meat, he wrapped it in its hide, deciding to leave the rest here.

Jason glanced down at his frozen bow, hefting it and discovering that it was restored. He wiped the surface and restrung it, finding that it flexed just as it had before. It was strange that the ice would hold, that it wouldn't break as the bow was drawn, and yet it seemed to still function.

At least he wouldn't be unarmed.

He made his way out of the cave.

The day had grown long, the wind and snow had begun, and it would be a long walk back to the village. He glanced back toward the cave mouth, wishing the dragon could bring him back home, but if he did, he would draw attention, and the people in the village might think to attack. It would be better if Jason went alone, even though he would rather have the dragon with him.

He trudged up the slope, and in doing so, he focused on the dragon pearl, the power within it, wishing he had some way to move more quickly. After a while, he found he was gliding along the surface of the snow faster than he had before, and by the time he neared the village, he was barely making any footprints.

It was similar to how Therin and Henry had walked, and yet they had far more control over their connection to the dragon pearls than Jason did. In time, and if he had an opportunity to continue to work with the dragon pearl, he hoped he would understand the nature of the power he could draw through it, but for now, all he had was the ability to generate some magic.

He reached the outskirts of the village. In the distance, he thought he caught sight of Reltash and the others, but he ignored them, turning toward his home.

Once inside, he closed the door tightly and glanced toward the hearth glowing with heat.

"Kayla? Mother?"

Kayla appeared in the doorway. Her eyes were drawn and the shadows seemed to cling to her, darkening everything around her. "I heard what happened."

"What do you mean?"

"I stepped out. I heard you fought with Reltash. Your bow broke."

Jason clenched his jaw. Were they starting rumors about him already?

He pulled the bow off his shoulder, holding it up. "You mean this bow?"

Kayla's eyes darted to the bow and she fixed it with a long stare. "It didn't break?"

Jason debated what to say. If he told her that it had and that the dragon had restored it, then it was possible she wouldn't even believe him, and yet, he could see the hope fading from her with each passing moment.

"It didn't break. And I found something."

"Rabbit?"

He shook his head.

She lowered hers.

"A deer."

Kayla jerked up, looking at him. "You found another?"

"I did."

"But you know what's happened—"

Jason shook his head. "I didn't bring the whole thing back. I don't want to risk anyone stealing from us again." He pulled the wrapped steak from his pocket and handed it over. It was large enough for several days' worth of food, and she eyed it hungrily. "I made sure you had enough for a few days."

"Just me?"

"You and Mother."

"What about you?"

"I need to keep hunting," he said. He motioned for her to join him at the table, pulling the chair out and taking a seat. He still hadn't taken his coat off, and he found that he was holding on to his bow, gripping it tightly. The irritation that had bubbled up within him at learning how the others had shared the story of his bow remained. It was bad enough that Kayla had to deal with everything she did, but to worry about him, to worry that he might have lost his bow, and to worry that he might not have any way to hunt for their family, wasn't fair to her. "I found a herd. I can gather more. It's not far from here, but it will require that I'm gone for a few days."

"A few days?" Kayla lifted her gaze from the steak to meet his eyes. "You can't survive that long away from the village."

"I've done it before."

"But you got lucky. What happens if one of the storms moves in, enough snowfall strikes, and you get buried by it?"

"I won't get buried by it," he said.

"What happens if there's an avalanche, and it carries you down the mountain?"

He hadn't told her that he'd already survived one avalanche. She wouldn't understand, and she wouldn't even believe that he had managed to return. No one had gone all the way to the base of the mountain and come back. The distance was too far, the climb too treacherous, and had he not had Henry with the dragon, he would likely have had to try to wind around to the back face of the mountain to return, a journey that would've taken weeks, possibly longer—if he managed to survive it.

"I'll be careful."

"If you don't return, how will we eat?"

That was perhaps the most important question she asked, and Jason sighed. "If for some reason I don't come back, you need to find the cave near the stream. Make your way inside. Move carefully, stay close to the wall, and once inside, you will find the rest of the deer."

"You left it there?"

"It's safest. No one's going to go in there."

"You don't know that."

"I know it's difficult to get in there. You have to press yourself against the wall of the cave, and if you don't, you run the real risk of falling into the stream. I've seen it happen."

She looked up at him. "I thought you found Angus downstream."

"What?"

"I heard what happened. The stories are that you found him downstream."

"I was in the cave when it happened," Jason admitted.

"Why were you there? I thought you were out hunting?"

"I was. Sometimes there are creatures in the cave."

"If there are animals there, then the deer isn't safe."

"It will be safe," he said.

She opened her mouth to object, and he wasn't even sure how he could convince her otherwise. It would be safe, and yet, it involved the dragon, something he couldn't reveal to her. Not yet. There would come a time for that; he was certain his sister was going to need to know about it. If she didn't, then she might not believe he could offer the help that he intended.

"Just trust me that it's going to be safe. There's more than enough for you and Mother to eat." If it came down to it, she would find the other deer, and she would realize they had plenty of meat for a long time. It was more than he'd left them even the last time.

"You don't have to do this," Kayla said.

Jason took her hands. "I do. I want to make sure that you and Mother are provided for."

She took a deep breath. In that moment, some spark returned to her eyes. Maybe it was hope, though it seemed fleeting. He hoped he could keep it there for longer than just that moment, and he wished there was some way for her to maintain that sense of hope, and yet, he understood why it would be difficult. It was the same reason it was so difficult for him—or had been.

"I'm going to check on Mother," Jason said.

She got to her feet, taking the wrapped meat to the stove. "I will prepare this for us."

"Not all of it," he said, offering a smile.

She shook her head. "Of course not."

When he headed to the back room, he found his mother lying on the bed, staring straight ahead. Her eyes were open and she breathed steadily.

"Mother?"

She didn't respond to him. Any hope she might have returned to the woman who had been up and active the day before was gone. Whatever had happened, it seemed to have been more than she could withstand.

Jason pulled the chair over, sitting next to her. He took her hands and squeezed. There was no strength in her hands as there had been before, and he found them frail, bony, the same way he found his mother.

"I'm going to have to leave for a little while," he said.

It might have been his imagination, but it seemed as if her breathing quickened.

"I found enough food for you and Kayla to have while I'm gone. She's preparing some venison now."

His mother blinked.

"When I return, I hope there will be enough of a supply for us to not have to worry about food again."

If he did this, if he found a way of deepening the connection between himself and the dragon, then hopefully the dragon would be willing to hunt with him more often. Thinking about how effortlessly the dragon had captured those two deer, Jason could imagine just how easy it would be for them to continue the hunt, to not have to worry about finding enough food. He might be able to capture enough that he could trade. Maybe he could even acquire a dragonskin coat. Not for him, but for his sister at least. Jason no longer needed the warmth a dragonskin coat would offer. He wasn't even sure what would happen if he attempted to wear one. It might be too much for him, far warmer than anything he could tolerate.

"Kayla knows that I'm going. And she will make sure you're safe."

As he started to stand, his mother squeezed his hands.

It was the most emotion he'd seen from her.

Jason sat back down, remaining alongside her. She

held on to his hands. Occasionally there would be another squeeze, but even that faded over time. She closed her eyes, breathing steadily.

When she did, he couldn't help but wonder if he was making a mistake. Could he have been wrong about going on this journey? It meant leaving his family. His sister already struggled, and with his mother in this shape, Jason didn't know if leaving was even something he should be doing. Yet, for them to have a future, he thought he needed to. It seemed the right thing to do, and it seemed as if it would provide a way for them to not have to worry the way they had every day for the last year.

It was more than that. The dragon needed his help.

For some reason, he could feel that. He might not be able to sense the hatch mates the same way that the dragon could, but Jason could detect that urgency and desire from the dragon.

If he didn't do this, he understood what would happen if the Dragon Souls managed to reach the hatch mates before he did. They would gain control over a creature that could tolerate the ice and snow. How long would it be before they were able to completely subjugate these lands? To bring them into the rule of Lorach?

Jason doubted it would be all that long. Saving those dragons was another way of helping his family. It was the same reason he'd gone after the dragon before, working with Henry, and now he felt as if he needed to do it because he wanted to ensure there was safety for them.

He took another deep breath, sitting next to his

mother, his mind made up. After a while, his sister called to him, letting him know the food was ready, and Jason tore himself free from his mother. Despite her frailty, she had a strong grip, and he had to pry his hands free.

Hopefully Kayla could get his mother to eat. Hopefully the two of them would be able to survive while he was gone. And hopefully he wouldn't be gone all that long.

Despite that, he couldn't help but worry that something would happen to them.

The people in the village had turned a blind eye to their needs ever since his father had died. They might recognize how they suffered, but they hadn't done anything to help, not as they had for others.

With his mother's sickness, it had made people even less inclined to help. Her helplessness was part of the problem.

Before heading to the kitchen, Jason pulled the dragon pearl from his pocket, pressing it on his mother's chest, and focused on the heat within him. He shifted that, instead feeling for the cold all around him. That had been a source of even greater power. He drew upon that, letting it flow through him and into his mother. There came a surge, and it washed over her, sweeping through her.

As before, there seemed to be some sort of resistance, but with the ongoing pressure of the cold, he managed to override that resistance, and he felt something change within her.

Maybe it was that her breathing eased, or maybe it was

something else, but either way, he recognized that something had just shifted.

Pocketing the dragon pearl, he straightened, looking around, and headed out to eat.

"How is she?"

"Resting," Jason said.

"What were you doing in there?"

"Just sitting with her, why?"

"I don't know. It's just that I thought I felt..." She shook her head. "It doesn't matter. Why don't we eat, and you can get some rest before you do whatever it is you plan for tomorrow."

"I'm doing this for us," he said.

"I hope so," she said.

"I am. For you. For Mother." Even for Father, but he couldn't say that to his sister. Not yet. When this was done, then he could introduce her to the dragon. Then she could know the power that Jason had encountered. And she would understand why they wouldn't have to fear any longer. But only after this was done.

She watched him as he started to eat but said nothing.

6

J ason made his way through the village, moving quickly toward the outskirts when he came across Tessa again. She was dressed in dragon skin, and she had a slingshot in hand. He frowned at her.

"What's that for?"

Tessa glanced down, flushing slightly. "It's nothing."

"It looks like more than nothing."

She flashed a smile, glancing to his bow before looking up and meeting his eyes. "Well, I'm going with my father to hunt close to Varmin."

"*You're* going hunting?"

"You don't have to say that as if you don't think I can do it."

Jason shook his head. "That wasn't what I was getting at." He wished he could take it back. It was more about Tessa leaving the village, the fear that she would have in doing so. How could she not, after what happened the last time she'd left? Jason didn't think that she had left the village in the time since.

"My father wanted me to come. The hunting parties haven't had as much luck lately, and..."

"I'm sure you'll have luck. If anyone will, it will be you."

"You could go with them. Us."

There was a time when Jason might have agreed to it. That was before.

"Maybe next time," he said.

"Are you sure?" There was a hint of hope in her voice, and it pained Jason to be the one who would take that hope away, but it also surprised him that she would even want him to be a part of any hunting party.

"I..."

He trailed off as he caught sight of Reltash making his way toward him.

Tessa looked to Reltash, and she nodded slowly. "I understand. Next time." She left him, and Jason experienced a pang of sadness.

Reltash was dressed in his dragonskin coat and had a sword strapped to his side and a bow slung over his shoulder. Angus wasn't with him today, but neither was Marl. It was a rare time Reltash was alone.

Jason approached. "Are you going off hunting again today?"

Reltash turned toward him slowly, and Jason made a point of pulling the bow off his shoulder, holding on to it.

"I'm going," Jason said. "I thought I found something yesterday, but there were others who scared it away."

"Dreshen. Where did you find that?"

"You mean my bow? You weren't nearly as strong as you thought."

Reltash frowned. Jason could imagine the way his mind was working, trying to sort through everything he had experienced, and it was almost as if Reltash were trying to decide if he actually had been responsible for damaging the bow. It was enough for Jason to smile.

And yet, he was careful not to say anything. He didn't want to draw too much attention to the fact that he had restored the bow. He still wasn't entirely sure how he had done so. If Reltash examined it too closely, he would find it was covered by ice, and that layer should render it brittle, and yet it seemed just as flexible as it had been before.

"I imagine it's more effective than the one you carry." Jason flashed a dark smile and pushed past Reltash, heading out of the snow. He could feel Reltash's eyes burning on his back and he took off, hurrying down the slope. Every so often, he would pause and glance back, but there was no sign of movement coming out of the village.

Move carefully to avoid falling.

This time, he *wanted* to fall.

He dropped down to his backside, sliding, trying to pick up speed. If he was going to meet the dragon, he wanted to do so as quickly as possible. Now that he had committed to this, it was time for them to get on their way.

It was the middle of the morning by the time he reached the stream and the cave.

Jason darted inside, moving carefully along the lip of earth, and paused to ensure that the two deer he'd caught were still where he'd left them.

They were untouched.

He glanced down at the stream. There was no sign of the dragon.

Here he had committed himself to this, telling himself he would be taking off for the day, but what if the dragon wasn't interested in that any longer?

He knew the dragon had been off hunting, and it was possible that he had disappeared again. If that were the case, then there might not be anything Jason could do to reach him.

How had he called the dragon the last time?

It had something to do with using the dragon pearl.

He took a seat, focusing on the dragon pearl and on the cold within him. It was the same thing he'd done the night before when he had tried to use that power on his mother, and as he did, he could feel energy radiating from him, striking the pearl and flowing outward.

The dragon pearl began to glow with a soft white light which intensified, striking the crystals overhead and reflecting off them.

It was blazing, illuminating the entirety of the cave, and as it did, he had to worry that doing so might have been a mistake. What if he was alerting others of his presence? If anyone saw the cave mouth glowing like that, they would know something was taking place inside it. It wouldn't surprise him for Reltash and anyone with him to come down here, not after they had been searching for something.

And he didn't even know what they had been searching for.

Jason let out a frustrated sigh.

There was no sign of the dragon. The more he focused, the more uncertain he was that he would even come across it.

Reaching the dragon involved some way of communicating, and yet he wasn't entirely sure what it was going to take. It was possible he didn't know enough about how to reach out to the dragon. It was something to do with his way of calling to it, but what was that going to require?

He pushed power out, sending it through the dragon pearl.

A stirring in the water caught his attention. Jason glanced over. The dragon poked his head out, letting his eyes press against the surface of the stream, and when his gaze locked on Jason, he crawled out, shaking free. This time, small shards of ice did come splattering off him. It was almost as if the dragon were angry with him.

"You returned," the dragon said.

"I told you that I would."

"I wasn't certain."

Jason glanced over at the deer. "I had to make sure that my family was provided for."

"What about my family?"

"You still haven't told me whether the hatch mates are your family."

The dragon sat up. It might be Jason's imagination, but it seemed almost as if the dragon were even larger than the last time he'd seen it. The top of his head brushed the ceiling of the cave. As he propped himself up on his crystalline wings, they spread out, making it so that the dragon filled the entirety of the cave.

"I don't know."

"I'm ready to go," he said. "I told you that I needed to see if there was anything my family needed. I made sure that they had enough to eat, and hopefully they are as prepared as possible for however long it takes us to find the hatch mates."

The dragon lowered his head, and Jason climbed on.

There was a chill from the dragon, and he wasn't sure if it came from the creature himself or from the water the dragon had been in. Either way, that chill was almost overwhelming, pressing in upon Jason, and he wrapped his bearskin jacket around himself. Most of the time, he didn't need the jacket any longer, and yet, with the dragon behaving like this, he had an even greater need for it.

It surprised him. It was almost as if the dragon was angry with him, and yet, Jason didn't know what he could do to temper that anger. He had left the dragon, yes, but he had needed to. His family had needed him. The dragon had to understand that.

Only, it didn't seem as if it did.

They glided along the surface of the snow. It was the same thing they had done the day before, and as they slid along the snow, picking up speed the faster they went down the slope, the wind whistling around them, Jason closed his eyes and clung to the dragon's back. There was nothing else he could do.

He took a deep breath, drawing in the cold air, letting it fill him. In doing so, he managed to ignore the cold he felt through the dragon. It was almost as if he was able to disregard the way the dragon pressed upon him, sending chills rolling through him.

All of a sudden, the dragon stretched out his wings, and they took to the air.

The change was drastic and sudden, and the power with which the dragon used that shift caught him off guard. There was a surge of his muscular wings, and then they soared higher and higher into the air. Unlike the other dragon Jason had flown with, this one did not spiral up. He simply streaked straight up, almost as if angling against the wind gusting against him.

The power of the dragon was almost alarming. They streaked higher and higher, and as they did, Jason gripped the dragon's back, squeezing with his legs, trying to ensure that he didn't fall.

Still, there was a sense of joy in flying with the dragon. There was something relaxing about the change, the energy the dragon used, and he cried out in surprise.

The dragon twisted in the air, banking, and they changed directions, angling toward the mountain peak. For a moment, Jason thought they might be visible, but the color of the dragon blended into the bleak gray sky. They were high enough up that he could see nothing other than the snow reflecting up toward him. As they crested the top of the mountain, he looked down, hoping to catch a glimpse of the village, but they were within the clouds and he could see nothing.

And then they angled down.

The dragon hurtled toward the ground, moving more and more rapidly, power surging from his massive wings as he streaked downward.

Jason squeezed, terrified, and yet there wasn't anything else to do. The dragon wasn't going to harm him—he didn't think.

"Where are we traveling?"

The dragon spread his wings and they slowed, catching a current of air and gliding. It was almost peaceful that way, certainly more peaceful than when they had been powering straight ahead, and as Jason clung to the dragon, feeling the way his wings moved beneath him, the entire body flexing as he flew, he experienced that surge of joy.

"I search for the sense of my hatch mates," the dragon said.

Jason breathed out, letting the cold air circle around him, trying to welcome it, but with as fast as they were moving, he felt nothing more than the cold working over him.

"Is there anything I can do to help?"

The dragon rumbled beneath him. "I have been hunting for the last few weeks."

"This is where you've been going?"

"It is."

They dove, hurtling toward the ground, and as they did, Jason realized the dragon streaked toward a horned creature that was unlike anything he'd seen before. When the dragon neared, the creature darted, and rather than shifting, the dragon spread his wings and glided after the horned creature, snapping it in his massive jaws and swallowing it.

There was a brief spray of blood that stained the snow, but then they were climbing again.

"How often do you need to eat?"

"When I hunt, I eat."

"And you're hunting now?"

"*We* are hunting."

They continued flying, staying above the ground, Jason clinging to the dragon's back, feeling the movements of the creature beneath him. With each moment, he started to unwind, letting the sense of the dragon fill him. There was power to it, and yet, the chill he'd been experiencing began to ease. It was almost as if the dragon had finally come to accept that he wasn't going to run off again.

"What should I call you?"

"Call?"

"I'm sure you have a name. I'm Jason Dreshen. Do dragons go by anything?"

"There has been no need to call me anything."

"Have you interacted with anyone else?"

"Only you."

As they flew, there was something about that which

troubled Jason. It took a moment to realize why that should be. "How is it that you've only interacted with me, and yet you know how to speak my language?"

"I understand the words you know."

"You can understand my thoughts?"

"We are connected," the dragon said.

Jason hadn't realized that, and yet, did it surprise him? It seemed the dragon had had some connection to him ever since he'd first found it, and yet Jason had not been able to know the dragon's thoughts.

"How is it you can know my thoughts but I can't know yours?"

"Because you have not tried."

"I have to have something to call you."

"Then choose."

It seemed so simple, and at the same time, it was not. Anything he chose would have to fit the dragon. He wasn't entirely sure what would be suitable. What could he call a creature like this? He didn't know anything that might fit with the right language, and yet, he realized something else. He didn't know the dragon well enough to choose anything for him. Perhaps in time he would.

Rather than calling him anything inappropriate, it might be better for him to simply refer to the dragon as dragon. Eventually, he would have to come up with a name. If they were going to travel together, then the dragon deserved a name. More than that, he probably *needed* a name. It would be easier for them to communicate.

Perhaps he should have asked Henry how the dragons were named. At least then he would have some idea of what the naming conventions were, and yet, he hadn't even revealed the dragon's presence to Henry or any of the others.

There was a part of him that felt a little guilty at hiding the dragon from them, but he thought he owed it to the dragon as an attempt to protect him. The moment the others knew about the ice dragon, they would want something from him. Perhaps they would attempt to use him. It was part of the reason he'd not revealed the dragon's presence to anyone.

The dragon rumbled again.

"You knew what I was thinking just then, didn't you?"

"I did."

"Can I keep anything from you?"

"Perhaps you can learn to, but why would you want to?"

"Why would I want you to know everything that I'm thinking?"

"Are you thinking anything that would cause harm to me?"

"I think I've proven I am not."

"Then you would have no need to fear."

Jason grunted. It seemed so simple to the dragon, and yet he knew it was not. There was nothing simple about any of this.

"The other dragons can't tolerate the cold, but can you tolerate heat?"

"I haven't tried," the dragon said.

"What do you think would happen?"

"I don't know."

"Do you enjoy the mountains?"

"Enjoy?"

"Do you mind it here?"

"It's all I've known."

The answer surprised Jason. "And yet you can feel your hatch mates."

"I can feel them. They are there within me."

What must that be like? What would it be like for him if he could detect his sister and mother? If he knew how they were feeling and how to help them?

Family, then village.

The hatch mates were the ice dragon's family.

In some ways, feeling his family would be beneficial. He might be able to use that knowledge to determine whether there was anything they needed of him, but it might also make him suffer more. Knowing the agony they experienced might be more than he could bear. Perhaps it was for the best that he wasn't connected the same way that the dragons were.

"If you can feel them, is there any way you can determine where they are?"

"What I feel is what you feel when it comes to detecting my energy," the dragon said.

"But I don't really feel anything."

"You're aware of the power you can draw from me."

Jason reached for the dragon pearl. He held on to the

dragon with one arm, squeezing his legs, and found the pearl within his pocket. He pulled on the energy within it, drawing it through himself, using the cold as a focus.

"Like that," the dragon said.

"I can feel it," Jason said. "The only difference is I don't know whether it's coming from you or from something else."

"The power you're drawing now is from me."

"Are all dragon pearls connected to the dragon in the same way?"

"I don't know."

"How don't you know?"

"How many dragons do you know?"

"I've met you, and one other." That wasn't completely true. There were some other smaller dragons that he had encountered, but they weren't very large, and he didn't have as much experience with them. Certainly not enough to discern whether there was anything to their powers. He barely knew about the power Henry was able to draw from the dragons.

"You know more than I know."

"How many other dragons do you know?"

"None."

They angled north. They followed the line of the mountaintops, soaring above peaks, traveling farther and faster than Jason could ever have imagined doing. After a while, he lay back, resting, but he had to wonder. If the hatchlings were out there, he didn't think Therin would have scattered them too far. They might have been within a certain radius of where this dragon was.

"We could go after the Dragon Souls," he suggested. It wasn't something he was eager to do, and if he did, he ran the risk of encountering danger. The Dragon Souls knew far more about their magic than he did, and anything he might attempt would be fraught with that danger. It was better to search for the hatchlings with this dragon, but if anyone would know where to find the other hatch mates, then he thought it might be the Dragon Souls, and Therin in particular.

Ever since they'd defeated Therin, there'd been no sign of the man. The first few weeks after defeating Therin had been the hardest. Jason had kept vigilant, worried Therin would come after the village, the dragon, and that Jason alone would know enough to withstand him. With each passing day when there had been no sign of Therin, Jason managed to relax further, though he still wasn't completely convinced Therin was gone. Maybe he hadn't survived the journey down the stream. With as cold as the water was, it was possible he had not. Even with a dragon pearl to draw energy from, to keep himself warm, it might not have been enough to overpower the natural cold.

In Jason's mind, it was better if Therin had not survived. They didn't need the Dragon Souls' attention upon the village. The fact that they had come there once had been enough, and if they believed there was a dragon, then it was dangerous for not only the dragon, but for Jason and the others he cared about—and cared about protecting. There would be no way to protect them if the Dragon Souls returned.

"What if we're searching too far away?" Jason asked.

"I've searched closer," the dragon said.

"If you can reach through me and detect something, maybe I can reach through you and detect something."

The dragon rumbled again. It seemed to be his way of agreeing with Jason, but even if the dragon agreed, Jason still wasn't sure what it would take to detect anything. More than that, it was possible he would never learn. It was possible there was no way for him to detect anything. He didn't understand the connection between himself and the dragon. Only that he had some way of using the dragon pearl.

Could he draw through that connection?

If he couldn't, there had to be some other way to see if he could help the dragon. What did he know about power and the Dragon Souls?

He thought about what Therin had said to him. There were other eggs that they had placed, and as far as Therin knew, none of them had hatched.

And maybe that was true, but Jason trusted the dragon. He trusted that the dragon would be aware of his hatch mates and would be able to detect the others.

But there was an advantage Jason had that the dragon did not.

Therin had revealed something to him.

Could he use that?

Understanding what Therin had done required knowing the man.

More than that, it might involve going someplace that Jason didn't want to go.

"We need to head back," he said.

"You have abandoned the search already?"

"No. I think we need to approach it differently."

"How so?"

He inhaled deeply, letting it out. "When my father was killed"—his voice caught, the same way it did each time he spoke of his father—"there had to have been other eggs involved. The man who was responsible for moving them would have done so there."

"You no longer blame the dragons for what happened to him."

"I don't. I understand the dragons aren't responsible for what happened to my father." He swallowed. "I want to do whatever I can to help you."

He forced down the pain of thinking about his father. It had been easier in the days since learning what had really happened. Living with the belief that the dragons had been responsible for his father's death had been hard, and for some reason he found it easier knowing his father had died for a different reason. Seeing this dragon, getting to ride him, and knowing the cave his father had once shown him was the reason the dragon had survived made it all the more bearable.

It still wasn't easy. Losing his father was never going to be easy, but he had to think that his father would have appreciated what had happened. He had to believe that his father would have wanted the dragons to thrive, even without knowing them himself.

"Where was this?"

Jason wondered how much the dragon was aware of what he was thinking. It was possible that he could connect to all of it and know everything Jason was thinking about, but it was equally possible that he didn't understand the emotion. He might know the language, but he might not comprehend the reasons that Jason suffered as he did.

"There's a village on the back slope of the mountain."

"Back slope?"

"The side with less snow."

"That will be more difficult for me to reach."

"I understand."

"I will bring you as close as I can. And you will search."

"I will do what I can," Jason agreed.

"When you find something, you will summon me."

"I'm not sure I know how to summon you."

"You will summon me the same way that you did before. You will call upon my power."

Jason reached for the dragon pearl, squeezing it in his hand. "That summons you?" He thought about the way that Henry had called the dragon.

"Drawing upon my power alerts me of your need."

"And you can find me?"

"I can."

They began to descend, and as they did, the snow

shifted. Wind was whipping around, obscuring them, and there was something else, something Jason had realized when they were flying. The dragon had changed course, heading back toward his home mountain. From here, they would be able to reach the village, but they had descended down the back face of the mountain. Snow stretched through here, though it wasn't nearly as treacherous as the snow on the front face.

The dragon dropped, reaching the snow, and then began to glide, skiing above the surface of the snow. Jason remained on the dragon's back and said nothing as they glided farther and farther down the mountain.

There were parts of this mountain that were more heavily traversed. There were sections of it where roads had been built, easier ways of traveling between the villages dotting the back side of the mountain. His village was the highest point on the mountain, and it had been the most difficult to protect, but at the same time, it held a certain level of prestige among the villages because of its role in defending against the dragons—along with their access to tellum. He wondered what the people of the village would think if they knew that such protections were unnecessary. They probably wouldn't believe it. Had he not experienced the dragons the way he had, and had he not seen what the Dragon Souls were willing to do, he would never have believed that the dragons were not interested in harming their people.

The ground began to change. Smaller shrubs dotted the surface.

This was what most people in the village used for firewood, if they were able to bring it upslope. It was difficult to carry most of this wood up the slope, so they relied upon dung, which was far easier to acquire.

The longer he traveled, the more the landscape changed, though it did so in a way that was similar to the front face of the mountain, giving everything a familiarity, though he rarely traveled in this direction.

And then the dragon skidded to a stop.

"This is as far as you can bring me?"

"There are others not far from here," the dragon said.

Jason nodded. He climbed off the dragon's back and patted the creature's side, then stepped away.

"You will summon me when you need me."

He reached into his pocket, feeling for the dragon pearl, and sent a surge of power through it. "You can feel that?"

"Yes."

"Then I will summon you."

With that, the dragon pumped its wings and took to the air.

As he did, Jason watched as his form became ever more distant. Eventually, he became lost in the clouds, nothing more than a memory.

Jason breathed out, squeezing the dragon pearl, hoping he'd be able to reach the dragon when it came time to leave, but if he could not, at least from here, he thought he might be able to find his way back to his village.

It would be a long climb, and potentially treacherous,

but there were plenty of people who had come down from the village to this part of the world. From here, Jason knew he'd be able to return.

He started down the slope, clutching his bow, holding his bearskin jacket around him, trying to ignore the chill, and yet, it wasn't the chill that sent a shiver through him. It was the idea that he was going someplace dangerous—a place where his father had been lost—and going without any protection other than his bow.

It was a mistake, he thought, and yet it was something that needed to be done.

7

It was late in the day when he saw light flickering in the distance. At first, he thought it was someone's campfire, and he moved carefully, slowly, thinking that if he approached too quickly, he could raise the wrong kind of attention. He'd expected to come across others long before now. The dragon had detected someone, so he'd expected he'd find that someone, but there'd been no sign of anyone else on the road with him. And it was more of a roadway than a vast expanse of snow. The wind wasn't nearly as harsh as it was on the front face, and though the evening brought snow, it came in softer flurries rather than the violence he knew from the front face of the mountain.

It might've been easier to have come this way and hunted, and yet the longer he'd been down here, the less he'd seen signs of life. There were some birds flying overhead, but that was about it. There was nothing else.

Certainly no signs of a herd of deer or any other creature that might've been valuable to him. He passed a few copses of spindly trees, but within them he found no trace of squirrel or rabbit or anything that would have been edible.

These lands were overhunted. It was for that reason that he preferred to hunt the front face. The work might've been more difficult, and he rarely caught something, but coming this way would force him to compete against the others from his village.

Could that be who he'd come across?

There were times when people from the village would descend far down the mountainside and come back empty-handed.

At least when Jason returned empty-handed, it wasn't quite the same climb. And when he did find something—which was increasingly common these days—he didn't have to share it with as many people as the hunting parties did.

Maybe that was why someone had been stealing from them. It was possible the hunting parties had been splitting too much, making it so those who'd been out hunting had to go hungry. If that were the case, Jason would've expected to have heard something more about it, and yet there had been no sign of others suffering starvation.

He approached the light slowly, and when he did, he realized there was something off about it. It wasn't just a campfire, not as he had believed.

He had found the town of Varmin.

Jason had visited here once before with his father, but it had been a long time and he could barely remember what it had been like. The journey down with his father had taken the better part of several days, and the return had been nearly a week. That had been a time when he was much more willing and interested in venturing out of the village. He remembered how hard it was to travel this way. His father had worked with him, training him to hunt, and had used it as an opportunity to explore a part of the world they didn't visit as often.

He recalled the buildings themselves. Many of them were made of wood, something not nearly as common up in the village. There they preferred to use ice, and packed it against stone dug out of the mountain itself.

More than that, in Varmin they were far more eager to light fires than they were in the village. There was less of an issue with acquiring the necessary firewood.

Seeing the flickering lights lifted his spirits, if only for a moment.

It reminded him of the festival, and yet knowing what he now did of the festival and the purpose behind it, he couldn't help but think that was a mistake. There was no reason to try to taunt the dragons. And there was no reason to fear them, either. The dragons were only a threat to them because of the Dragon Souls, though he doubted anyone within the village would know that or understand why.

He continued down the mountainside, moving cautiously. Doing so meant he ran the risk of questions, and though there were enough people from his village who visited this far down the mountain, the fact he'd come this way by himself would raise questions.

Jason paused at the outside of the town. Varmin was a large town, spread out over a flattened section of the mountainside and along the slope, built in such a way that it flowed downward.

Not only was there the light from flames inside of buildings, but there was the scent of smoke, that of firewood rather than dung, all of it filling his nostrils. Other smells were there, food baking, the scent of strange spices, and every so often, the sound of a steady thundering.

The first time he heard the thundering, Jason paused. It had been a long time since he'd heard that, and it reminded him of the cannons used by his people during the festival, but he didn't think this thundering came from cannons. It was something else, though he wasn't entirely sure what.

When it came a second time, rumbling beneath him and reminding him of the dragon, he reached for the dragon pearl, gripping it for a moment as he worried there might be some need for its protection.

He needn't have been concerned.

There was no additional rumbling.

He reached the outskirts of the town. He didn't have any money, and he hadn't come with anything to trade. He should have brought the coin pouch he'd taken from Gary, but that remained in his room, hidden.

Jason took a deep breath and started into the town. He

passed a couple of widely spaced buildings. The snow was not nearly as deep here as it was higher up the mountain. His boots crunched in the snow nonetheless, and the longer he made his way, the more he felt the snow beneath him shifting. It was unlike anything he was accustomed to in the higher reaches of the mountain.

He followed the trail into the village, making his way between a series of buildings, and searched for anyone who might be out in the growing darkness.

There was nobody.

So far, he had encountered nothing. The more that he traveled, the more he thought there would be someone here, but he didn't find anyone.

Could everybody be in for the night?

In his village, it was uncommon to come across people out at night. Jason enjoyed the crispness of the evening air and the rarity of stars twinkling overhead. Others feared the snow and storms that came each night.

When he had come here before, he had done so with his father, and they had visited a market, but he saw no sign of the market now.

Perhaps it was closed for the evening.

As he wandered through the street, he didn't find any place to go.

The rumbling came again.

It was close, but more than that, there was something about it that tugged on an awareness within him.

It wasn't the dragon. The ice dragon wasn't going to approach the town of Varmin without Jason summoning him, which meant it was something else. He paused as he reached the southern edge of the town. He still hadn't encountered anyone else, though there were plenty of homes with lights glowing within.

There was a part of him that was tempted to knock on doors, to ask questions, but that wasn't going to get him any answers.

Instead, what he needed was to find a place to settle for the night. In the morning he could venture out, and he could ask the questions he wanted. It would be easier in the daylight rather than the growing darkness. At night like this, he would only raise suspicion.

It would be easier to find others who would recognize he came from the village. There was no harm in revealing that fact, and more than that, he thought it would be beneficial. He might be able to uncover more information that way than he would otherwise.

Where would he settle for the night?

That was his big question. When he had slipped down the mountainside and ended up in the town, he'd had some idea of what to do. He'd traded for the dragon pearl, using that to get money to stay someplace.

He wasn't about to trade the dragon pearl now. He understood its value, and there was more than that to it. He had no interest in losing his connection to the ice dragon, the only thing that would help him find his way back up to his village.

He was empty-handed. Which meant he was going to have to sleep out in the night. With his bearskin coat, he had protection. With the connection to the dragon, he wasn't about to freeze, and if it came down to it, he thought he could use the power through the dragon pearl, though he wondered if doing so would draw the dragon to him.

Shelter.

He wandered, finding a towering pine forest growing near the southern border of the town. The trees were narrow and stretched like fingers toward the sky, covered by fragrant pine needles. He wandered between them and decided that he could stay here. If nothing else, the forest would offer a certain protection, and at least there was less wind here. As far as he could tell, no snow was blowing in, so he wouldn't have to worry about that, either.

Weaving through the trees, he looked for one that might offer him more protection than the rest. Maybe he could find some fallen branches and create a hut for the night.

More than just that, he could start a small fire.

Jason smiled to himself. It had been a long time since he had used wood for a fire.

With the dragon pearl, it would be an easy enough thing to start the fire. He thought the dragon would understand that, and hopefully it wouldn't draw his attention, summoning him.

Nothing his father had ever told him would help him here.

Jason began to gather the fallen branches that he

found. Some of them were little more than strips of needles, and others were larger, and after he had wandered for an hour, he had a sizable pile. He dragged them toward a clearing within the trees. While the pine trees might provide some protection, the fire would offer protection of a different sort.

Jason leaned over, using the dragon pearl, and summoned warmth.

It was a different sensation than when he had drawn through the dragon, trying to use cold. In this case, he was focusing on the warmth within himself, and pulling that out. He thought he was able to do so, that he had enough strength, and in doing so, he could feel the connection to the dragon.

Heat rushed out of him, and it flowed into the dried branches, catching fire. The flames burst upward, tearing through the kindling, and within a few minutes, he had a warm and glowing fire.

Jason sat back, staring at it. He didn't have enough knowledge of how to control fire like this. It was possible he might lose control, but out here where he was, as long as he kept the flame confined within the snow, he thought he would be able to prevent anything worse from happening.

Heat built, crackling through the branches, and he sat in front of it, enjoying that warmth. There was something comforting about it, in a way that he had rarely known comfort, and Jason relaxed.

He started to drift, letting that warmth caress him.

There was no reason he couldn't sleep. He hadn't seen anyone in Varmin, and once coming to the forest, he hadn't encountered anyone here either, so he didn't think he would be disturbed.

As he drifted, he heard a rumbling again.

This forced Jason to sit up. He looked around. It was closer than it had been. When he had detected the rumbling before, he hadn't known where it was or what it indicated, but now that he was here, he couldn't help but think the rumbling came from something nearby.

Getting to his feet, he held on to the dragon pearl, glancing over at the fire. It had burned down a little bit but was still blazing quite brightly, smoke drifting from it and spiraling up into the night sky before disappearing on the wind gusting over the treetops.

Jason backed up, getting near the border of the trees, and he focused on everything around him. He wasn't sure what he might be able to uncover, only that there seemed to be a sense of energy, though that might just be him.

As he focused, he couldn't help but think there was more to it. There was power.

The rumbling came again.

As soon as it did, the power disappeared.

What was he detecting?

Maybe it was nothing, but he couldn't help but feel as if the rumbling were similar to the cannons fired off at the festival—or similar to a dragon.

He had come here looking for evidence of the dragons,

and of hatch mates, but he hadn't really expected to find something so soon.

He focused on the sense of power. Now that it was gone, he wasn't sure there would be any way to locate its origin, but he tried to think through it, concentrating on what he could uncover. There had to be some aspect to it he could detect and trail after.

Slowly, that sense of power began to build again.

This time, Jason closed his eyes, and he drew on a trickle of energy through the dragon pearl. He used the warmth, thinking the cold summons might be a different way of calling to the dragon. And he had used the cold summons before; that had been when the dragon responded, and at this point, he didn't want the dragon to appear. It was possible that whatever was out there, whatever power existed, might be dangerous.

It was even possible it was Dragon Souls.

Jason froze.

Could that be it? He hadn't given it much thought before, but now that he made the connection, he couldn't help but think that the Dragon Souls might be out in the night, searching, and he couldn't help but think they might be responsible for the energy he felt building.

If that were the case, he would need to be much more careful.

He closed his eyes, focusing on that energy again, and let the sense of it continue to build around him. There was a distinct signature to it. That power was there, radiating, but Jason couldn't pinpoint where it was coming from.

He drew upon more energy through the dragon pearl, using his own heat, but that wasn't enough. What if he could use the energy he detected?

There was no reason he shouldn't be able to draw upon that. He could feel it, and it pressed outward upon him, and the more that he felt, the more certain he was that there was something there for him to pick up on. He focused his mind, using as much as he could to reach for the awareness out there. It had to be there, but what was it?

Taking a deep breath, Jason pulled in that power.

At first, there was no change.

But gradually, the sense of energy he detected began to stir around him.

As he focused on it, it began to draw toward him.

And then the rumbling exploded.

It wasn't far from him.

He veered off the path and headed down the slope, making his way carefully. He held on to the dragon pearl, maintaining a connection to it, using his sense of warmth and channeling it through the pearl. All he needed was a possibility of power, though he wasn't entirely sure he would be able to use it in anything other than a destructive sense.

When he'd used the dragon pearl before, he'd destroyed, attacked. The only time he'd done anything differently was when he had connected to the energy within the pearl to repair his bow.

There had to be another way. As he focused on it, he

could feel that energy rising.

He brushed past a pair of pine trees and ignored the needles as they pressed against him. Jason took a deep breath and focused on the energy building. If he could pull that and borrow from it, then he could use it again. What he wanted was to pinpoint the location of the energy rising around him.

Whatever was out there was important.

Jason turned toward the sense of it and had started to draw upon that power when it exploded again.

This time there was a definite rumbling, and it was only a few paces from him.

He started running.

A distant part of his mind knew he should be more careful, knew he should be running away from power like that, not toward it. Whatever power was out there, whatever energy was causing this rumbling, was dangerous to him; and yet, he couldn't help but head toward it, knowing that whatever power he was detecting was something he needed to be a part of.

He wasn't sure whether it was another dragon or whether it was something else entirely. The longer that he ran, the more certain he was that he was going to find something. Dragon Souls or dragon, either would be beneficial to discover.

He began to detect the buildup of energy once again.

This time, he froze, using everything in his being to draw upon that power, feeling the magic surging within him. It flowed through him and he pushed outward with it at the same time, trying to use what he could detect of the magic in order to pinpoint its location.

The rumbling evolved from it, much like it had either time before, and this time, Jason thought he knew where it was.

Below him.

How could that be?

As he focused on it, he couldn't help but think that it had to be below him, but how was that even possible?

The tunnel. A mine.

While his village had tellum mines, Varmin had iron mines.

Could that be what he detected?

Maybe it wasn't anything other than mining activity and not anything magical. They could be using the same explosive powders the people of his village used in the festival. He didn't know enough about the mining process to be sure whether or not that was the case, but it fit.

Jason slowed, looking around, and this time when the power began to build again, he focused on it. Rather than trying to draw upon it, he just listened to it.

It pulled on his senses. It was a strange sensation, almost as if the air became charged with energy. Were his coat off, he suspected the hair on his arms would stand on end. The longer he was here, the more certain he was that the power was continuing to build, and he let it work through him.

He was certain of the source. He had channeled the energy, drawing it through him, and in doing so, he was able to determine the location with much more clarity. What he was looking for was some way to reach the mines.

There was a part of him that worried it was coming from a Dragon Soul. He would need to be careful. He had to keep them from finding the dragon pearl he carried, and he would need to protect the ice dragon as much as he could.

Making a steady circuit, Jason found the darkness outlined near a hillside. Trees grew up on either side of it, and he approached slowly. As he did, he realized what it was. A cave.

If it was the dragon, then he had to investigate.

Family, then village.

This was the reason that he had come here. If only the dragon was able to help him. Then again, the dragon *was* able to help him. He had the dragon's pearl. He had access to that magic.

He focused on the power flowing through him and pushed it outward through the dragon pearl. It began to glow, and he started forward into the cave.

The walls were smooth, leading him to think they might be naturally formed. The ground was slick, though not quite icy. Could this be a stream heading through here? Many caves were formed like that. Not only the cave near his village, but there were the remnants of another that was not nearly as large as the one he had once explored with his father.

He held on to the dragon pearl, holding it up, letting

the light flow over everything. In doing so, he could feel the energy that filled him, flowing away from him and into the length of the tunnel.

Power began to build again. This time, Jason paused, waiting. He hadn't been within the tunnel before when it had exploded, and there was a part of him that worried what might happen, but when the rumbling occurred, he felt it only vaguely.

It was almost as if the tunnel itself served to protect him.

More than ever, he was certain that the power came from underground. He probably should have put out the fire overhead, keeping the forest from burning down, but he didn't think there was anything to be worried about. The flames had been surrounded by the snow, and they were distant enough from the rest of the forest that there shouldn't be any danger there.

Jason followed the contours of the tunnel. It angled downward and then veered off to the right. As it did, and as energy continued to build, he hesitated.

That power was near.

Now that it was near, he was certain it wasn't caused by an explosion. It was almost as if there was an intention behind it.

He started forward, creeping carefully, and when he rounded a curve in the tunnel, light caught his attention. He stuffed the dragon pearl into his pocket, blinking out the light he carried with him.

Someone else was down here.

Jason crept forward, moving slowly, keeping his head and body pressed against the side of the cave. Energy built again and he resisted the urge to pull upon it, to let it flow through him. If he were to do so, it would only run the risk of alerting whoever else was down here, summoning that energy.

That had to be the key. It had to be that someone was summoning it.

Jason reached another branch point. Down one side of the tunnel, it was dark. He tried to peer down the darkness, but his eyes struggled to adjust, even though he had dragon sight. It was almost as if the brightness near him made it more difficult to see. He focused for a moment and then turned his attention away from that tunnel, looking toward the other section. Where the light was coming from.

As he stared, he saw no sign of movement. The only thing he was aware of was the buildup of energy.

He moved carefully.

With every step, he thought he might encounter someone along the tunnel, but there was no sign of anyone.

He noticed the building power again and pushed against it.

It was a strange sensation, partly because the power was rising so quickly, and it began to fill him with an awareness.

He wanted to draw upon it, but he had to ignore it.

When the rumbling occurred, he found it was nearby.

Where, though?

It had to be near enough that he could feel it, but he saw no sign of anything. There was a light somewhere, but even that was faded, so distant that it was difficult for him to determine its location.

There was no one else in the tunnel with him, and Jason began to move more confidently and quickly. As he hurried along the tunnel, a door caught his attention.

He frowned at it. It was made of iron and a swirling pattern of metal created a spiral along the surface, a massive lock hanging on it. He paused, pressing his hand on the door for a moment. Heat radiated from behind it.

That was strange.

He moved on, heading along the tunnel a little farther, and as he did, he came across another door. This one was similar.

It was barred closed and he focused on it, pressing his hands on it as he had the first one, and as before, he could feel the heat radiating from it.

Strange.

He didn't realize that iron mines were warm, and yet, he hadn't spent any time in an iron mine and knew nothing about what was involved.

Maybe they were all hot like this.

The energy began to build again.

This time, it was close. It filled him.

As much as he tried to resist, he couldn't, and the power he detected started to push against him. Jason found himself pushing back, though he worried about doing so.

When the rumbling occurred, it seemed to come from everywhere.

Not just everywhere, but mostly in front of him.

The door.

He had to know what was behind the door.

He might not have a key, and as he looked along the hallway, he found no place where a key might be located. What he had was a dragon pearl, and he knew how to use the energy within it. It was possible he might be able to focus enough power into the lock that he could destroy it. But whatever was on the other side of the door might be dangerous.

If it was, he would have to be prepared to either run or attack.

Jason pressed the dragon pearl up against the lock. He focused on the power within himself and pushed out through the pearl.

It exploded into the lock.

The sound rang out along the tunnel. It was like a bell tolling, the iron ringing, and he covered his ears.

He looked around. There was no one else here, but something like that would draw attention. What was happening on the other side of the door was different, but it wasn't drawing nearly the same attention that he was.

As Jason pulled on power again, letting it flow through him. He thought there had to be some way to use what he was detecting.

He drew upon that power.

It exploded again.

Once more, the sound of a bell ringing echoed along the length of the tunnel.

At that point, he was tempted to turn around and head back out of the tunnel, but the energy built from the other side of the door. This time, it grew quickly, and when it rumbled, it did so with a violent sort of energy.

It was almost as if that energy were calling to him, demanding he open the door.

There was some intention behind it, and he thought he had to find out why.

Jason pushed the dragon pearl up against the lock again, and he started to pull on his own energy. The power that he detected from the other side of the door began to build once more, and rather than ignoring it or pushing it away, he decided to draw upon it. He would use that power, whatever it was, and he would see if he could summon that in a way that would allow him to unlock this door.

When the power flowed through him, he slammed into the door. It exploded.

The lock snapped.

There came another tolling of a bell, a ringing much like before, but he ignored it as he pushed on the door. It swung open. Heat wafted out, almost more than he could take.

Jason looked around the inside of this room. There

was a softly glowing orange light, and it permeated everything.

He was in a narrow hallway. It ran parallel to the hall he had been in, and behind it were rows of bars.

At first, he wasn't sure what the bars were for. Then the light began to dissipate, enough that he was able to see more clearly, and as he did, he realized what it was and why he was seeing it.

They weren't just bars. They were cells.

And on the other side of the cell was a dragon.

8

He froze in place, staring at the dragon. This one looked nothing like the ice dragon, and it looked nothing like the dragons he'd seen with Henry near Dragon Haven. This one was all dark scaled, and there was something off about it.

It turned its head toward Jason, eyes blazing a bright orange, and energy began to build. As it did, the darkness on the dragon faded, becoming a matching orange, glowing with an intense heat.

The dragon exploding power against its cell had been what he'd felt.

There was incredible heat. More than he could bear. When he had been around Henry and his dragon, there had been nothing like that, and when the dragon had taken on heat, it had not become unbearable to be near, but this was something else.

Jason took a step back. "I'm here to help."

He didn't know if the dragon was able to understand him, didn't know if it could read his mind the same way the ice dragon could, but if it could, he wanted the dragon to know that he meant it no harm.

The heat began to fade.

"Can you understand me?"

"Yes," came a deep, rumbling voice.

"How long have you been held here?"

"Long."

That didn't help him. The ice dragon didn't have a good sense of time, so why should this dragon?

Either way, he knew what he had to do.

Family first...

"Is there any way I can help you get out?"

He didn't see any sign of a lock or any other way of freeing the dragon. It was almost as if the dragon had been dropped in here, and yet, there had to be something. The bars were all of stone, slatted so narrowly that the dragon wouldn't be able to escape, and Jason walked along the outer edge, searching for some way to get to the creature, but there wasn't anything.

There had to have been a way of getting the dragon in, so there had to be some way of getting the dragon out.

He looked at the bars, and yet he couldn't find anything.

"You can't escape, can you?"

"I cannot."

He pulled out the dragon pearl and pressed it against the stone and focused on the heat, pushing it into the stone. It exploded against the bars, but nothing else happened.

Then again, why would he have expected anything to happen? It would be the same thing that the dragon was doing. It was trying to draw heat, and that was what Jason was doing.

"I'm going to do what I can to get you out of here, but then you're going to have to hide."

He had no idea where the dragon could even hide. If the ice dragon preferred the cold and the snow, what would this dragon prefer? There was nothing like this. Even when he had been with Henry, he'd never experienced a dragon like it, which told him that whatever Therin had been attempting with the ice dragon had been done to this one. Again, an environment had been used to influence the dragon.

Jason took a deep breath, focusing on the bar, and tried to push power out again, but once again, nothing changed.

What about cold?

The more that he focused on heat, the less likely it was that he would be successful, but he hadn't tried anything with cold yet.

He wasn't even sure if he'd be able to call upon the cold here. It was possible he wouldn't, but as he considered it, he thought that there had to be some way to use it. There was no cold within him, not here, but could he draw it through the dragon pearl?

It would be power coming from the dragon, and if he

did it wrong, it would run the risk of summoning the dragon, but in this case, he thought that was necessary. This was the reason they had come here.

Family first.

Jason focused, and as he did, he tried reaching for the power within him, the sense of cold, and when it didn't come, he tried again.

There was no sense of cold.

If he was wrong, and if this failed, then an opportunity to return and help the dragon would fail. He doubted he would be given another chance to get down here without others observing him. And even if he did, there would be the likelihood he would have to battle to find his way down.

It had to be now.

He squeezed his eyes shut, focusing on the ice dragon. He forced an image of what he had encountered into his mind, thinking about the connection he believed was there between them, even if he wasn't able to access it. The ice dragon could reach it. And in doing so, he could understand what Jason needed, and he would recognize that he needed that power, the connection, and the cold.

The sense of it began to build deep within him.

Jason pulled on it, drawing everything that he could, focusing it through the dragon pearl. He held his hand out, pushing the pearl up against one of the bars, and let that energy, that cold within him, continue to expand.

Sound came from somewhere nearby, but he had to ignore it.

He needed to focus.

How could he focus when there was this sense coming near him? If they knew about the dragon and if they knew what he was doing, then they might be here to stop him.

Which meant that he had to work fast.

Jason continued to focus on the sense of cold, trying to draw something toward him, but there was no response. The longer he focused, the less likely it was he'd be able to get anything to work. There was too much distraction near him, and as much as he wanted to break the dragon free, he wasn't sure if he'd be able to.

"I'm trying, but I don't know if I can do anything more," he said.

The dragon rumbled and there came another surge of pressure, this one reminding him of what he had experienced when he had been around the ice dragon. He focused on that sense, trying to use whatever he could to uncover some way of reaching for the cold he would need. How could he do so?

Attempting it was challenging, and as much as he wanted to, as much as he strained against it, he couldn't find any way to reach what he needed in order to save the dragon.

Jason looked up. He wasn't going to be able to stop this, and whoever was coming moved quickly. The sound of them hurrying along the hall called to him, and yet, he didn't know what else he could do.

He gripped the bars, trying to look through them,

wishing there was something he could do to help the dragon, and yet there didn't seem to be.

"I don't have anything more," he said.

The dragon rumbled and he focused on that power, knowing there would have to be something, some way to reach for it, but he couldn't figure out what it was going to take. If it wasn't the cold, then what was it?

The heat hadn't worked for him, either, and though he thought there had to be some way to use that, he couldn't determine what it would be. He couldn't determine what it would take.

Fear set his heart to fluttering. He had come here chasing the sound, but if he thought about it, he had never really expected to find a dragon.

Somehow, Jason had to do whatever he could to release the dragon, and he had to find it within himself. It was a matter of chasing down that strange stirring, that sense of cold that he was so accustomed to.

That was the key.

It was a familiarity with the cold, and he was more than just familiar with it. It was a part of him. It was everything that he knew, and the more that he thought about it, the more certain he was that he could find some way of reaching for it.

The only question was how.

Jason focused, drawing on that energy, that sense within him, and the more he homed in on it, the more he could pull upon it, and he reached for it.

It flowed through him.

He continued to call upon it, to draw it forth, and he pushed it into the dragon pearl. As the cold leached out, washing away from him, into the dragon pearl, the bars of the cage began to grow colder.

He didn't know if it would be enough.

His connection to heat hadn't been enough, but now that he was focused on the cold, he was certain it should work.

But cold alone wasn't going to be enough to shatter the bars.

The dragon turned toward him. Its body started to glow and heat began to radiate from it.

"I'm trying to help," Jason said.

It was harder and harder to hold on to the cold as the dragon began to glow with an increasing intensity. He was pulling on the power of the cold, on the ice that flowed through him. He was as much a part of it as the dragon now was.

The heat continued to radiate from the dragon.

Jason tried to ignore it, to focus on anything else, and yet he could not.

All he could feel was the heat coming off the dragon.

Without wanting to, he took a step back.

The dragon belched flames where he'd been standing.

Noise near the doorway caught his attention, and three figures appeared.

Jason clutched the dragon pearl, trying to focus on the cold, on some way of attacking, and yet, power didn't flow through him as it had before. He was growing tired, and everything he'd used in order to draw power had begun to overwhelm him.

Something shattered.

Jason spun to see the dragon shoving his head through a crack in the cell. It swiveled toward the three men, and flames streamed toward them.

When the fire was gone, nothing was left but ash.

The dragon backed up but kept his head partway through the bars of the cell.

"Again."

Jason looked at the dragon pearl. The combination of the ice and then the heat had allowed the dragon to explode outward. He had not been strong enough with the heat, and he doubted he'd even be strong enough with the ice, but combining his connection to the ice and the dragon's to the heat, he'd managed to do it.

He hurried forward, choosing a different section of the cell, near enough that if it worked, he might be able to break free a large enough section for the dragon to escape.

If it worked, the dragon would be freed. Jason would have succeeded in this step.

And then what?

Then he would have to find some way of summoning the ice dragon, though Jason wasn't even sure if he had any way of doing so.

He thought about what he had done before, feeling the way the cold had fluttered through him. It was a part of him, and he could use that. He had to use that.

As he focused, he could feel that cold working its way through him.

He breathed it in and then pushed it out through the dragon pearl.

Once again, cold began to work its way along the bars of the cage, and he continued to push, sending as much power as he could through it, more and more working its way out from him, through the dragon pearl, and into the bars blocking the dragon.

Ice began to form beneath his hand, and it spread all along the cell. Without the fear of someone approaching, he was able to push even more power through it than he had before.

Then he could feel heat radiating from the dragon again.

Jason stepped back, knowing what the dragon wanted from him.

Heat exploded. The dragon's body began to glow orange, almost like molten metal.

As he looked at the dragon, he realized that was exactly what it was. That was why he had thought it so strange before.

It wasn't so much that the dragon was glowing with a bright orange flame as it was heating up like metal.

Like iron.

His breath caught as he thought he understood.

Much like the ice dragon had taken on characteristics of his village, the iron dragon had taken on aspects of this place.

How many others would the Dragon Souls have placed? How many other dragons would there be like this?

Hatch mates. That was what the ice dragon was after. Others like him.

Family first.

Jason let out a shaky breath.

It seemed impossible to believe that the dragon would be made of iron, and yet, how would that be any different than the dragon made of ice?

The bars exploded.

He raised his arm, covering his face, but the shards parted around him. Some of them were hot, and they sizzled, hissing in the air as they passed him.

When they were gone, he looked over to see the dragon poking its head through the bars. The hole was almost large enough for his body to come through.

"Again," the dragon demanded.

Jason nodded, and he approached another section of the cell.

As he began to focus on the cold, he wondered if he was going to be strong enough. Having pulled enough power through himself like this, it was possible he'd already expended himself far more than he could withstand. He had no idea what limitations he might possess when it came to using this power. It might be he had no real limits, but it might be that he had significant restrictions that would prevent him from being able to draw upon as much power as he wanted.

As he felt the cold working through him, as that power

was flowing, Jason continued to pull upon it, drawing it through him, and he let it out. The bars turned to ice, no different than they had before.

Heat radiated from the dragon's side as it stepped forward. It pressed its body up against the cell, and as before, those bars shattered, exploding outward with a violent force.

When the dust and haze cleared, he looked around. The dragon was able to fold his wings in and make his way out, squeezing between the bars of the cell, and he stepped out toward Jason.

With a loud roar, flames erupted from the dragon. The entire body of the creature glowed. It seemed as if his body flowed, like metal shifting.

It was quite beautiful.

"Come on. We need to get you out of here."

He wondered if the dragon would let him lead, and yet, if he didn't, Jason wasn't sure that he would be able to help as much as he wanted to.

The dragon stepped off to the side and Jason hurried to the door. He held on to the dragon pearl, though fatigue began to work through him. If it came down to it, he would use whatever power he could, but it might be up to the molten dragon to handle things on his behalf.

The hallway was empty. It was narrow, and he hadn't considered that before, but how would the dragon be able to get out of there?

Jason needn't have worried. The dragon folded his wings in and slithered along the hall behind him, moving almost like a snake. The entire time he did, his body glowed. It was difficult for Jason to even look at, and he had to hurry to stay ahead of the heat radiating off the dragon.

When he'd come through here before, it had been darkened and he'd had only the dragon pearl for light, but this time, he was working through here with the light of the dragon guiding him, and he moved far more rapidly than he had before.

The dragon rumbled.

It reminded Jason of what he had tracked, the sounds that had brought him here.

There were shapes in the distance.

The dragon pressed his face up to Jason. He could feel heat radiating from his nostrils, steam that burned, hot through his bearskin coat. His face felt painfully sharp. "Move over."

Jason jerked himself off to the side, getting away from the dragon. He pressed against the wall and heat exploded.

Flames scorched along the hallway, illuminating everything in front of him. Briefly Jason could make out figures along the hallway, but then that moment passed and whatever figures were there disappeared, burned in a cloud of ash.

He shivered.

He ran forward, racing toward the end of the hallway. The dragon slithered behind him, the sound of it strange, a squealing, and it mixed with a steady hissing.

By the time he reached the entrance to the cave, Jason was exhausted.

He peeked his head outside, worried that he might encounter someone he had wanted to avoid, and yet the night was calm. It was dark. A hint of a cool wind gusted, welcome relief after the heat inside the cave radiating off the dragon.

The dragon pushed behind him, and Jason staggered out into the opening.

When he did, the dragon followed, slithering behind him.

And then light exploded all around them.

9

J ason shielded his eyes. Within the cave, the light had been behind him, allowing him to better make out what was in the distance, and his eyes hadn't fully adjusted to the brightness. With the overwhelming light all around him, he struggled.

For a moment, he thought it came from lantern light, but the longer he stared, the more certain he was that wasn't it at all.

Dragon Souls.

That had to be the source of the light, and as Jason looked around, he could practically feel the power radiating off the Dragon Souls. They were near him, and he steadied his breathing, worried they might attack, but there was no sign of an attack.

"What is this?" the dragon rumbled.

"I don't know."

Heat exploded from the dragon.

As it did, Jason counted five dark-cloaked figures surrounding them. They had taken up positions all around them, and each of them carried a dragon pearl. How many had something *more* than just a dragon pearl?

It was possible the Dragon Souls were prepared to try to control the dragon. Wasn't that what they did? When he'd been working with Henry, he had understood the Dragon Souls used their power and their magic in order to dominate the dragon, and Jason was determined to try to prevent that, and yet, he wasn't sure he would be able to do so.

He glanced back at the dragon. It was hard to tell whether the creature was fighting or not, or whether there was anything else taking place, but the glowing of his scales continued.

"You're going to have to fight," he said to the dragon.

The heat continued to build, radiating off the creature, and flames erupted from his nostrils. He spread them around the clearing, and when they burned off, the figures remained standing.

Dragonskin.

That wasn't good.

Jason focused on his dragon pearl. It had worked inside the cave, and he had to wonder if he could do the same thing out here. If he could, maybe he and the dragon could work together.

As he began to focus on the cold, something changed.

The dragon began to retreat, the heat radiating from it

shifting, the molten nature of his skin and scales beginning to lighten.

"You have to fight whatever it is," Jason said.

He focused on the cold, the familiarity of it, the way it caressed him. He was able to draw upon the wind out here, thinking about how it gusted out of the northern mountain, and the snow and ice that came with it. He was filled with the power of it. He connected from that cold to the ice dragon, and pushed power out from the dragon pearl.

He let it explode from him.

It washed outward, a wave of it, and he looked at the iron dragon.

"You need to use your power now."

The dragon seemed to ignore him.

"Now, or you'll be captured again!"

That seemed to shake something within the dragon, and the heat built once more. It exploded outward. In doing so, it slammed into the others, and combined with the cold that Jason had been summoning, they were able to pull upon enough power to overwhelm the Dragon Souls.

They were thrown back.

Jason scrambled toward the dragon. When he reached it, he wondered if he would be able to withstand its heat.

"I'm going to need you to fly us out of here."

"Fly?"

"You're a dragon. You have wings. You need to fly."

"I've not flown."

Jason swore under his breath. How was he supposed to teach a dragon how to fly? That wasn't supposed to be his responsibility, but if the dragon had been captured and trapped since he'd hatched, it was possible the dragon had no idea how to fly—or even whether he *could* do so.

The Dragon Souls were beginning to get up.

There wouldn't be much time before they realized he was as much of a threat as the dragon, and if they realized he'd used ice, the cold from the ice dragon, then they would know that dragon existed.

He focused on the cold again, drawing it through him, and pushed outward.

The effect wasn't nearly as strong as before. The dragon reacted, pushing outward, using his connection to the heat and flame, and as he did, the Dragon Souls were thrown backward once again.

The combination of ice and fire had been enough, but how much longer would it last before the Dragon Souls were able to figure out some way of withstanding even that? Jason had seen how Therin and the other Dragon Souls had navigated the northern cold, but suspected that it took some amount of time before they were able to do so.

He reached the dragon. He held his hand out, worried it would be too hot for him to withstand, and as he felt the heat radiating off the creature, he hesitated. Surprisingly, he was able to tolerate it, and he touched the dragon's neck.

"Let me climb on," he said.

The dragon swiveled his massive head toward him, his eyes glowing, and he regarded Jason for a long moment.

"I have no reason to hurt you. I want to help you. I want to make sure no one else can hurt you."

The dragon lowered his head and Jason quickly climbed on.

Its body was hot, though not unbearably so. He worried what would happen if it became molten again, but for now, he was able to grab on, and he could withstand the strange heat, the metallic feel to the dragon, and he gripped the creature.

"We can go," Jason said.

The dragon turned his head, looking at him, and as he did, the Dragon Souls began to move.

"Flap your wings," he said.

The dragon stretched out his wings and tried to flap them, but nothing happened. And as an iron dragon, it was possible that he might not even be able to fly. Maybe this kind of dragon was incapable of that.

Jason frowned to himself.

"Run," he said.

The dragon understood what that meant, and he took off, squeezing between the trees, and as he neared some of the Dragon Souls, his tail swung around and carved through two of the nearest ones.

They were split in half, and Jason turned away from the gore.

Not just an iron dragon, but one with a tail like a sword.

The dragon ran, the ground rumbling beneath his giant claws, and he continued to hurry, but Jason spun on his back, looking behind him. The Dragon Souls were chasing, and they were moving quickly.

Of course they would be. They understood the nature of their power, and they understood what it took to use their power, so it shouldn't be surprising at all that they would be able to keep pace.

There had to be some way to keep ahead of them, but what was it?

Jason focused on the dragon pearl, clutching it tightly, and pulled upon cold.

Maybe the ice dragon would recognize his need, but if he did, then it was possible he would be summoned and then two dragons would be in danger.

It was best if only one dragon struggled.

Jason released his hold.

"Run down the slope," he said.

All of this to find the dragon, and he still hadn't the opportunity to ask anybody about dragons. Here he'd thought he might come here and find answers, and yet he'd had no idea that he would be rescuing a dragon like this.

They struck a tree. The dragon bounced off but Jason started to slide. He grabbed tightly, holding on to the dragon's back, clinging to it. His fingers slipped between its scales, and he felt heat radiating from that spot, so he jerked his hands back, sliding along the dragon's spine.

He scrambled forward.

That was a mistake. What he needed was some way of holding on to the dragon, but without burning himself.

It was possible the dragon couldn't be held on to, not by him. Given how much heat radiated from the dragon, it might be more than he could withstand.

Jason hurried, scrambling up the neck of the dragon, and latched on once again. The heat radiating from the dragon was immense, but somehow didn't burn him. The dragon bounced off another tree, and this time, his tail swung around, catching one of the tall pine trees. It spun all the way through, cleaving it as if it were a giant axe, and the tree began to fall, dropping behind them.

A barrier.

"Keep doing that," he said.

The dragon growled and yet his tail flipped from side to side, and each time it struck a tree, it cleaved all the way through it.

Heat surged as it did, and Jason couldn't help but feel as if the dragon understood exactly what he needed. The trees were knocked down as they went, leaving destruction, but better than that, blocking the Dragon Souls from easily reaching them.

They had to find some way to escape, some place to hide, and yet out here, Jason had no idea where the dragon could hide. He had no idea what he could do to help protect the dragon, if there was anything at all. It was possible there wouldn't be any way to protect it.

He allowed the dragon to keep running, saying nothing, just clinging to its back.

The dragon raced forward, scrambling, and then it dropped to its belly and started slithering. It was the same way the dragon had moved through the tunnel, and surprisingly, it was able to move even faster. It was flowing along the ground.

It left a trail, and that trail would be easy to follow, but he suspected there would be a trail regardless. It wouldn't matter whether the dragon was running or whether it was sliding. There would be a path behind him either way.

Jason could do nothing else but hang on.

As he did, he focused on the ice dragon. He thought about the power he needed, and he wondered if the ice dragon might have some way of helping him hide.

"We need to find someplace to disappear," he said.

The iron dragon rumbled again, and heat exploded from his mouth.

They had reached a denser part of the forest and they bounced between trees, though not nearly as violently as Jason would've expected. It was almost as if the dragon were able to slither between them, to avoid most of them, but every so often, they would fully slam into one and Jason would go jostling along the dragon's back. Thankfully, he'd uncovered a way of holding on to the dragon by gripping the spikes along his neck, but it was almost not enough.

As he gripped the dragon's back, he squeezed, wrapping his arms and legs around the dragon, clinging as tightly as he could, afraid of being tossed off. If that were to happen, Jason doubted that he would be fast enough to be able to catch up to the dragon again.

"There is a place," the dragon said.

It came like a hissing sound and the creature jumped forward, getting back to his legs, and then went running. The dragon moved far faster than Jason would've expected given his size, and he scrambled within the trees, managing to avoid most of them, and when approaching those that he couldn't, he lowered his head. Jason learned to drop down, and when the dragon crashed into the trees, he no longer felt them with the same force. He was able to let the dragon absorb most of it.

When the dragon struck the trees, they trembled before falling.

It was amazing how powerful the dragon was. The way the dragon was able to crash into the trees, knocking them down, left him marveling at his strength, but it also left him wondering how much destruction they would leave in their wake.

It would be enough reason for the Dragon Souls to chase the dragon.

"You have to find some way of moving without leaving a trace," he said.

"Why?"

"These others who are after us will try to use you."

"They would not be able to use me."

"They have some way of influencing dragons. Perhaps controlling them. I don't really understand it, but I do know they will try to take your power. That's the reason you were brought here."

"What do you know about it?"

"I'm guessing you were brought here as an egg. The mine influenced you."

"Why would you think that?"

"You're different than other dragons."

"How many dragons do you know?"

"Not enough, but enough to know that you're different."

The dragon managed to slither around the trees, and as he looked behind him, Jason didn't see any sign of their passing. It was almost as if the dragon was doing exactly as he asked, trying to keep from leaving any footprints as they ran through the forest. The trees began to thin out and it was easier for the dragon to work his way around them. He reached a stream and ran alongside it. The dragon avoided stepping into the water, and Jason couldn't help but wonder what would happen if the dragon did go into the stream. Would the water affect him the same way that it affected metal?

It was possible it would, which was reason for the dragon to avoid it. It was different than the ice dragon, a creature that could tolerate the cold in the water, but they would have to explore that distinction later, to try to understand just what everything meant for the dragon. For now, they needed to find a way to get him to safety.

"Where are you going?"

"You suggested a place," the dragon said.

"No. I suggested you find a place that you know would be safe."

"A place calls to me."

"How does it call to you?"

"I feel it."

Could it be another of the hatch mates? It was unlikely the dragon would be able to detect that so clearly, especially as the ice dragon couldn't. Then again, what did Jason know about this dragon at all?

The dragon began to run more rapidly.

They were on open ground, and there was no snow on the ground. That was a strange thing, but even stranger was the way the dragon suddenly dropped.

The change was jarring, and he hadn't expected it, but the dragon swept his wings out and they glided, though they slid along the surface of the ground nonetheless.

Below them was darkness.

Jason wasn't able to determine what it was, only that it was blackened, and yet, the dragon seemed comfortable, familiar with it in a way that Jason was not. As they descended, he clung to the dragon's back, thinking that if nothing else, if they were to crash, he would be protected by the dragon.

Then they glided to a stop.

The dragon scrambled forward. Walls surrounded them.

Jason kept his head down, clinging to the dragon's neck, and when the dragon began to slither forward again, sliding along the surface, he stayed there, afraid to move.

They slithered for an impossibly long period of time, moving deep underground, and then the dragon came to a stop.

Jason lifted his head, looking around, afraid of what he might find. Surprisingly, they were in a massive cavern.

Heat began to build from the dragon and Jason scrambled down, not wanting to get burned, and he looked all around, taking in the sight of the walls and of everything else, and realized what this was.

An iron mine.

He'd never seen one, and even though he'd been near one in Varmin, he wasn't sure the cell the dragon had been in represented a typical iron mine. This, on the other hand, had to be one.

They were in a massive chamber, and all around were other side tunnels. There was nothing but darkness in them, and yet, he had a sense the dragon knew exactly where they were and whether there was anyone else around them to be worried about.

"How did you know about this place?"

The dragon continued to glow, the heat radiating off his body giving off enough light to illuminate the entirety of the chamber. The walls were artificially made, scraped by pick and hammer, and yet the inside of the space was enormous. In the distance, it seemed as if there was a drop-off, and Jason feared to get too close to it. For all the time that he had lived atop the mountain, he'd never expected to go inside of it.

"I could feel it. It draws me."

"I don't understand what that means."

"This place calls to me."

Jason looked around. "Are there any others here?"

He studied the walls, the markings that were on them, and wondered how long ago it had been occupied. There had to be others here, and yet he didn't see anything that signified another presence. The mine itself was completely empty, and because of that, he had to believe they were relatively safe.

Perhaps he could call to the ice dragon.

Then again, he wondered if the ice dragon would be able to tolerate a place like this. He needed snow and cold, and in coming here, the ice dragon might be somehow diminished.

"There are no others here."

"Are you sure?"

"I would know."

He nodded. He wasn't about to challenge the dragon, especially as he suspected that it would know.

How long would they stay here?

It was possible one of these other tunnels would lead back out, and if so, then Jason could use it to explore.

"Is this the only way in?"

"No."

"How do you know?"

"I just know."

He maneuvered so that he could stand right in front of the dragon. He looked up at the massive creature, meeting the dragon's eyes. "How is it that you know?"

The dragon took in a deep breath, and when he let it out, there was a mixture of steam and a faint orange glow to it. "The knowledge is there. I don't understand why I should have it, but I do."

Jason thought he understood. The dragon was born to this place, the same way the ice dragon had been born to the upper mountains. He had an innate knowledge of the tunnels, of the mine, and because of that, he would know all of the ways through here.

That was valuable to them, considering they didn't know how long they would be trapped here and whether there would be others coming.

"There's another dragon out there I need to get word to."

The iron dragon looked down at him. "Is this one controlled by those others?"

Jason shook his head and held up the dragon pearl. He pushed as much cold into it as he could. Within the mine, as humid as it was, he found it more difficult to do so, but the longer he tried in places like this, where he shouldn't otherwise be able to reach the cold, the easier it became. He was connected to that cold, probably the same way that the dragon here was connected to the mine. He was able to use that connection, that power, and because of it, he was able to push through the dragon pearl, using that to summon a sense of cold.

It was barely more than a hint of cold, nothing more than that, and yet as he summoned it, the pearl took on a pale white glow.

"He's not controlled by the others. The dragon allows me to borrow from his power."

It was a strange thing to think of, and yet that was the truth. The dragon did allow him to borrow from it. Because of it, Jason couldn't help but think he should be able to do more with that power.

The dragon knew of him. The dragon knew he had his dragon pearl. If Jason could continue to control that, if he could use that, then he might be able to summon the dragon down here. It would involve somehow showing the dragon where he was, and unless he knew, it was possible that he wouldn't be able to do so.

"You may bring him here."

"I don't know how to show him where this is."

The dragon breathed a streamer of fire from his nostrils, illuminating one of the tunnels. "Take that shaft. You can use it to reach the surface quickly."

"How quickly?"

"Quickly."

"Why didn't we take that way?"

Jason leaned forward, pushing the dragon pearl in front of him and letting more power flow from him, and as he did, he realized why they hadn't taken that route. The shaft was far narrower than the other ones. It was possible the iron dragon couldn't make his way out through the narrow tunnel.

"I would not have fit."

Jason took a step back, regarding the iron dragon. The iron dragon might not fit down that tunnel, but the ice dragon wasn't nearly as large, at least not yet. In time, it was possible the iron dragon and the ice dragon would be the same size, and yet, for now, the ice dragon was smaller.

He hurried forward, reaching the tunnel, and he crawled through it.

As the iron dragon had said, the tunnel was narrow, but not so narrow that he couldn't make his way along it. He hurried forward, and every so often, he glanced back, worrying the dragon was unsafe. He didn't like the idea of leaving the dragon behind him, not when the Dragon Souls were out, though there were fewer than when they had first been attacked.

How long would it take for them to summon other Dragon Souls here? Once they knew there was an iron dragon in existence, they would bring reinforcements.

It was the same thing that would happen when they realized the ice dragon existed.

And here Jason had thought all he had to worry about was the ice dragon, but now with the iron dragon, he had to be concerned about much more. He had to worry about what the Dragon Souls might do and how much more they might attempt, and yet, he was even more determined to ensure that the dragons remained safe.

The tunnel led up at a sharp angle, and he found himself holding on to the wall as he climbed. There was no sense of movement, but a breeze began to drift along the length of the tunnel.

Jason remained motionless for a long moment, watching, and as he did, he wasn't sure if there was something there he couldn't yet see. The longer he remained, the more uncertain he was about what was there.

The tunnel stretched in front of him, far longer than he cared for, and he felt it begin to narrow, leaving him to wonder if the ice dragon would even be able to make it along the tunnel. It was possible it was far too narrow for the ice dragon to be able to get through here safely.

And then it widened again.

As soon as it did, Jason tested to see whether there would be enough room for the dragon to maneuver, and as he stretched his arms apart, he thought that there would be.

He hurried along the length of the tunnel, and when he felt a gust of breeze, he knew he was getting close to the very end of it. He moved faster and focused on the dragon pearl, using the cool breeze it was gusting through here, letting it flow over him, knowing that if he could reach the power within the dragon pearl, he should be able to summon the ice dragon.

And yet, he didn't want to call the ice dragon too soon. It was possible there was a Dragon Soul out there, and he would need to be careful. He didn't want to draw their attention to the fact that he had an ice dragon.

Unless they already knew. How many times had he used the dragon pearl in order to rescue the iron dragon? It had been quite a few, and because he'd drawn on the cold flowing through the dragon pearl, he had to think they would be aware of what he had done.

If they knew that, then they might know there was an ice dragon, and that was counting on the fact that Therin hadn't survived. If he had, then it was even more likely that they were aware of the ice dragon.

Jason stood at the end of the tunnel.

There was nothing more than a drop-off in front of him.

An enormous gorge opened up. Far below, he could hear the sound of rushing water, and he imagined that the stream that originated in his mountain emptied out here, though he didn't know if that was even possible. He did know the stream wrapped around, winding along the back face of the mountain. As it did, it gained additional power, flowing faster and faster before becoming a water-fall down to the base. As far as he knew, that would be where Therin had ended up, and if he had—and if he had survived—then Therin might know what had happened to him, how he had come to be encased in ice.

Jason looked all around, focusing on the sense of the dragon.

From here, there was enough of a chill to the air that he didn't feel as if it were unsafe to summon the dragon. He thought that he could call to it, and in doing so, he could alert the dragon to the fact that he still lived.

He pulled on power. He called slowly through the dragon pearl, letting that energy increase, growing in intensity. The more he pulled upon that power, the more he felt it flowing through him, and the more certain he was that there was something to it.

At first, he detected nothing. The energy swirled around him, and Jason was certain something was there for him, but he didn't know what it was.

Gradually, that energy began to build, and he realized that it represented the dragon.

It was getting closer.

Movement in the sky caught his attention, and it surprised him that the dragon was much closer than he would've expected. It was swooping down, darting from high overhead, and it blended in with the gray skies.

Then the dragon appeared before him.

"I found one of your hatch mates," he said.

The dragon rumbled. "Where?"

"Up near that city. You should know something, though."

"What should I know?"

"The dragon isn't anything like you."

"How is he?"

"Much like you took on features of the ice and the mountains, this dragon took on features of this place."

"Such as what?"

"He has taken on characteristics of the metal mined here."

He waited for the dragon to respond, and he worried about what response the dragon might have, but there was none.

"I think you can fit down this tunnel, but it is going to be tight," Jason said.

There might be another way for the ice dragon to

reach the iron dragon, but it involved taking a pathway that Jason didn't fully know, and then he would run the risk of getting lost trying to reconnect with the iron dragon.

"Move back," the ice dragon said.

He backed down the tunnel, and within a moment, the ice dragon squeezed into the mouth of the cave. As the dragon's wings folded, he slid in, reminding Jason of how the iron dragon had slithered across the ground. The ice dragon pushed out with cold and the ground began to crackle, forming a slick surface. The dragon slid, forcing Jason in front of him.

They moved with increasing speed, and the dragon glided all the way down through the tunnel. It was an interesting technique, and almost more impressive than the way the fire dragon had slid. At least with the ice dragon, there wouldn't be any long-term effects for anyone to know that they had been here. The ice would melt, and there would be nothing more than water.

They shot forward, and when they staggered free into the cavernous opening, Jason rolled to his feet, looking all around.

Where was the iron dragon?

He found no sign of it.

10

The ice dragon was near, and cold glowed from him.
Jason held out the dragon pearl, drawing upon the power of the dragon, igniting the pearl so the cavern glowed with a soft white light.

"He was here," Jason said.

"Could the others have reached him?"

"There were Dragon Souls nearby, but we stayed ahead of them. They wouldn't have been able to catch him."

The dragon rumbled and Jason looked around, a growing irritation filling him. Had he made a mistake? It was possible that he could have summoned the ice dragon from in here, and if he had done that, then nothing would have happened to the iron dragon.

Would there be any way of detecting the heat from the iron dragon?

It was possible, but perhaps not without a dragon pearl.

He looked around, staring at the ground, and he found a small nugget of metal.

When he crouched down in front of it, he realized it reminded him of a dragon pearl.

The surface was smooth, still warm, and yet as he held it out, it was almost perfectly round, far more round than it should be for anything natural.

He turned toward the ice dragon. "I think this is a dragon pearl from the iron dragon."

"Then something happened."

"That's the only way a dragon pearl would be left?" Jason honestly didn't know. When he had come across the ice dragon's pearl, he had thought it had been intentional, but perhaps it had been left accidentally. If so, then this being left behind indicated that something was wrong.

If that were the case, then Jason would need to focus. It was possible he could use the energy within the dragon pearl, and then maybe they would be able to determine what had happened to the iron dragon.

He held on to the metal and focused on the heat within it, connecting to that heat which was within himself, and he strained.

He might not be a full Dragon Soul, and he might only have a partial ability with that power, but he thought he should be able to reach for that heat. He had done so before, and that was when he wasn't even that familiar with the dragon paired with this pearl.

No sense of heat responded.

It was emptiness. Nothing.

Jason looked around. There were nearly a dozen different tunnels. The iron dragon could have gone through any of them. The Dragon Souls could have summoned the iron dragon, dragging him free, giving the dragon no choice but to follow. They had been lucky to escape, but perhaps they hadn't really escaped as well as they had thought.

He breathed out. "Do you have any way of detecting your hatch mates?"

"He is near," the ice dragon said.

"How can you tell?"

"I can feel him."

"If you can feel him, then tell him it's all right to return."

The ice dragon rumbled.

There was no response.

Jason hadn't really expected there to be, though he had been hopeful that there might be something. The longer he sat there, feeling the iron dragon pearl in his hand, the more he hoped there might be some way of using that power, and yet, he wasn't at all surprised that there wasn't.

He thought about what he knew of the dragons and realized that the connection to the iron dragon would be different. It wasn't just heat, it was that of molten metal. Jason might have a link to the other type of dragon pearl, but this dragon, and this pearl, was something else.

He frowned to himself. Perhaps that was the point.

He couldn't connect through the iron dragon's pearl. At least, not in that form.

He held out the ice dragon pearl. Focusing on the energy within it, he borrowed power from the ice dragon and sent it surging into the pearl. As he did, the power flowed. It went slowly at first and then picked up intensity. It was almost as if the ice dragon had resisted, waiting to see what Jason might do. And all he was doing was sending energy skirting along the various pathways. He wasn't attempting anything else, and he didn't have the necessary control to do much else, but he thought that he might be able to hold on to what he could detect. And if he could, then perhaps he could uncover a sense of the dragon.

As he pushed outward, the power was uncontrolled. A circle of cold, and yet, he was aware of how it washed through the various tunnels. It radiated away from him, rolling down the tunnels, and as it did, Jason focused on it, feeling that power.

There was something there.

He turned, focusing on only one of the tunnels now. He continued to draw cold through the ice dragon, letting that power wash through him, toward the tunnel, and then beyond.

In doing so, he thought he still felt something. At first, he wasn't entirely sure what it was, but the more he pushed, the more certain he was that something resisted him.

He nodded to the tunnel.

The ice dragon nudged him and Jason climbed onto his back. They jumped and glided into the tunnel.

Much like before, the ice dragon pushed out with cold and the ground formed a glaze around it that the dragon slid upon. Surprisingly, the dragon managed to slide upward almost as fast as he had slid down the tunnel. They glided, his wings folded in and wrapped around his body and power propelling them forward. Jason continued to hold on to the connection to the dragon pearl, the energy that flowed through him, and as he did, he was increasingly certain that there was something up here. He just had to reach it, though he wasn't sure if he would be able to do so.

He focused, sending energy forward, drawing upon the ice dragon.

When it reached the resistance this time, Jason continued to push.

It was a strange resistance, and he had no idea what it was, only that it was unpleasant, grating against him, as if it were unnatural.

He pushed harder, using the power from the ice dragon, and found that wasn't enough. He had to draw from within himself, and so he focused on some of the heat within him and pushed.

It was always strange to Jason that he could use the ice dragon pearl by drawing on heat, but for whatever reason, he had managed to do so. He did so again now, letting that power flow outward.

When it struck the resistance, he continued to push, recognizing that whatever he was feeling was unnatural, and he had to believe that he could overwhelm it. It would take force and strength, and yet he was convinced that he could do so.

The resistance fell.

They surged forward even faster.

Somehow, whatever resistance was out there had restricted them from moving as quickly as they could otherwise, and now that the blockage was gone, the ice dragon practically streaked through the tunnel, like an arrow loosed from a bow.

And then he saw a darkened shape in the distance.

He tapped the ice dragon and they started to slow, but not nearly fast enough.

The shape in front of them was blocking the tunnel, and as they streaked forward, they were going to hit it.

Jason gripped the neck of the ice dragon. Had he not been experienced with riding on top of the iron dragon, he might not have known how to brace himself against the impact, but having done so, he recognized what he needed to do. Holding on to the ice dragon's neck, he ignored the impact. When it struck, he rolled forward, tossed free of the ice dragon.

He struck something hard, metallic.

The iron dragon.

He wasn't glowing, not as he had before.

But why was he here?

The ice dragon got to his feet and rumbled, the sound of his irritation filling the inside of the cave, and yet Jason worried about how much notice the ice dragon might draw. It was possible he would be attracting far more attention to them than they wanted.

The iron dragon stirred.

Jason backed up against the wall of the cave. He hesitated, not wanting to move too far forward, not wanting to get in the way of the iron dragon if he were somehow controlled by the Dragon Souls, and yet there was no sense of that. The only sense he had was that of heat still radiating off the iron dragon, and yet, he understood that if the iron dragon were to awaken and summon his power, he could blast Jason with his heat.

It was possible he could do the same thing to the ice dragon.

It would be a dangerous—and deadly—combination.

Jason crawled forward, holding on to the dragon pearl.

When he reached the iron dragon's head, he frowned, looking him over. The iron dragon had his eyes closed, and though he moved, he didn't seem to do so with any real intention.

What had happened here?

He crawled past the iron dragon, moving down the hallway. He pushed a hint of cold into the dragon pearl, looking around, hesitating as he did, worried that perhaps he might draw too much attention, and he saw a pair of figures lying motionless on the ground.

Jason approached slowly.

He held out the dragon pearl, ready to push power through it, and yet he didn't know if he would be able to overwhelm a Dragon Soul if it came down to it.

There was still no movement.

When he reached them, he saw that one had his neck twisted irregularly. He wasn't getting back up. The other lay with his leg bent, obviously broken from the way the bone jutted through the skin, pressing up against the side of the dragonskin he wore.

Jason kicked the man.

There was a groan, but nothing else.

They were both dressed similarly. They both had dark pants, a dragonskin cloak, and a jacket underneath that matched. One of the men had a medallion attached to his jacket, likely some signifier of rank, but he hadn't had the opportunity to speak with Therin enough to know what the different ranks of Dragon Souls would be.

He glanced back at the iron dragon, but the other creature hadn't woken yet.

Behind the iron dragon, the ice dragon rumbled.

"I'm fine. There are two Dragon Souls here, but they're both incapacitated."

The dragon rumbled again.

"I'm going to search them."

"What do you expect to find?"

"I don't know. Money?" Jason laughed to himself. Money was basically useless in his village. They operated on trade and bartered what they could. Yet, as he searched through the pockets of the Dragon Soul, he found something even more valuable.

Dragon pearls.

The man had three of them, and Jason pocketed them.

As he did, a different idea came to him.

The man was roughly his same size. And there might be some benefit in wearing dragonskin rather than his bearskin.

Before he did so, he decided it would be better to question the ice dragon as to whether the dragon would mind. If he did, then Jason wasn't about to do so. He didn't want to anger the ice dragon by putting on a dragonskin jacket.

Checking to make sure the other man was still down, he hesitated a moment before peeling the cloak off, and then pulled off the man's jacket. The man moaned as Jason undressed him, but he ignored it. He moved on to his pants, and at least here he was all the more careful, not wanting to cause too much pain. It would be bad enough that the Dragon Soul would wake up without dragon pearls and without his dragonskin clothing and find that he had no power remaining.

As he pulled the pants off, he glanced down at the man's boots.

They were just as fancy, and also made of dragonskin.

Was everything they wore dragonskin?

He carried it back to the ice dragon. When he sat it down in front of the ice dragon, the dragon glanced over. "What do you think?"

"You undressed him?"

"His clothing. Would you be offended if I wore it?"

"Why would I mind you wearing it?"

"It's dragonskin," Jason said.

The ice dragon rumbled, the sound filling the inside of

the cave, and he flicked his tail. When he took a deep breath, he looked over at Jason, and then rumbled again.

"Why would you wear this?"

"The dragonskin offers some protection from heat. It provides some protection from the cold as well."

"I have offered you protection from the cold."

"You have," Jason said, realizing that the ice dragon had provided him far more protection than he had ever realized. "It's about the heat. I find I have a harder time with it now than I ever did before. And there's something else."

"What is it?"

"Your dragonskin is impervious to weapons. At least, more so than my bearskin is."

Jason didn't know what he might encounter, but having a dragonskin jacket and cloak might offer more protection than what he had otherwise. He could imagine the benefit it would provide.

Then again, he didn't want to upset his companion.

"You may wear it."

Jason tipped his head.

"I'm going to keep the bearskin jacket," he said.

"As you should," the dragon said.

Jason quickly changed, pulling off his jacket and pants, and slipped into the dragonskin clothing. It had been many years since he had tried on dragonskin, and he marveled anew at the suppleness of it. It fit remarkably well for clothing that wasn't made for him, and when he slipped on the cloak, he could feel body heat clinging to him.

He shifted the contents of his pocket, moving the dragon pearls from one to the other, and then made his way back up to the two fallen men. The now mostly naked man was starting to awaken, and Jason summoned power to the dragon pearl and released it on him. It exploded into him, knocking him out once again.

He glanced at the dead man and frowned.

There was a difference between the two. The dead man carried a sword.

Jason unbuckled that and strapped it to his waist. The sword was only as long as his forearm and felt awkward, but that might be only because he was unaccustomed to wearing a sword.

He debated a moment, but then stripped the dragonskin off him as well, folding it neatly, and carried it back to the ice dragon.

"We'll bring this with us, too." He wrapped the bundle and tucked it under his arm.

He moved back to stand in front of the iron dragon.

The dragon remained unconscious, as if slumbering, and the longer they'd been here, the more Jason began to worry that something worse had happened to him. The Dragon Souls must have summoned him, and yet, now that they were gone, unconscious and dead, the summons should have abated; and yet the dragon still seemed affected.

He pushed power through the dragon pearl, focusing on the iron dragon, and as he did, there was no resistance as there had been before.

He released that power and tapped the dragon on the side of his head, running his hands along his massive jaw.

"Time to wake up," he whispered.

He touched the dragon, feeling the warmth of the dragon's jaw, the strangely metallic texture, and on a whim, he pushed outward, doing the same as he would if he were holding on to a dragon pearl. Yet with the iron dragon, he was only trying to connect to the dragon itself, not to a pearl.

There was a strange surge, but then it faded.

Jason wasn't even sure if that surge was real, but if it were, then the connection had formed. Could he use the power of the iron dragon? Whatever power he detected was that of molten metal.

He caressed the dragon's cheek again.

There came that strange surge again, almost a reverberation, and as he felt it, Jason couldn't help but wonder if something was happening between him and the iron dragon.

He pushed again. He had no idea what he was doing, only that it seemed to be working. More than ever, Jason had to wonder if he shouldn't have spent more time with Henry, learning what it meant to be at least a partial Dragon Soul. If he had learned that, would he have known enough to use that power now?

He'd probably know no more than he did now.

It wasn't as if he would gain anything more. He had a connection to the ice dragon, and he had kept the ice dragon alive, but he had also now rescued the iron dragon —twice.

He had to think that was something beneficial, even if it meant he'd been a part of several of the Dragon Souls dying.

It was difficult to think about that.

Living in the village, death was a constant companion and a real possibility for so many of the people, and yet Jason had never directly experienced death until his father had passed. Seeing the Dragon Souls die was far more real.

All things must die. Don't fear it, but don't chase it.

He pushed the thought out of his mind. There was no point in thinking like that, and it was easier to focus only on what he could control.

And that was helping the dragon as much as he could.

He pushed again, sending a surge of warmth toward it.

Warmth didn't seem to work, but would cold?

When he had been focusing on the iron dragon, he'd been using whatever connection to the cold he had, and yet there had to be something else to it. He pushed on the cold sense that flowed through him, sending that into the iron dragon.

In doing so, there came an echoing sense.

With it came a jolt.

The dragon rumbled.

Heat began to radiate off the iron dragon and he shook his head, whipping his tail. Jason ducked underneath it, afraid of the force of that tail, knowing the way it could cut through someone.

He glanced back and noticed that the ice dragon had moved back as well, and cold was radiating off him.

Between the two of them, there was fire and ice, the contrasting nature of the two filling the inside of the tunnel with a strange sensation.

"What happened?" Jason asked as the iron dragon awoke.

"You were gone," the iron dragon said.

"I was gone to find the ice dragon," he said, pointing to the crouching ice dragon. Sharp spikes protruded from the entirety of him, and it was the first time that Jason had seen the dragon so prepared for battle. He had seen the dragon fight before, and he had witnessed the way he could use the ice spikes and push them out, but he hadn't seen him do so in quite some time. They were almost beautiful. Deadly, but beautiful. The spikes protruded, glistening sharp points that Jason suspected the dragon could shoot, targeting anything within the cave.

"I felt drawn," the iron dragon said.

"How did it feel?"

"You would draw me the same way?"

"I wouldn't, but I would like to know how it felt."

"It seemed as if they were adding to the song."

Jason tipped his head, wondering what sort of song the iron dragon would even hear. "What did it sound like?"

"It sounded like bells tolling."

It was the sound of metal ringing. Of course it would

be. And it shouldn't surprise him that the Dragon Souls would have some way of using that power to draw the iron dragon. It wasn't unlikely that they would somehow uncover the key to it. The Dragon Souls were powerful, they had quite a bit of experience with the dragons, and it would be easy enough for them to know what it would take to attract the iron dragon.

"And that song called to you?"

"That song drew me. I followed it here, and then something else happened."

"What else happened?"

"I felt resistance."

Jason glanced back at the ice dragon. His spikes were still protruding, and though it might only be his imagination, they seemed to be retreating.

"What sort of resistance did you feel?"

"I don't know that I can explain. The resistance was there, and it allowed me to know the song was wrong."

"That was us," Jason said.

"You fought them?"

"I didn't know what it was, but I felt something. I thought there was resistance in the tunnel, and when I began to feel it, I realized I needed to push against it. As I did, I felt that resistance fade." And now that he knew what it was, he wondered if he could recreate it. If he could counter what the Dragon Souls did, if he had some way of overpowering the way they summoned them, would he be able to free dragons?

It seemed impossible to even consider, but then again,

a year ago, it would've seemed impossible to even be speaking to a dragon.

Now he was speaking to not just one dragon but two. He had saved not just one dragon but two. And if the ice dragon was right, then there might be more for him to find.

Would they all be like this?

He frowned, looking past the iron dragon, and he couldn't help but wonder if perhaps he was going about things the wrong way.

If they found dragons that had specific tendencies, they would be able to understand just what Therin and the others had been up to.

They weren't typical dragons.

But then, Jason had known they weren't going to be typical dragons. That was the whole point of what they were doing, the way Therin had used them, thinking he could harness the abilities of a different land. Therin had wanted to conquer these lands, to add them to the Lorach kingdom.

"I don't know how long we can stay here," Jason said.

"Those two won't pose any challenge," the ice dragon said. His words were clipped, and they were spoken with a little more harshness than he usually used, as if he still wasn't sure what to make of the iron dragon.

But then, it was possible that he didn't know what to make of the iron dragon. The ice dragon had wanted Jason to find another, to find the hatch mate, and now that they had done so, it wasn't at all what he had expected.

Of course, Jason wasn't what anyone would've expected. The ice dragon wasn't what anyone would've expected. Why should the hatch mate be anything different?

"We should still move. I don't how many more Dragon Souls will be out there."

There had been five, and now four were gone, and yet... Jason had a hard time thinking that was all of them. There had to be more, and if they had brought down only a few of them, how long would it be before they realized and sent reinforcements?

It meant that Jason and the dragons would have to find reinforcements as well.

Doing so involved taking a risk that he hadn't necessarily wanted to take. It involved doing something he hadn't necessarily wanted to do.

When he had agreed to remain in the village, he had done so because he'd believed he could offer a certain protection to the ice dragon, and he'd thought he could help his mother and sister. Surprisingly, even though he'd remained, he still didn't feel as if he had helped them nearly as much as he had wanted to.

Now there was something else that needed him.

The dragons needed him.

Hopefully his sister and mother would be all right with him being gone a few more days. *Family first, then village.* The dragons were now his village. If this worked, if he went to Dragon Haven, then it was possible he could help save more than he had intended.

"I think I'm going to need help rescuing your hatch mates," Jason said.

"I thought you were the help," the ice dragon said.

"I was going to be the help, and I still am going to help, but I wonder if perhaps we need more than what we have."

"What more?"

"Others who understand—and respect—the dragons."

The ice dragon rumbled. "I don't know if I will be able to remain."

"You need the cold?"

"Even this place is difficult."

"I understand." He glanced over at the iron dragon and could not help but wonder if the same would be true of him. He needed something similar to the mines, and without them, Jason had to wonder if the iron dragon would suffer the same way the ice dragon did in this place.

There was only one way to find out, and yet, trying to bring the iron dragon with them posed a different set of challenges.

"He doesn't know how to fly," Jason said.

The ice dragon rumbled and turned away, but not before shooting a pair of icicles. They both struck Jason, though he suspected they were intended for him.

The ledge leading out to the gorge had a steep drop-off. In the daylight, it was far easier for Jason to see what was far below them, which was the water rushing through the gorge and flowing with a violent energy.

The ice dragon flapped his wings, hovering in front of him, just out of reach.

The iron dragon clutched the edge of the ledge, his body glowing, almost unbearable heat radiating from him. Were it not for the dragonskin cloak and jacket that Jason now wore, he wasn't sure he would even be able to tolerate it.

"You just have to glide," Jason said.

"You don't have wings," the iron dragon said.

"I don't, and you do. Look at how he glides."

"I am not like him."

Jason had hoped that the opportunity to work together would help bring the two dragons closer, and yet it seemed almost as if they were more irritable. The ice dragon seemed upset because he hadn't found someone who understood him, and the iron dragon was upset because the ice dragon was able to fly.

As he watched, he couldn't help but wonder if perhaps the iron dragon was right. The ice dragon *was* different. It was possible his means of flying was different. Certainly the ice dragon flew differently than the other dragons Jason had experienced. When those dragons had taken off from the mountain, they had spiraled up, almost as if circling on the wind, whereas the ice dragon would glide down the mountain, catching the breeze before shooting up into the air.

What if the iron dragon *couldn't* even fly?

He was different, and because of that, it was possible there was nothing he could learn from the ice dragon. They were fire and ice; how could either one understand what the other was going through?

And yet, Jason felt quite strongly that the iron dragon needed to learn how to fly. In order to safely reach Dragon Haven, he would need to fly. So far, there had been no more sign of the Dragon Souls, but even that wasn't likely to last. The longer they lingered here, the more likely it was that the Dragon Souls would return. If they recognized the dragon was freed, they would go hunting for it.

He didn't know what had happened, or why the dragon had been captured, or even who had been responsible for capturing it, but he doubted it would take long for the Dragon Souls to get word that something had taken place.

"How do you move usually?" he asked.

That seemed to be the key. The ice dragon glided along the snow, whereas the iron dragon was different. He writhed, wiggling along the surface, so different in his movements.

"How do you move?"

"I walk, but I'm not a dragon."

"No. You are not."

"I'm just asking so we can figure out what might help you understand how you can fly."

Jason stared at the iron dragon. There was something about the heat and the way his entire body seemed to glow, the way the molten nature of his scales appeared to flow.

That had to be the key, didn't it?

If that were the key, what was it going to take? If it were about using the molten nature of the dragon, Jason would have to find something within the dragon himself to latch on to, but didn't know if there was anything he could do that with.

He focused, staring at the dragon, thinking about his experience in traveling with the creature and watching the surface of his scales as he rolled.

An idea came to him.

"Try slithering through the air."

"Slithering?" the ice dragon asked.

"I know you fly differently, but then, you fly how you

needed to in the ice and the cold. The iron dragon will need to travel differently. When I traveled with him, I felt him practically slither." There wasn't any other way to describe it, and as he considered it, he thought that he was right.

Only, how was the iron dragon going to slither out into the air?

"Open your wings and slink forward as you did through the forest," he said.

If that worked, he would be amazed. If it didn't, then the dragon would drop, and though he didn't think the creature would be harmed by the fall, he still did not want to be responsible for something happening to him. He had no idea if they would be able to climb back down to help the dragon, though he had to believe there would be some way of reaching him if it were necessary.

The iron dragon clutched the ground. Slowly, he began to spread his wings, separating them out from his body, and as he did, the heat billowed off him. It was enormous and almost unpleasant, and on a whim, Jason crawled up on the iron dragon's back.

"What are you doing?"

"I'm going with you."

"And if I slither to the ground?"

"I'm still going with you," Jason said.

"You're that sure this will work?"

Jason shrugged. "I have no idea whether it will work or not, but I believe your way of moving is different enough that it could—and should."

The dragon swiveled his head, looking at Jason, his eyes glowing a bright orange. As Jason stared at him, he noticed that the way his eyes glowed seemed to mimic the manner in which the heat radiated off his body. It was flowing, the same way his body seemed to flow, and it was a strange thing.

The dragon turned his head away, and heat began to build from him.

Jason looked away, staring across the distance, watching the ice dragon. His crystal-blue eyes met Jason's, and they stared at each other. For a moment, Jason could practically feel the disappointment within him. It was almost as if Jason were betraying the ice dragon, but that wasn't it at all. Why couldn't the ice dragon see Jason was trying to help? Wasn't that what the ice dragon had wanted? He had wanted for them to find the hatch mates. And now that he had, now that they were trying to help one, the ice dragon didn't want him to do so?

Jason focused on the iron dragon.

"Slither," he said.

The dragon pushed off. They fell.

Then the iron dragon began to slither, sliding forward as he had through the forest. His wings remained open, motionless, and yet, strangely, the way he slithered, the heat radiating, stretching from his head down toward his back, seemed to propel them forward.

Then they glided.

It wasn't quite the same as flying with the ice dragon, but Jason hadn't expected it to be. The iron dragon was different, and yet, as they glided, he realized it was successful. This was flying for the iron dragon.

"Try using your wings," Jason said.

He didn't know if it would make a difference, but the iron dragon pumped his wings. It was a strange sensation, the stiff, metallic movements so different from the way the ice dragon flew, and yet there were similarities. Iron and ice weren't all that different, were they?

Gradually they began to ascend. The heat continued to ride along the surface of the iron dragon, radiating from head to toe, and power surged, propelling them forward.

They were flying, and he patted the iron dragon's side.

The ice dragon took a position in front of them.

"Where is he going?"

"I suspect he intends to take us to Dragon Haven."

"And where is Dragon Haven?"

"Dragon Haven is a place of dragons. Free dragons."

And they were more than just free dragons. If his experience had been representative of Dragon Haven, the dragons were practically worshipped.

He had a marker that Henry had given him, and Jason thought he should use it to summon the man, to let him know they were coming, and yet if he did that, he wondered if the Dragon Souls might be alerted to their presence. It was better if they simply appeared.

Then again, if they simply appeared, it might look as if *they* were Dragon Souls. With Jason dressed as he was, they might come across the wrong way. He had a bundle of other clothing on the ice dragon, his bearskin coat and the other dragonskin clothing, but he wasn't sure if that would make a difference.

They gradually gained altitude.

As they did, it seemed to Jason that the iron dragon became more confident in his flying. Every so often, he would pump his wings, but not nearly as often as the ice dragon. It seemed as if the heat radiating along his body propelled him almost as much as his wings did. It was a strange and undulating way of flying, as if he slithered through the sky, yet there was something rhythmic about it.

It was different than the ice dragon, and different than what he had experienced when traveling with Henry, but it was no less powerful and no less impressive.

He clung to the iron dragon's back.

As he did, he stared down at the ground.

The whole purpose of coming here had been to find other hatch mates. They had found one, but how many others would be like this? Would there be any way of finding them before the Dragon Souls?

Perhaps that wasn't the right question.

Jason frowned, swiveling on the dragon's back, looking toward the cave they had come from. "I think we need to go back." He patted the side of the iron dragon. They moved forward a little faster, and when they got within range of the ice dragon, he shouted out, "We need to speak to the Dragon Soul."

"What would you say to him?" the ice dragon asked.

"I would ask where the other Dragon Souls are

searching."

The ice dragon regarded him with those blue eyes for a moment before rumbling. The sound filled the sky like thunder, and with a swish of his tail, the ice dragon spun.

The iron dragon did not change direction nearly as easily. It was a sign of his discomfort flying that it took him several more moments to turn, but when he did, he quickly kept pace with the ice dragon, and they flew alongside him.

The edge of the cliff loomed in view and Jason held himself down, pressing his body up against the dragon, waiting for the inevitable collision.

The ice dragon slithered into the opening, and there was a certain grace to the way he did so. Jason could imagine the ice forming, his body gliding along the surface.

When the iron dragon struck, there was a loud gong, the metallic sound of the dragon colliding with the stone, his wings folding in, his legs tucked up, and then he slithered forward.

Jason kept himself low, clinging to the iron dragon's back, until they came to a stop.

They reached the small clearing where they'd left the living Dragon Soul. He was unclothed, and in the time they had left him, he'd barely moved. Anytime he had threatened to wake up, Jason would strike him with another attack through the ice dragon, and yet, now that he was traveling with the iron dragon, he wondered if the ice dragon would even allow him to borrow his power again. It was almost as if the ice dragon were angry with Jason.

He had to be careful. The dragon might be temperamental if he ignored him.

As he approached the Dragon Soul, the ice dragon crawled alongside him. He was able to roll himself up within the tunnel, sliding alongside Jason, tilting so that he fit within the cave more easily.

"What do you think to find from him?"

"They knew about this dragon," Jason said.

He glanced back, looking at the iron dragon. He sat on his legs, his head practically filling the entirety of the tunnel. He was a large dragon, and it might be Jason's imagination, but it seemed almost as if the dragon were getting even larger the longer they traveled together.

How much more time did they have before he was too large to fit even in a tunnel like this? How would they ever hope to hide him?

That seemed to Jason to be the greatest challenge. If they couldn't hide him, then it would be far too easy for the Dragon Souls to find him. And already the Dragon Souls had proven they had the ability to use whatever their call was to summon the dragon, to control him. It wasn't hard to believe that they would be able to continue to do so, and eventually overwhelm the dragon's ability to prevent them from using him.

So far, Jason had protected him, but what would happen if he weren't there?

Perhaps that was why they needed to get to Dragon

Haven. If they could reach it, and if they could get the people there to help, then they wouldn't have to fear what might happen to the dragon.

He crouched down next to the fallen Dragon Soul.

"We keep attacking him, but I wonder if we can wake him up."

"You can," the ice dragon said.

"How?"

"Do you think my power is only destructive?"

"I know it's not."

"Use it," the ice dragon said.

Jason focused on the cold, on what he could feel as it flowed through him, thinking of that chill. As it usually was when he was so close to the iron dragon, finding that chill was difficult, and yet, as he was closer to the ice dragon as well, it was a little bit easier. The proximity made it so that he could feel the cold. He called upon that, drawing on it, and let it fill him.

He pushed it out, using the dragon pearl, summoning that magic. It flowed through him, through the dragon pearl, and out and into the Dragon Soul.

He had no idea how to use the power, but he found that he didn't need to.

It seemed almost as if that power were directed, and when he looked up at the ice dragon, he realized that it was. The ice dragon controlled it. He guided Jason, controlling how the power flowed from him, into the Dragon Soul.

The other man gasped.

He blinked open his eyes, looking up at Jason, beyond him, and then something changed.

"Don't try to harm the dragons," Jason said.

He had no idea whether the Dragon Soul would even be able to do so without a dragon pearl, but he didn't want to risk it.

"Who are you? Are you with the rebels?"

"Rebels?" Jason smiled to himself. "I think you've got it wrong."

"Where did you find this dragon?"

"How did you know about this dragon?" Jason said, nodding to the iron dragon.

The Dragon Soul turned his head slowly, and when he saw the iron dragon, his eyes widened.

The iron dragon glowed softly, the heat undulating along the surface of his scales, radiating along his body, the metal seeming to flow as it often did when he used his heat.

"He lives."

"He does, and he will live free."

"There is no free, not when it comes to these creatures. You don't understand how dangerous they are."

"I think he's dangerous, but I also don't think he deserves to be controlled by you. Now, where are the other Dragon Souls going?"

"You wouldn't even begin to understand."

"I understand better than you think. I met Therin."

Jason watched the other man as he said Therin's name, curious whether that would elicit much of a response.

There was a part of him that wondered whether Therin lived and if he did, then perhaps this Dragon Soul would know; but the man didn't show any emotion, so it was possible that Therin had truly disappeared.

It would be best if he had. That meant that the village would be left alone.

"Therin is but a part of something much greater," the Dragon Soul said.

"And by that, you mean placing dragon eggs where they can take on characteristics of their environment?" When the Dragon Soul's eyes twitched, Jason realized he was right. "How many others are there?"

"There have been many attempts."

"And yet, you knew that this one had succeeded. How?"

"We were sent word."

"There isn't a Dragon Soul presence here. There would've been no reason for them to get word."

Jason hadn't visited Varmin very often, but there had been no Dragon Souls, so for them to be here, and for them to have someone they could count on to get word to them, suggested they had more influence than he realized.

Would it be like that in other places?

"As I've said, you can't begin to understand."

Jason sat back on his heels, staring at the man.

They needed answers, and he had no way of finding them short of tormenting him, but that wasn't something he thought he could do.

"I guess we leave him here," Jason said.

He got up and the ice dragon shifted, twisting in the cave, and they started away.

A sharp cry told Jason when the Dragon Soul was trying to move.

He swallowed back the nausea rolling through him. He couldn't imagine trying to move with a broken leg like that, and couldn't imagine how much pain the other man experienced when he did so, but with everything the Dragon Soul was willing to do, he thought the man deserved it.

"You will find you won't get very far with that leg," Jason said. He had a sense that the ice dragon could have healed even that, and yet leaving the man broken made it easier for them to walk away. "If you would like to live, then perhaps you could share with us where the other Dragon Souls are heading."

"I'm prepared to die," the Dragon Soul said.

"I am sure you are."

Jason continued through the tunnel, resisting the urge to glance back. As he reached the iron dragon, he pushed on the creature. He moved forward, slithering ahead, and the ice dragon pulled up the rear.

"Wait!"

Jason tensed.

"Bring me with you and I will share what I might know."

"I thought you were ready to die," Jason said.

"I would like to see these creatures."

"You can see them now."

"I would like to understand them better."

"Why?"

"Because there have been none like them before."

Jason frowned, and yet he understood. It was the same thing Therin had said. They were accustomed to a specific kind of dragon, the typical ones, and that was part of the reason they'd brought the eggs out here, to a different part of the world. And Jason doubted this was the only place where they had brought dragon eggs.

As he looked at the man, he debated what he was going to do. He wanted information, and he thought the only way he could acquire what he wanted was to bring the man with him.

The idea of having one of the Dragon Souls traveling with him troubled him. Jason didn't care to allow that, but at the same time, he didn't know that he could do anything differently. He needed the Dragon Soul in order to find what he wanted.

"You aren't going to do anything to harm the dragons."

"You fear for them?"

"I'm determined to keep them safe."

The Dragon Soul stared at him, and there was a strange look in his eye, but Jason continued to watch him carefully. He held on to the power of the dragon pearl, pushing outward with that cold energy, ready for an attack were it necessary.

The broken man lay there, watching, and finally, he took a deep breath. "You have my word I will not harm the dragons."

Jason smiled. "That's not going to be good enough for me."

"Then what will be good enough for you?"

"I need you to make a vow."

"Is that not what I did?"

There had to be some way to have the man commit to not harming the dragons. Would there be any way to use his connection to the dragon pearl?

"You are going to promise not to harm them. You're going to promise not to attempt to use them. And you will help us in any way that we need in order to succeed."

The man watched him, and for a moment, Jason thought that he might refuse, but then the silver-eyed Dragon Soul pressed his fingers together and brought his arms up to his chest. He bowed his head slightly. He touched his lips to his fingers and said, "I, David Arnson, speak the words of the flame to you. I will make no attempt to harm the dragons. I will make no attempt to train the dragons. I will make no attempt to abuse them in any way. I offer you my help, at the price of my life."

A surge of energy washed away from David at the words, and Jason frowned. He had never experienced anything like that before, but he had to believe that whatever David had done was powerful. And it was a vow, the kind Jason had asked of him.

"Will that be sufficient for you?"

Jason stared at him for a moment. "We will see."

David regarded him with a frown. "You don't understand what I just did."

"I don't, but that doesn't matter. What I do understand is that I want to make sure you won't do anything to harm the dragons."

"The rebels would have... no matter. I have given you the promise you asked for and much more."

He glanced over at the ice dragon. There was something to his blue eyes that was difficult for Jason to read, but he thought that the dragon could discern something.

Turning toward the dragon, Jason frowned. "What is it?"

"When he spoke those words, I felt... something."

"He called them words of the flame."

What was it about the words of the flame that was significant to the Dragon Soul? Was there anything that would be useful in understanding that?

"We can't bring him with us like that," Jason said, nodding to the nearly naked man.

"We cannot."

"Do you think we should let him have his dragonskin back?" Jason asked.

The ice dragon rumbled softly, and Jason understood.

Grabbing the folded pack off the ice dragon's back, he handed over his bearskin clothing. "Put it on."

"What is this?"

"Put it on," Jason said.

The Dragon Soul stared at it, and then nodded to his leg. "I'm going to find it difficult to do anything in this shape. You can change that, though."

Jason muttered under his breath. He might be able to

change it, but he didn't know if he *wanted* to. It involved healing the Dragon Soul, but if he didn't, then bringing David with him wouldn't be all that useful. They needed to have him in good enough shape so he could travel. Unless they did something to help him, they wouldn't be able to use his knowledge. He would slow them down.

Clutching the dragon pearl close, Jason pulled on power from the ice dragon, funneling it through the pearl. He pushed it out, letting the power wash over the Dragon Soul. As before, the energy seemed guided by the ice dragon, and it flowed out from him and into David.

David gasped, and when the power rolled through him, he sat upright, holding his leg. He looked around and gradually, the leg began to straighten.

Jason released his hold on the energy within the dragon pearl and the ice dragon turned away from him, heading down the tunnel. It left him and David alone.

The Dragon Soul got to his feet, testing his once broken leg.

"That was... interesting," the Dragon Soul said.

"You aren't going to attack now."

"I wouldn't dream of it," he said.

"Why was it interesting?"

"The nature of the healing was different than what I'm accustomed to."

"How is that?"

"Typically, there is a warmth, but then with that dragon, I can understand there would be no warmth."

"The warmth comes from the type of dragon or from the dragon pearl?"

The Dragon Soul stared at him. "The power comes from the dragon, but it comes through the Dragon Soul. When you begin to understand the nature of your power, you will be better equipped to funnel it. Then again, I thought that's what you were doing there."

Jason said nothing.

The Dragon Soul smiled. "You aren't controlling it. The dragon was guiding it. Interesting. That indicates the dragon has far more knowledge than what one would expect of it." The Dragon Soul pushed past Jason, staring toward the distant sight of the ice dragon. "I hadn't expected to find one so powerful here."

"Why would it have to be powerful?"

Despite himself, Jason found he could learn something from this Dragon Soul. And if the man was going to answer, then perhaps that was a reason to continue to speak to him. He had no idea how much David would share, and yet, he wanted to know the answers to these questions. He wanted to learn how much the Dragon Soul would know about his abilities, and if there was any way to gain an increased control over them.

For what they might be facing, Jason understood that he might need that knowledge.

"Not all dragons have the ability to heal. We treat those that do with a different measure of respect."

Jason laughed bitterly. "Respect? You abuse the dragons."

"You will find none of my dragons are abused. They are trained. Taught. And kept from violence. All that is true. But none of them are abused."

Jason shook his head, glancing down the hallway. He held on to the dragon pearl, holding a hint of power through it. If the Dragon Soul attempted to attack, he was ready to respond. "You don't understand anything about the dragon. You think you do, but everything that you believe you know is wrong."

"I doubt it," David said. He glanced down at the pile of bearskin clothing. "I don't think I can wear that."

"You will wear it."

"It's unlikely to fit."

Jason shrugged. "It fit me just fine."

The Dragon Soul looked up at him, regarding him for a long moment. "You? The rebellion wouldn't..." He turned his attention back down to the pile of clothing. After a moment, he leaned down, grabbed the clothing, and lifted the bearskin pants. He shook them, and then tentatively slipped them on. There was a part of Jason that didn't want David to wear his clothing, but he thought it was beneficial for him to continue to wear the dragonskin. At least with dragonskin, Jason would be able to withstand the warmth of the iron dragon much better than he had while wearing the bearskin.

"Where is your home?" the Dragon Soul asked as he was slipping on the jacket. He tested it, ensuring that it fit, and when he had it all the way on, he shook his head. He muttered something softly, but Jason wasn't able to hear what he said.

"No place that matters," Jason said.

The Dragon Soul looked up. "I believe it matters quite a bit. You have the look of... well, you have the look. And yet, here you are, dressed like this," he said, sweeping his hand across the bearskin, "and with dragons like those. I am quite curious as to where you are from and how you came to be here."

"You're going to have to remain curious," Jason said.

"And you speak of Therin."

"I did," Jason said.

"Therin has not been seen for many months."

"He's either frozen and dead or he's hiding from you."

At least that answered something. Jason hadn't been sure what Therin might've been doing. It was possible that he had managed to survive, and if so, he could have returned to Lorach, though Jason had expected if that were the case, he would have marshaled the dragons and brought Dragon Souls to bear on the village. That they hadn't seen anyone left him with the sliver of hope that Therin hadn't survived the fall.

Even now, he wasn't entirely sure. It was possible this Dragon Soul was misleading him. He had to be careful of what he told him, and had to expect the Dragon Soul would lie to him. He had no reason to believe the man would speak the truth, but he could be cautious. He could anticipate that David would try to lie to him, to betray him, and he could be ready to respond.

The only problem was that he wasn't entirely sure what he would need to do.

"Are you ready?"

The Dragon Soul grunted. "Dressed like this? I suppose I'm as ready as I can be."

Jason let David get in front of him, and they headed out of the cave. At the entrance, he found the ice dragon and the iron dragon flying, circling outside. The iron dragon was turning, spiraling in the air much more efficiently than he had been before. He'd been practicing.

"They are unusual," the Dragon Soul said. "Misfits of a sort."

"I wouldn't call them that."

"What would you call them, then?"

"I would call them dragons."

"Indeed."

"Where else were you looking for dragons?"

"Like those? There would be no other dragons like those."

Jason frowned. "If you aren't going to be helpful, then you can remain behind. There's no reason for you to have to come with us." He focused on the cold, using the dragon, prepared to shatter the man's leg again. He didn't like the brutality, but he also wasn't about to leave this man behind to continue to cause trouble for the dragons.

"There's only so much I was privy to."

"Where do you think the others are looking?"

"There is a valley not far from here."

"Why would they have gone there?"

"Look at them," the Dragon Soul said.

"What about them?"

"You can see how unique they are. There's something impressive about them. They have taken on aspects that traditional dragons have not. They are different. Misfits."

Jason frowned. He didn't want to think of the dragons like that. They might be different, but they certainly weren't misfits. The ice dragon had saved him and had changed things for him. He didn't know the iron dragon as well, but he was powerful, and there was something about him that would be even stronger in time.

"They shouldn't be. The great Sol knows there should be nothing about them that could exist, yet here they are."

"The eggs have taken on characteristics of the environment," Jason said.

"Perhaps," David said.

"You think there's another answer?"

"I think there is the possibility of another answer," David said. He continued to stare, looking outward. "There have been attempts at something similar over the years. None of them have been successful."

"Why this one, and why now?"

David glanced over, watching Jason. "Exactly."

It was more than just the fact that the experiment was successful at this point. It was successful with more than one dragon. And if it had worked with more than one dragon, and if what the ice dragon said about his hatch mates was true, then there were several others they had to find.

He looked outward, watching as the ice dragon circled, watching the way that he regarded the iron dragon. There was still hesitancy to him, but even so, Jason noticed how the ice dragon tilted his wing, getting closer to the iron dragon, before shifting course and flying higher into the air.

There might be some uncertainty, but there was also a desire to understand.

It was that desire which had brought him here in the first place. It was that desire that had motivated the ice dragon. And it was that desire that Jason needed to help see through. He understood what the ice dragon was after, the knowledge of who he was and how he came to be, but more than that, there was an understanding of where he belonged.

The dragons were powerful, and despite that, they didn't want to be alone.

More than ever, Jason felt that with a certainty.

He pulled on the power of the dragon pearl, summoning through it, and the ice dragon turned toward him.

When he landed near them, Jason climbed onto his neck, and he waited for David. David hesitated only a moment before following Jason onto the ice dragon.

"You will guide us to the next place," Jason said.

David held on to the ice dragon, and there was something about the way he looked at the creatures that both unsettled Jason—and gave him a glimmer of hope.

12

They soared high over the sky. The air took on a bit of a chill, and the longer they flew, the more that chill began to work its way around the ice dragon. The cold seemed to strengthen the ice dragon, empowering him, and Jason clung to his back, holding tightly, worried that something would change. He'd flown without saying a word the entire time, and next to him, the iron dragon continued to fly, moving quickly, his wings arcing in a strange fashion. Yet the longer he flew, the more certain Jason was that the iron dragon was beginning to understand what it took for him to do so.

David had been silent throughout their travels. Eventually, Jason would need to get him to say something, but for now, the silence was fine.

He thought instead of his sister. His mother. He couldn't help but wonder whether his sister had tracked down the slope, finding the cave, and had managed to acquire more of the venison.

Leaving when he had troubled him. He would not willingly have abandoned his family at a time when things were uncertain. He had no idea who was trying to steal from them, and when he returned, he would have to be prepared for the possibility that he would need to resolve that situation.

That was *if* he could return.

Learning about these dragons, and the possibility of others, left Jason wondering what he would have to do moving forward.

Maybe his task would be about serving the dragons.

Family first, then village...

There was another way to take care of his family. He could move his sister and mother down to the town at the base of the mountain. There was nothing for them in the village, not any longer, not without their father, and with enough coin, Jason could ensure their safety.

Then he could continue to work with the dragons, no longer worried about what was happening to his family, no longer fearing they would not have enough to eat.

He sighed, and he noticed that David was watching him.

"What is it?" Jason asked.

"There is something about you I can't quite place," David said.

"Then stop trying," he said.

"I don't think that I will. Whatever it is, I haven't seen it in quite some time."

"I don't care for the way that you're looking at me."

"Call it curiosity."

"You can call it whatever you want, but I don't care for it."

David watched him for a moment before turning away. Despite that, Jason noticed the way he was turning toward him, how every so often, his gaze would drift. He wanted to force David to ignore him, but how could he?

The landscape below was difficult to track. He tried to focus on that, to pay attention to only what was below them, but it was hard to see anything from where he sat on the dragon. His dragon sight wasn't helpful when it came to peering over the edge. Everything was different. There were swatches of dark green and brown. There wasn't the usual undulating banks of snow, though every so often, he did catch pockets of white, as if there were snowier sections of the ground below.

He had no idea where they were heading, and the longer they flew, the more he began to wonder whether David was leading them into a trap. He might have spoken the words of the flame, but what did that really mean?

"When you said the words of the flame, what is that?"

"The words of the flame are a sacred vow. It's spoken with the Dragon Soul's power, and it is meant to convey a commitment. They are not spoken lightly."

"How?"

"How did I speak them?"

"How is it something of power?"

The Dragon Soul watched him. "I find it amazing that you have survived as long as you have without knowing these things."

"I haven't had any experience with your people before recently."

David glanced over before turning away again. "You should have been brought to Lorach and trained."

"Trained or enslaved?"

"There are things done for safety," he said.

"Whose safety? Yours or the others?"

David frowned. "You can't understand. You don't know what we have been through."

"No. I don't, and I have no interest in knowing what you've been through. Not if you're going to use the dragons like this. All I know is that you've tormented them. You've abused them. And because of that, you've made them into something they should not have been."

David watched him, saying nothing.

After a moment, he turned his attention away and pointed toward the ground. "There," he said.

"What's down there?" Jason asked, reluctantly turning away. A part of him wanted to know more, to discover what they might be encountering, but another part didn't want to continue the conversation with David. He had no idea what he might do, and because of that, he wanted to be careful with him.

"There's the sense of something."

Jason turned to the ice dragon. "Can you feel it?"

"I can feel there's something there," he said. "I cannot tell what it is."

"Does it feel like your hatch mates?"

David pressed his lips together and frowned.

"It feels similar," the ice dragon said.

If it was similar, then it was probably the hatch mates, but why wouldn't it be the same?

Everything about this felt off. The longer he flew with the dragon, the longer he traveled, the more he began to wonder whether what he detected down there would be another unusual dragon.

A misfit.

He stared at the ground and, clutching the dragon pearl, he pushed out a hint of cold, letting it wash away from him. It was nondirectional, and when it struck the ground, it diffused away. There was strength behind it, the strength of the ice dragon, but there was no real purpose to it.

He needed to be more careful with using power like that. Anything he might do would potentially waste any energy he—or the dragon—possessed. And he needed to ensure that they had enough strength to pull through this.

David shook his head. "You should not be so casual about that."

"Casual about what?"

"About using your power in such a way."

"You can tell what I do?"

David nodded thoughtfully. "Surprisingly, I can."

"Why is that surprising?"

"I would not have thought I would have been able to do so. And yet it seems that when you draw upon this ice dragon, I'm able to tell." He twisted and looked over toward the iron dragon. "Can you use his pearl as well?"

Jason considered ignoring the question. It revealed too much about him, he thought. And yet, if there was any way to better understand the nature of the dragon pearls, and to better understand if there was something he could do differently in order to borrow that power, then shouldn't he pursue it?

"I haven't figured out the key."

"Some dragons are difficult. It takes great training to draw power from them."

"You're not training this dragon."

"Be that as it may, it is unusual for me to be able to detect your use of power."

Jason thought he understood. "You think you could use it."

David glanced down at Jason's hand. "I suspect I could, only I don't know if I would understand what is necessary."

That was a key piece that Jason was not about to reveal. He wasn't about to share with David that it would involve pulling on the cold, the familiarity of it, and he wasn't about to reveal that in knowing that cold, letting it flow through him, he could...

Was David somehow influencing him?

He looked over, watching David.

He didn't think so, but he wondered if the meandering

nature of his thoughts was related to something David was doing.

He had to be careful. He didn't want to be used—and he really didn't want the dragon to be used. At this point, his control over the ice dragon and the dragon pearls was the only thing keeping David from overpowering him. That and his promise made through the words of the flame.

As they descended, the ground began to take on form. The trees were a bit different than what he had experienced before. Humidity wafted toward them, warmth that wasn't present in the upper air. It was almost overbearing, and the ice dragon surged with cold, as if he were attempting to fight it.

"Will you be all right?"

"I will need to resist," the ice dragon said.

"Do you think that you can do so?"

"For now," he said.

"If you need to return—"

"I'm not returning," the dragon said.

Jason wasn't about to argue. When it came to this, and when it came to what they would need to do, he thought the dragon needed to decide for himself. He would know the limits he had, if there were any real limits.

He held on to the dragon's back, clinging to him, and the cold continued to radiate away from him. The iron dragon descended more rapidly, plunging toward the ground. His body began to glow, more so than before, and yet, as they neared the trees, the glowing retreated.

They circled, finding a clearing and coming down in the middle of it.

Once down, Jason looked around. The trees were tall, with broad leaves, and there was heavy underbrush all around. This was nothing like the forest he had seen near Varmin, and it was nothing like the forest he had seen near the town at the base of the mountain.

David climbed off the ice dragon and looked up, breathing in deeply. His eyes closed and he held his hands out to either side, palms facing up. As he took those deep breaths, he looked all around.

"Do you know where this is?" Jason asked.

"This is Saren. I haven't been here in quite some time."

"The forest or this place?"

"These lands. All of this. There will be several towns scattered throughout."

Jason frowned. He hadn't seen any sign of towns, and yet, from above, it would've been difficult to do so.

Strangely, the dragonskin seemed to protect him even here. There was less of a sense of the heat, and he was able to tolerate it much better than he probably would've in his bearskin. He glanced over at David, looking to see how David was handling it, and he seemed to be doing fine.

"Well?"

David pressed his lips together. "I will do what I can."

"I thought you said you detected something here."

"I thought that I could, but I will need some time to focus on it."

"That wasn't what you said."

"It might not have been what I said, but it will take me some time to determine if there's anything here I can uncover."

Jason wanted to argue, but it wasn't going to change anything. The longer they lingered, the more he suspected the ice dragon was going to suffer. He looked over and studied the ice dragon. There seemed to be a shell of ice around him, and it glistened, water dripping from it.

"If you suffer too much—"

"I will stay until this is done."

"You don't need to torment yourself."

"I wasn't there with you for him," he said, looking toward the iron dragon.

For his part, the iron dragon slithered between the trees. He moved quickly, gliding along the ground, almost as if this were his element, though even here, Jason didn't think the iron dragon was particularly comfortable. There were no mines, and there was no iron, and there was nothing that was familiar to the dragon.

He could tolerate the warmth, but he would be unlikely to tolerate much else.

"You didn't have to be there physically to be there," Jason said.

"I will be there this time."

Rather than arguing, Jason turned and studied David. David was focusing, and rather than concentrating on the trees, or on the sky, he was looking down. He made a steady circle, his feet dragging through the fallen leaves and debris. He murmured something softly, his lips moving, though Jason didn't hear anything coming from him.

As he approached, he looked to see if he might be able to understand anything about what the man was doing, but he couldn't identify anything.

"David?"

"Quiet," the Dragon Soul said.

Jason debated arguing, saying something back to him, but what would the point in that be? He needed David's focus, and if he had some way of finding the dragon, then they needed to use it.

Instead, he turned to the ice dragon.

"Can you feel your hatch mates?"

"There is something here, but I'm not able to determine what it is. I have a sense of energy, and it reminds me of what we felt near him."

The iron dragon continued to move, winding through the trees.

"Do you think you could work with him to pinpoint it?"

"I doubt it," the ice dragon said.

"Is that only because you don't want to, or because you don't think that you can?"

"I think the two of us are different enough that it will be difficult for me to effectively work with him."

"You're both dragons."

"We are both dragons, but we are different."

It reminded Jason of what David had said. Misfits. Was that really what the dragons were? He didn't think so, and yet, they were unusual. Unusual wasn't necessarily bad, but perhaps when it came to these dragons, unusual was... unusual.

And they needed to work together, regardless of what the ice dragon said. If they could work together, if they could connect to each other, then they could better understand their purpose. And in understanding that purpose, they could find some way of uncovering the other dragon.

There had to be another dragon here. He might not be able to feel it, not the same way as the ice dragon or David, but there was something about this place that suggested there would be a dragon. And rather than searching for the dragon, he could try to uncover what about this place would fit the dragon. What traits would it take on from here?

If he could discover that, then he could help the dragon when they found it. Assuming they did find one.

What did he know? There was humidity. There were trees. There was nothing else.

Perhaps there wouldn't be any way to determine anything from here.

He didn't know enough about this land to know whether anything here would be helpful. It was possible that though he had found the ice and the iron dragons, there would be nothing like that here.

Jason took a deep breath and noticed something strange to the air.

At first, he wasn't sure what it was. An energy seemed

to fill the air, and he looked around, searching for the source of it, but found nothing.

There had to be something here.

He turned toward David. David was still walking in a circle and muttering to himself. The ice dragon was slowly making his way over to the iron dragon, but neither was saying anything.

As far as he could tell, there wasn't anything here, and yet, there was something to the air. There was an energy, and he thought he could use it.

Jason ignored the dragon pearl he was holding on to, focusing instead on that energy. If there was anything he would be able to uncover, it would be in drawing through that energy, not any other way.

He focused, and that sense came to him, drifting slowly at first, but then as he continued to pull upon it, with an increasing intensity.

It was near the other dragons.

Jason made his way there, holding on to the dragon pearl, that energy similar to what he detected from both the ice and the iron dragons.

There was another possibility, and it troubled him the most. As he approached, he looked around, glancing at the sky, half afraid he might come across one of the Dragon Souls—or more. What if David had betrayed them? He might have spoken the words of the flame, and the ice dragon might have detected something within them, but what did that really mean? It was possible that whatever connection he claimed, whatever bond he said came from it, meant nothing.

He reached the ice dragon.

It was watching the iron dragon as he slithered around the trees. There was something strange about the way that he watched, and it took Jason a moment to realize that the ice dragon was attempting to slither the same way that the iron dragon did.

He stood watching for a moment.

If only there was some way that the two of them would be able to understand each other. It was possible they were different enough that they wouldn't be able to do so. Jason wanted them to try to find some common ground. If they could, then they would be stronger for it. They were hatch mates.

The energy continued to increase, building with a violence.

"Do you feel that?"

The ice dragon turned toward him. His sides glistened and the layer of ice over him was not nearly as thick as it had been.

"There's some sort of energy here."

The dragon rumbled.

He sniffed the air, turning his long-fanged snout toward the ground, and sniffed again. Cold radiated from the dragon, and as it did, he formed a thicker barrier of ice around himself.

"I don't detect anything," the dragon said.

It could be that the effort of trying to withstand whatever was taking place around here was too much for the dragon, but it could be something else. If it came from whatever energy Jason detected, he would need to act more quickly. He focused on what he could detect, and yet nothing was clear to him.

The iron dragon continued his slithering course through the forest, and Jason watched, focusing on the energy from the dragon, wondering if there was anything he might be able to learn. It was unclear to him.

The Dragon Soul remained near the center of the clearing. Jason watched, searching for any sign of what David might be doing, trying to understand just what it was, but he couldn't tell. The man was making his circle, muttering, and yet... There came an energy from him, too.

That was the source of what Jason was detecting.

He headed back over to the Dragon Soul, stopping just outside of the circle he formed. "What are you doing?"

"You cannot disturb this."

"What are you doing?"

The Dragon Soul flicked his gaze up. His eyes had taken on an orange hue, and sweat dripped down his brow. "I am trying to summon the creature."

"You want to control it."

"Not control. The dragons need to be trained."

Jason wanted to lash out, to strike the Dragon Soul, but if he could draw the dragon to them, then perhaps he could try to find some way of connecting to it.

The only problem was that if the dragon reacted the

same way the iron dragon had, then it might be angry at how it would have been summoned.

"How are you summoning it?"

"I am calling to its nature."

"We don't know its nature."

"We know enough about it to be able to call to it," David said.

The circling continued and the muttering persisted. Jason stood on the other side of the circle, debating whether or not he should interrupt what the Dragon Soul was doing, but decided to let him continue.

He stood back a step, watching, feeling the energy David was producing.

Would there be anything he could do to add to the Dragon Soul's efforts?

Not to try to summon the dragon, but perhaps to prevent David from harming the creature if it finally appeared.

He focused, pushing power out through the dragon pearl.

That was a mistake. He couldn't use the power of the ice dragon, not as the dragon was straining to overcome the effects of this place.

Was there another way he could do it?

There were other dragon pearls. The Dragon Souls had carried them, and he could use one of those.

He reached into his pocket, feeling one of the dragon pearls, and pulled it out. It had a bluish color to it, streaks of black running along its surface, and it was perfectly smooth and round. It was slightly warm and he squeezed it, attempting to push a hint of power through it.

As he did, he felt a strange reverberation.

David looked up. "What did you do?"

"I was going to help," Jason said.

David glanced down at the pearl in Jason's hand. "You just alerted them."

"Alerted who?"

"The others."

"How do you know?"

"Because I felt it."

"This is a dragon pearl. It's connected to the dragons."

"And which dragon do you think it's connected to?"

Jason's breath caught. He had made a mistake. Here he had thought he was going to borrow power from the dragon pearl, and yet in doing so, he'd only done what he'd been trying to avoid. The Dragon Souls would now know that they were here, searching for the dragon, and how long would it take for them to arrive? They wanted to avoid the Dragon Souls, and yet he might be the reason they drew their attention.

He pushed the dragon pearl back into his pocket, ignoring it. There would have to be another way.

"I must act quickly," David said. He looked around the clearing for a moment. "I need his help." He pointed to the ice dragon.

"I don't know that he will help you."

"Then we will not be able to act before the others come."

"How do we know you would even help us?"

"Have I done anything to prove otherwise?"

"Other than attack me? Other than trying to summon the iron dragon? Other than attempting to summon this dragon?"

"All of those things were necessary. And I have given you the word of the flame. I will not attack."

Jason flicked his gaze over to the ice dragon. "We need your help," he said. He pushed a hint of power through the dragon pearl.

The ice dragon looked over. There was a glaze over his eyes. He was growing tired.

They wouldn't be able to stay here much longer, and if the Dragon Souls appeared, the ice dragon was unlikely to help much at all.

It was going to require they find some other way to escape. Thankfully, it seemed as if the iron dragon was still fine, and yet Jason didn't have any way of knowing how to use that dragon's abilities. He might have the iron dragon pearl, but even with that, he didn't have anything he could use it for.

"What do you need?"

"I made a mistake. I attempted to use one of the other dragon pearls, and now the Dragon Soul claims I have alerted the others."

The ice dragon regarded him. For a moment, clarity returned to his icy blue eyes. "Why would you use another?"

"Because you're struggling here."

212 | D.K. HOLMBERG

"I have more than enough strength."

"I'm not doubting your strength, but I'm doubting what you're experiencing, and I worry you don't have enough power remaining to withstand all of this."

"What do you need now?"

"The dragons will need your help in order to try to finish what he's doing."

The ice dragon regarded David. "He's trying to control the dragon."

"Can you feel it?"

"Indirectly. I understand what he's attempting to do, and yet, I'm not subjected to the same influence."

"If you can feel it, you can add whatever you can to help it be effective." Jason didn't know if that would matter, but if it worked, then they might be able to summon the dragon, and then... He had no idea. All of this was predicated on the idea of finding the dragons, gathering them together, and then what? He knew the Dragon Souls were out there, hunting for these so-called misfits, and yet, if they were so difficult for this one Dragon Soul to summon, it seemed to him they would be difficult for the others to summon as well.

The ice dragon perched with his wings spread out. Ice began to form on the ground around him, creating a circle. It appeared around the place on the ground where the Dragon Soul had dragged his pattern. As the ice dragon pushed outward, ice continued to form, pressing inward. The power that the Dragon Soul was summoning increased, drawing with increasing energy. The longer that Jason focused on it, the more he could feel that.

He understood the reverberation within it. There was additional power, a response, and yet he didn't have any idea what it came from.

The dragon, most likely, but where was the dragon?

They had been here for a little while, long enough that they should have seen something.

He focused on the ground, thinking that perhaps it would be underneath him, the same way the iron dragon had been under the ground. The ice dragon had even been underground, though he had been within the stream and the cave, the cold surrounding him.

Where would they find this dragon?

If it had taken on traits of the forest, traits of this humid place, then...

Jason jerked his head around, studying the trees.

That was the key. This place was alive with forest energy.

The trees swayed, moving with the breeze, and yet, the air was heavy and still.

That wasn't a breeze at all.

He breathed in, focusing. He felt the power, the energy of this place, and the more that he focused on it, the more certain he was that it was there. He could use it somehow.

He let that energy fill him, that sense, and tried to think of how he might be able to better call upon it.

From what he could tell, there was no way to do so.

The energy was there, the power was there, and yet, there was nothing else.

The branches high overhead continued to sway.

That was where he needed to focus his attention. He stared, looking through the shadows and the darkness, and he searched for any sign of the dragon.

There wasn't anything moving.

Other than the trees.

Heat pressed in upon him, and it took a moment to realize it came from the iron dragon. He'd settled in near Jason, and much like him, he was looking up at the trees.

"I can feel it," the iron dragon said. His voice was a hiss, little more than a whisper.

"Do you know what it is?"

"It is one like me—and not like me."

Heat writhed along his leg, undulating and then dissipating.

Jason turned his attention back to the top of the trees, and as he did, he began to make out a shape. It was up there, though it wasn't moving.

He stared, looking for anything that would remind him of the dragons, anything that would reveal the presence of it, and then he saw it.

Two eyes that glimmered. They were a deep green, so deep he thought he imagined them at first and that they might be nothing more than the leaves on the trees, but those were a fainter green than what he saw now.

"You can come down," he whispered.

He had no idea if his voice even carried, but in this

place, he had to believe that the tree dragon would recognize him. And if it did, then he had to hope there would be some way to call the dragon down.

There was no movement.

And yet, he was certain of what he saw. He was certain that he noticed the green eyes looking down at them, watching. The dragon was aware of everything.

And there was something else within it that he realized.

The dragon was able to resist.

The Dragon Soul summons persisted, and as it did, Jason could feel the way it was radiating out, the power added to it by the ice dragon, but even with that, the dragon managed to ignore it.

"I want to help you. You can come down here."

This time, he pushed a hint of energy with the words, wondering if it would make a difference. If it did, then perhaps he might be able to draw the dragon down, and yet, there came no response. It was almost as if the dragon couldn't even hear him.

Somehow, he would have to get up there.

He looked over. The Dragon Soul and the ice dragon were caught up in what they were doing. Was there anything Jason could do?

Short of reaching the dragon, he didn't know if there was.

There might be a way to reach the dragon.

He looked over at the tree. It was wide, but he thought he could climb along it.

Taking a deep breath, he wrapped his arms around the trunk and started up.

The bark of the tree had a smooth surface, and it was difficult for Jason to keep his grip. Every so often, he started to slip, and that forced him to dig his heels into the tree to maintain his position. He struggled against it, and yet, as he climbed, he could feel the presence of the dragon overhead. There was something about the dragon that called to him.

He glanced up. The deep green eyes stared at him, watching. The dragon hadn't moved. He was thankful that it hadn't, but what would happen when he reached it?

It was something he would have to consider when he got closer, but for now, Jason was content to continue to climb, trying to reach the dragon as quickly as he could. If the Dragon Souls came, he would be responsible for that, and he wanted to get to this dragon before they had a chance of reaching it.

He continued his climb, moving quickly. Every so often, he slipped, losing his grip on the trunk, and he struggled to hold on to his place.

As he climbed, he couldn't help but feel as if he were getting closer. He let the sense of the dragon draw him and squeezed as tightly as he could. Finally, he reached a branch he could hold on to if he were to fall, and then propped himself up. Jason took an opportunity to rest, catching his breath. He looked down, realizing how high he was, and resisted the urge to slide back down to the ground. The ice dragon continued his circle of power, pushing around the Dragon Soul. From above, there seemed to be a pattern forming in the frost, though it was difficult to tell what shape that pattern would take.

Taking a deep breath, Jason continued, climbing along the trunk. He worked quickly, moving his legs first, then his arms, and then repeating. He dragged himself up the trunk, and when he reached another branch, he paused. He hazarded a glance up, noting the way the dragon seemed to watch him. As he got closer, he was hoping to be able to make out more of the dragon's form, but there wasn't anything other than the eyes.

There had to be something more he could discern.

He was closer now, and even still, he wasn't able to tell much more about the dragon than he had before. There had to be something about the dragon that was concealing it.

Jason steadied himself, and when he had himself prepared, he started up the side of the tree again, climbing quickly.

Near the next branch, he paused, crouching once more. Surprisingly, there didn't seem to be more of a shape to the dragon than there had been before.

Not only were there the deep green eyes, but the scales of the dragon seemed to blend into the tree. It was why he hadn't seen anything at all. It was as if the dragon formed the canopy. The more Jason stared, the more he began to understand. The dragon's tail stretched down the trunk of the tree, and his massive wings were spread out, arcing overhead, blending in and looking like the treetops. The only thing that was visible was his eyes. As he got closer, he was able to make out the enormous size of the jaw and head, and in doing so, he almost slipped.

He was close—far closer than he'd realized he was.

Jason didn't move. He could scarcely breathe. He didn't know if any movement would draw the anger of the dragon, and yet the creature simply watched him, almost as if curious.

"I'm Jason Dreshen."

The dragon didn't move.

"I want to help you. There are others who will try to use you, but I don't want them to."

He wasn't sure how to explain the Dragon Souls, or how to explain his role with them.

"Can you feel what's happening down there?"

He glanced at the clearing, where the ice dragon and David were working.

The dragon stretched his head forward, moving slowly, and as it did, it seemed to be nothing more than leaves fluttering on a breeze. The effect was enough that Jason smiled, amazed at how delicately the dragon was able to move, the precision with how it concealed itself.

"They're trying to call to you. They want to help you."

The dragon pressed his head closer to Jason. In that moment, a hint of panic rolled through him. He was approaching an unknown dragon, a creature of enormous power, and he was letting it get so close that it could almost bite him. He'd seen the ice dragon hunting and knew the kind of power they possessed, the way they were able to rip apart enormous creatures with little more than a snap of their jaw.

He didn't have the sense that this dragon wanted to harm him. Whatever else happened, he believed the dragon was curious, much like all the dragons he had met.

"You could come with us. We want to protect you."

Jason tried to push, using his connection to the dragon, straining for some way of reaching the dragon, and yet he didn't think that there was any way to do so.

There was a resistance within the dragon.

"There are others who would love to meet with you. They want to understand."

The dragon inhaled. It practically sucked the wind out of Jason's lungs, and he held on to the branch, afraid of going anywhere. For a moment, he thought the dragon might come along with them, that they might be able to escape and figure out the rest of it, determine worlds they could escape to and hide within, but then an explosion struck.

It came again. And again. Each time it came, it was familiar to him, ringing through the entirety of his body.

Dragon Souls.

He looked back over toward the green dragon, but the dragon was gone.

13

J ason looked through the treetop, searching for signs of the dragon, anything that would tell him where the creature had gone, but he could make out nothing. Every so often, the upper branches would sway, and as they did, he couldn't help but feel as if that was a sign of the dragon moving through the branches, but then the motion stopped, leaving him watching, wondering.

How had he lost the dragon so easily?

There was a stealth to it that the others did not have. He'd lost all evidence of it. That amazed him. For the dragon to be able to disappear so quickly and so quietly was a marvel.

Another explosion thundered, then another.

Jason squeezed the tree, sliding down the trunk. He moved quickly, every so often digging his heels into the trunk to slow himself, and held on as he dropped to the ground. When he neared, he jumped free, racing toward the ice dragon.

"Something's coming," he said.

David looked up. "We aren't finished."

"What you're doing isn't going to work."

"You don't know that. I can continue to summon, connect to the dragon, and I can—"

"The dragon is gone."

David blinked. "Gone? Did they get to it?"

Jason shook his head. "When the Dragon Souls appeared, the dragon disappeared."

"Because of you," David said.

"Not because of me." Well, not entirely because of him.

He glanced over at the ice dragon. Water was streaming down his side. The heat of this place was almost too much for the creature, and if they stayed, he wouldn't be able to fight if it came down to it.

"Go," he said to the ice dragon.

"I can stay."

"If you stay, you won't be able to fight."

With a rumble that suggested how frustrated the dragon was, he lurched into the air. With a flutter of wings, he exploded upward, streaking into the sky and disappearing.

Jason held on to his connection to the dragon, using the cold flowing through the dragon pearl, testing whether he would return and whether there would be any sign of injury to the dragon, but he didn't detect anything.

Either the ice dragon had managed to move past the Dragon Souls, or they hadn't been aware of him.

He turned, looking toward the iron dragon.

"We need to get him out of here," he said.

"You can't control that one as well?"

"I'm not controlling any of the dragons. I simply ask."

He found the iron dragon still slithering through the trees, winding from place to place as he went, and Jason approached slowly, carefully, and stayed away from the heat radiating from the dragon's back.

"It's time for us to go," he said.

The dragon halted, turning his enormous head toward him. One wing struck one of the trees, and it rang like a bell. "What is it?"

"It's time for us to go. There's something coming."

The dragon rumbled. It was a different sound than the ice dragon had made, though similar enough. "I will destroy them," he said, looking past Jason and at David.

Jason shook his head. "I'm sure you would, but I don't think we should remain. If we do, it's possible they will come with greater numbers. We need to get moving." He took a step toward the iron dragon. "I found the dragon of this place. I spoke with him. Or her. It wasn't willing to come with us."

That troubled him, but even more troubling was the possibility that the others might gain control over that dragon. If they did, then he would need to do whatever he could to fight them off, but perhaps they wouldn't know of its presence.

And yet, if they did discover that there was a dragon of the forest, then it would be his fault. Which meant it was his responsibility to draw the Dragon Souls away.

How was he going to do that?

It would involve fighting. He wasn't interested in fighting the Dragon Souls, but he also wasn't willing to allow them to gain power over another dragon like this.

The iron dragon swiveled his head toward him, and a flash of orange burned through his eyes. "Then we go."

Jason crawled forward, waiting for David, and the two of them climbed on the iron dragon's back.

They hadn't tested whether the dragon would be able to take flight from here, and there was a part of Jason that worried whether the dragon would have the necessary skill to do so. What would happen if he couldn't?

They would be stuck. They could run through the forest the same way they had run before, and given the way the iron dragon moved, he thought they could outpace the Dragon Souls for a while.

Thankfully, the dragon managed to launch himself into the air, and as he did, he quickly took to the sky, using that strange way of his, his undulating form, the heat radiating from his back.

Jason had to grip tightly, and he was forced to ignore the heat from the dragon.

Next to him, David held on easily. It was almost as if he didn't mind the heat and the nature of the dragon, or perhaps it was more that he was impressed by some aspect of the dragon. Either way, David sat upright, holding on with one hand, gripping the dragon as if it were nothing.

Jason looked behind him as they pierced the canopy of the trees. He searched for any sign of the tree dragon, but there was nothing. He wasn't sure if he would be able to make anything out from here, anyway.

"We have to draw their attention," he said.

"You want to do *what?*"

"We need to draw their attention. If the Dragon Souls come after the dragon here, then…" Jason wasn't entirely sure what would happen if they pursued the dragon here, but he did know that it seemed as if the tree dragon had no interest in fighting. It would be easier for him and the iron dragon to do what was necessary.

"If you draw their attention, they will chase us. And if they come prepared with dragons—which I'm sure they will—we will not be able to overwhelm them."

Jason leaned forward. "How fast do you think you can fly?"

"I am still learning."

"Do you think you can outfly the ice dragon?" At least with the ice dragon, Jason had a sense of how fast that one was compared to the others.

When it came to flying with the iron dragon, he didn't know. He'd never seen the iron dragon challenged, and it was possible he wouldn't be able to outpace the other dragon.

"I might be able to," the dragon said.

"You're going to need to fly with as much speed as you

can summon." He reached into his pocket, grabbing one of the dragon pearls. He pulled out the one he had used before, the one with blue and black striations through it, and he gripped it tightly. Power began to surge in him, and he let it flow, exploding into the pearl.

It was the heat that burned within him, but it was also the heat that he borrowed from the iron dragon, and the longer he held on to it, the easier it was to issue the summons.

An explosion thundered near them. An enormous bellow cried out and he lowered his head. There was at least one other dragon.

It was coming toward them, and gauging the speed of it, it was coming quickly.

"Time for you to fly as quickly as you can," he said to the iron dragon. The heat began to radiate from the dragon, and it rolled along his side, flowing along him. As it did, Jason clung to him, holding on with as much strength as he could bear, and yet, he wasn't entirely sure he could maintain that grip without releasing the dragon pearl and putting it back into his pocket.

He looked behind him. In the distance, it appeared as if a small bird was approaching.

Not just approaching, but overtaking them.

It wasn't a small bird at all. It was a dragon, and it was moving with incredible speed.

He released his connection to the dragon pearl, putting it back into his pocket, and leaned on the dragon's back.

Had this been a mistake?

He was relying upon the iron dragon being able to outrun another dragon, one that understood its abilities. The iron dragon didn't know what it was able to do quite yet. In time, the iron dragon might be formidable, and it was possible he would grow to become powerful enough to overcome any of these other dragons, but for now, the iron dragon was still learning. He was so young, the same way the ice dragon was still young. The ice dragon believed he would've been able to tolerate staying in the forest, but Jason had seen otherwise.

Why hadn't he considered the possibility that the iron dragon would also view his abilities in a way that wasn't realistic?

They weren't going to be able to outrun the oncoming dragon.

Another roar exploded.

It was different than the first, and as he listened, he was aware that it came from something else.

A different dragon.

How many would there be?

The Dragon Soul sat stiffly on top of the dragon, and he stared straight ahead.

What must he be thinking?

He probably didn't care. If the dragons were captured, then he would have every opportunity to study them the way that he wanted, so if it were up to David, then none of this would matter.

They should've left him behind.

Then again, had he left him behind, Jason would never

have seen the forest dragon. Even though they hadn't been able to bring the dragon with them, he knew the creature existed, and knowing that was enough. If they could learn where any of the other hatch mates could be found, then it was another thing he needed to do.

The only problem was that Jason didn't know how many more they were looking for. How many more of the dragon eggs had the Dragon Souls set out throughout the world to take on features of their environment?

And why would they suddenly be effective? That was the part of all of this that Jason didn't fully understand, and perhaps it was the reason he needed to go to Henry and the others in Dragon Haven to get a better sense of why all of this was taking place.

Another rumble. This one was close. Jason looked over his shoulder; the dragon was speeding toward them. The creature was enormous. Deep red scales caught the light, seeming to glow, but not with the same intensity as the iron dragon. They needed to find some way to outrun the dragon.

Or to try to help the dragon.

Could he do the same thing he had when it had been about aiding the iron dragon? If there was some way to free the dragon from the other's influence, then maybe he could help.

What had he done with the iron dragon?

He had pushed, and yet, he had used the ice dragon's power.

Reaching into his pocket, he found the dragon pearl. It

was cold, as it often was, but not unpleasantly so. He gripped it and focused on the power flowing through him. As they got higher into the sky, he was able to draw upon that chill in the air more easily, and he let that flow through him and into the dragon pearl.

For a moment, he hesitated, waiting to see if there was anything he might be able to detect about the ice dragon. If he were somehow limited, if he were injured, then Jason would need to refrain from using that power. If not, then he would be able to draw upon it.

It seemed as if the dragon had been restored.

He summoned strength, letting that power flow through him, and sent it outward.

He targeted the maroon dragon, letting the energy flow into it. He drew through the ice dragon, the same way he had in the cave when he had been trying to help the iron dragon. In doing so, he could feel that power, and there was a strange resistance.

"What are you doing?"

"Quiet," Jason said.

David leaned close. "You will destroy her."

"Who?"

"If you try to take control of the dragon while she is flying, you will destroy her."

Jason swallowed, looking over at David. "How did you know what I was doing?"

"I told you I can feel it."

"How is it that you can feel what is being done with the ice dragon that well?"

"Because I can."

"What makes you think I will destroy the dragon?"

"A fall from the sky will kill even a dragon."

Jason glanced down. "We need to descend," he said to the iron dragon.

The dragon roared and then plummeted.

The sudden change was almost too much for Jason, and he gripped the dragon's back, squeezing onto him as they whistled through the air, steam rising all around him. As they went, he wondered if they would have enough speed, but a shadow formed overhead.

He glanced up.

The maroon dragon plummeted along with them, moving quickly, and Jason ducked his head, pressing his body up against the iron dragon.

David looked up, and Jason couldn't read the expression on his face. Was it happiness?

He had half a mind to throw the man off the dragon. A dragon might not survive a fall from that high, but a man definitely wouldn't.

Instead, he grabbed David, pulling him closer to the dragon's back, and they squeezed against the iron dragon.

As they descended, the dragon rolled, and did so at the last moment. Had he not, they would have been raked by the maroon dragon's claws.

There was another one out there. He had heard it, but he'd not seen it yet.

There was no time to look and see where the other dragon was, and it took every bit of Jason's effort to hold on to this dragon, to be prepared for whatever else he might do.

The iron dragon spun, rolling through the sky, hissing as he did so.

More power radiated from him.

The entire body of the iron dragon began to glow with an intense light.

Not the entire body. His whole thorax, extending out to his wings, but not his head and neck.

It seemed almost as if the dragon refrained, knowing Jason wouldn't be able to tolerate it. The dragonskin protected him. Where his body touched the dragon, he was able to withstand the heat, and he glanced over at David. David wasn't tolerating it nearly as well. Wearing Jason's bearskin, he was forced to shift, moving from place to place so that he didn't get burned.

The sudden change had made a difference, though. They spiraled toward the ground, like an arrow streaking toward the target.

As they did, Jason glanced up. He focused on the power through the dragon pearl, and then pushed.

He ignored David's objections, setting aside everything other than the sense of power he was pushing outward. If he could reach the dragon, he could eliminate whatever influence was obscuring it, and then he might be able to free it from whatever the Dragon Soul was doing.

The dragon roared.

Jason sent the power washing over the dragon.

He wasn't acting alone. Much like when he had tried to

help the Dragon Soul, trying to heal him, there was an influence from the ice dragon, guiding him, showing him what was needed to help. As he worked, Jason could feel that guidance, the way the ice dragon was helping, using his power.

Freeing the maroon dragon.

The dragon roared again and Jason didn't dare look up. He let that power flow through him, and as it met the resistance of whatever was injuring it, he continued to push, drawing power from the ice dragon, summoning it through him, through the dragon pearl, and outward and into the maroon dragon.

It struck and Jason pushed, letting that power flow through him, and it washed over the maroon dragon.

There was resistance, but much like he had with the iron dragon, he forced his way through it. Now that he understood what was necessary and how to accomplish it, he found it much easier to overwhelm that resistance. It came from somewhere deep within the dragon, an injury, a scar, and he forced it through the dragon.

In doing so, he found that he was able to remove that injury.

The ice dragon guided him, letting him direct the power, and as it worked through the maroon dragon, something changed.

The dragon didn't chase them with nearly the same speed.

As he looked back, the dragon started to plummet.

They weren't all that far off the ground. Only fifty feet

or so, but it was enough that Jason worried whatever he'd done had injured the dragon. It was the warning the Dragon Soul had given him.

Jason couldn't help but think that he had done what was necessary. If the dragon had been captured by the Dragon Soul, it was possible that whatever he was doing was freeing the dragon.

He let the power roll through the dragon, and strangely, as he did so, he felt a stirring, a connection that formed.

For a moment, he thought he shared the dragon's perspective, but then it passed.

As the dragon crashed into the ground, there was a thunder of sound. The dragon cried out, someone else screamed, and Jason looked down.

The Dragon Soul.

There was more than just one Dragon Soul.

Two had been riding on the dragon.

Where was the other dragon?

The iron dragon rolled and then began to climb.

"There's another dragon out here," Jason said.

"I can feel it," the iron dragon rumbled.

"Can you tell where it is?"

"I cannot."

He looked over at David. "What about you? Do you know where the other dragon is?"

"Why would I be able to tell where the other dragon is?"

"Because you're a Dragon Soul. You would have some

way of knowing where the other is. Where is it?"

"I only knew about the maroon dragon."

"You knew?" Jason sat up, facing David. "What do you mean you knew?"

"How do you think we got there?"

"How many other dragons were here?"

"There were three that carried us. One departed, heading back to Lorach."

"Then you knew that there would be two. The maroon dragon and—"

A shadow suddenly loomed overhead.

Jason dropped down, but he wasn't fast enough.

Something grabbed for the iron dragon.

The iron dragon screamed, a rasping metallic sound he'd never heard before, and it seemed as if steam hissed from him, squealing out into the sky.

The dragon burst into painful heat, his entire body beginning to glow, the redness working along his scales and then fading, but it did so slowly.

He twisted, and they managed to avoid the attack, but as he looked over, he realized David hadn't completely dodged it.

An enormous gash was torn through his arm. Blood poured down it and he slumped over.

Swearing to himself, Jason reached for David and pushed power outward, sending it from the ice dragon pearl and into him.

He summoned the ice dragon, letting that power flow through him. It rolled into David, hitting the wound, and yet the ice dragon wasn't guiding them as he had before.

He needed the help.

The ice dragon would help.

Unless freeing the maroon dragon had taken too much out of him.

Jason fumbled for the power within the dragon pearl, but he didn't have enough.

What about one of the dragon pearls he'd taken from David?

He grabbed for one, pulling heat through it, using the heat from himself, from what he felt from the iron dragon. As he did, it radiated outward, and it flowed into David.

The power was enormous, and he didn't know if it was because they were so close to the maroon dragon or because of the heat radiating off the iron dragon. Either way, that power flowed into David. It seemed as if David guided the flow, and the blood stopped pouring from his arm.

Jason didn't know enough to do more than that. If nothing else, he thought he could prevent David from bleeding out. It would involve holding on to the Dragon Soul and keeping him on the dragon's back, and he wasn't sure that he was able to do that.

He looked around but couldn't find where the other dragon had gone.

"Where did the last attack come from?"

"I don't know," the dragon rumbled.

How could the dragon not know?

Then again, Jason hadn't known. The attack had suddenly been there. It was almost as if it had appeared out of nowhere.

Was there some other way for the dragon to attack?

Jason looked up. He had to be here somewhere, but as he looked around, he saw nothing.

Power flowed. There was a steady rumble, and he focused on it, listening, and felt the source of it.

He pulled on power through the dragon pearl, letting it flow out from him, and he sent it through the dragon nearly upon them.

It struck, and rather than refraining, trying to push gently, Jason sent everything he could through the pearl, into the dragon, and felt the resistance there. As before, it was something of an injury, and now that he had worked with it once before, he thought he understood it. It was like a scar somewhere deep inside of the dragon. If he could smooth it over—

He didn't have an opportunity. Something struck the iron dragon again.

Surprisingly, the iron dragon was ready and its heat flared, rolling through it. It seemed as if the entire dragon roiled, and he whipped his tail around.

Another dragon cried out.

Somewhere, the dragon was here, but Jason couldn't see it.

How could a dragon be invisible?

These were enormous creatures, and it seemed impossible to him that one could simply disappear, and yet there it was. There was no sign of the dragon, no sign of where it had come from and where it had gone.

He focused on the power he was pushing through the dragon pearl, letting that flow through him, and as he did, he felt that ongoing resistance. He pushed again, allowing it to roll through him. It struck the dragon, and he pushed again.

The scar began to disappear.

Jason shoved again, this time drawing all the strength he could, all the power he had within him, and he let it flow over him, into the strange mysterious dragon, and it overpowered the dragon and its scar.

It also overpowered him.

Weakness washed over him and he slumped forward, trying to cling to the iron dragon's back.

Somewhere, he heard a deep rumbling, and he worried they were going to be attacked again, but then there came a loud crash, a roar of pain, and something else.

Another cry.

The iron dragon circled. Far below them, Jason was able to make out the form of a black dragon lying motionless on the ground. Three Dragon Souls scattered around it. Some of them were moving, but it was difficult for Jason to tell what they were doing. He tried to draw upon power, but he was wiped out, and anything that he might have left was gone.

He wanted to help. He wanted to ensure that the black dragon—and the maroon dragon—were not going to be harmed, but he didn't know if he had the strength to fight Dragon Souls.

He tapped on the iron dragon's back and leaned close to him. "We need to go."

"Are you sure?"

"No," Jason said, looking over the dragon's side. "But I don't know if I can handle another attack."

He hated the idea of leaving the dragons behind. If there was any way to rescue them, he wanted to do it, and yet, he didn't know if he had the necessary strength to do so. It was better for them to get out of here, survive, and move forward.

They angled upward, and as they did, Jason was forced to help hold on to David, keeping him pinned to the dragon's back. He was tired, more tired than he had been in quite some time, and as they plunged through the clouds, he found the ice dragon circling, watching. Locking eyes with the ice dragon, he nodded. They had survived.

David rolled over, looking over at him, and then he pushed Jason free of the dragon's back.

14

T his was how he was going to die.

All things die...

Jason had never really given it much thought, and yet living in the village, there was never a question that life was hard and that it would be all too easy to perish from the elements. Still, he had thought that he would get a few more years before something claimed him.

And he never would've expected dragons to be the reason he died. Despite what happened to his father, Jason thought he was going to have more time.

As he dropped, the wind whistling around him, the cold air blowing past him, he thought of his mother. His sister. The village. All of those were disappointments. He wouldn't get to return, and yet it was only his mother and sister that he cared about. He no longer cared to return to the village, not as he once would have. What he did care about was not helping the dragons. Disappointing them. Being unable to see them to safety.

It was his mistake. The Dragon Souls would now claim the ice dragon and the iron dragon, and had he been smarter, he might have been able to learn more than he had, and yet he had been too trusting.

What he should've done was go to Henry right away. He should've returned to Dragon Haven as soon as he knew there were other dragons. He should've gone for help.

He parted the clouds.

The ground loomed toward him, much closer than it had been. It was still far below, rapidly getting closer and closer. How much longer did he have until he crashed into it?

Strangely, there was a greater sense of flying by falling than he'd ever had riding with the dragons. He stretched his arms out, wondering if he could slow himself.

Even if he could, what point would there be? There wouldn't be any way to save himself.

At least he would die warm. He would die dressed in dragonskin. And maybe there was a hope that the dragons would survive this. He wasn't entirely sure if it was possible, but he had to think they could pull through it.

A chill began to work through him.

That was strange. Ever since connecting to the ice dragon, he'd never felt the same chill. Dressed in the dragonskin, he shouldn't be cold. The dragonskin should protect him, should keep him from that sensation, and yet here he was, cold in a way he hadn't been since finding the ice dragon.

It could be fear. He certainly was afraid, though strangely, he wasn't nearly as frightened as he thought he would've been. He would see his father again. And eventually, his mother and sister would join them. They would celebrate in the afterlife.

The cold continued to build.

Was someone calling out his name?

Jason frowned.

The ground was close, and yet he continued to feel the cold rolling toward him, the surge of it, and he looked behind him.

The ice dragon swooped toward him.

"Be ready," the ice dragon said.

He ducked his head, parted his wings, and streaked beneath Jason.

As he did, the ice dragon pulled up, and he grabbed for Jason.

Jason grabbed for the dragon at the same time and wrapped his arms around his neck, clinging tightly to the dragon.

He held on, but started to slip.

"I need something to grip," he shouted. The wind was loud, whistling around him, making any conversation difficult. That was why he hadn't heard the ice dragon in the first place, and yet, the ice dragon must have heard him.

Spikes began to protrude from the ice dragon's back. Jason grabbed on to two of them, holding tightly.

The dragon spun and shot toward the sky.

But not before drawing the attention of the three Dragon Souls on the ground.

They watched and Jason looked down, knowing that they saw him, saw the ice dragon, and saw what had happened.

"How did you fall?" the ice dragon asked as they pierced the clouds.

"David kicked me off."

The dragon rumbled.

As they parted the clouds, Jason looked, searching for the iron dragon, but there was no sign of it.

Where would they have gone?

He couldn't leave David with the iron dragon, and yet, he had no idea how to search for it.

"Can you detect him?"

"I feel that dragon no differently than I feel the others."

"How many others?"

"There are four others," the ice dragon said.

"How much of the others can you detect?"

"Not as much as I would like," the dragon said.

Jason wished there were some way to find the iron dragon.

And maybe there was.

He released one hand and searched through his pocket, sorting the various pearls he'd uncovered, and came across the iron dragon pearl.

might not understand how to connect to the iron dragon, but he had ridden the dragon, and he had worked with him, and if there was any way to find him, he would search.

And it was possible he didn't need to find the iron dragon.

He held the ice dragon and iron dragon pearl, and frowned.

"How much strength do you have remaining?"

"Enough."

Jason wasn't about to argue, so he called upon the cold, letting it roll through him. He was tired, but for the iron dragon, he needed to do this.

He sensed that power surging through him and connected, letting it flow outward from the ice pearl and into the iron pearl.

It was a strange way of attempting to heal the iron dragon, but what he needed was some way to connect, and he had the iron dragon pearl, which was a part of the dragon, even if it wasn't a complete part.

At first, there was a strange resistance, but then the power began to flow.

It wasn't just a power, it was a connection. It began to build, cold pouring from the ice dragon pearl into the iron dragon pearl. But then something changed, and it began to flow in the other direction. It was almost as if they were connecting.

Jason hesitated. He feared doing too much, and yet, he thought that he needed to do anything he could in order to help the iron dragon.

"Keep going," the ice dragon said.

"I don't know what's happening," Jason said.

"I don't either, but I think you're doing what must be done."

"Will this affect you in any way?"

"You are calling upon my power. It's possible it will."

And if it did, Jason worried that he was making a mistake. If he were somehow connecting the ice dragon to the iron dragon, fire to ice, then it was equally possible the Dragon Souls would be able to use that connection to reach for the ice dragon. It was possible they would be able to do the same thing he was doing now, and yet if nothing else, he was determined to try to free the iron dragon from any influence. As he pushed through the iron pearl, he continued to feel that power. It flowed outward, rolling from ice to fire, and yet it began to retreat.

There was no other influence.

He frowned, releasing his power.

"The dragon is not influenced," he said.

That seemed surprising to him, and yet, he was certain of it.

And if he wasn't influenced, then where was he?

Jason held on to the iron dragon pearl, looking around, and yet he couldn't feel anything.

"Where did he go?"

"I don't know."

They had been betrayed by David, but so far, David

hadn't influenced the other dragon in any way that would change him.

It didn't mean he wouldn't be able to. It didn't mean that he wasn't trying to. All it meant was that for now, he hadn't done so.

What if he wouldn't be able to? It was possible that with what Jason had done, the way the ice dragon had healed the iron dragon, there was no way for the iron dragon to be influenced in the same way. If that were the case, then where had the iron dragon gone?

He stared at the pearl, trying to find an answer, but there were no answers.

There were only more questions.

He breathed out, thinking of the molten heat he knew when around the iron dragon. There was nothing within him that understood that heat. There was nothing within him that flowed the same way the molten nature of the dragon flowed. There was no part of him that would be able to understand the dragon in order to connect to the dragon pearl.

Still, somehow he had to find that part of himself. He had to find a way to reach deep within him, to uncover the connection he had to the dragon. He wanted to understand what had happened. He needed to find the creature. He had no idea what it was going to take or where that knowledge was going to come from.

He imagined trying to flow the same way the molten metal of the dragon flowed, thinking about how that sense of metal rolled along his back, the way that the dragon seemed to shift, change, and as he thought about it, he was certain there was some way to uncover it. Jason had to find that within himself, only he didn't know where.

He held on to the sphere, the power of the other dragon within him. He knew it was there, that it was just a matter of finding it. If he could, then he could summon that connection.

Was there a part of him that worked the same way? He thought about how the dragon had slithered, the way he had used the undulating feature to draw heat through him, to power himself. There was nothing similar Jason could come up with. Try as he might, he came up blank.

The ice dragon circled, and Jason felt no closer to answers than he had been before.

Was this a mistake?

There was no way to find the answer. He'd been kicked off the iron dragon, and in doing so, David had made it so that he wouldn't be able to return, so he would lose his connection to the iron dragon.

It filled him with rage.

That anger flowed through him, slowly, and he was unsettled by it, but he wasn't about to let that rage consume him.

Still, it boiled up within him, burbling deep beneath the surface, and as it did, Jason understood. There was the connection to the iron dragon, and all he had to do was latch on to that rage, to that anger, and he could use it.

It filled him.

Jason let it. He welcomed that anger. It came to him

slowly, roiling through him in the same way that the molten nature of the metal had roiled through the dragon.

That couldn't be a coincidence. That had to be something real, and as he focused on it, he was more and more certain he needed to use that anger.

He pushed that connection into the dragon pearl.

Power flowed with it.

It seemed to unlock something within him, and it unlocked something within the pearl.

A soft bell started to toll.

Why should that make a difference? Why should anger seem tied to the dragon?

Maybe it was a matter of the dragon's captivity, or maybe there was something else to it, but either way, Jason knew that was what it had taken to connect him to the dragon.

Now that he pushed, he could feel that energy, and he let it roll out from him, and he welcomed it.

The power filled him, and he pushed through it, searching for some way of knowing what the dragon had done, looking for where to find the dragon, and the more that he pushed, the more certain he was that the dragon was nearby.

The tolling of the bell continued, loud and unabated.

There was something to that. Jason listened, leaning down.

Somehow, he had to focus on the tolling of the bell, the ringing, and if he could do that, then he might be able to uncover where the iron dragon had been dragged.

"Do you hear that?" he asked.

"I hear something," the ice dragon said.

"I think that I have figured out how to connect to the dragon, but I'm not completely certain."

The dragon rumbled and sniffed at the air, his head swiveling side to side, and Jason focused on the dragon, listening, and in doing so, he thought that he could hear the bell continuing. He focused on what he had done, sending that sense of anger and rage through the dragon pearl.

There was something unpleasant about using it, and yet, he thought he understood what was needed.

Distantly, he found the sense of the dragon.

It was below him.

After directing the ice dragon, they descended. They dropped quickly, the wind whistling around him. Jason didn't know how long he would be able to hold on to the power within the iron dragon pearl, and he worried that he wouldn't be strong enough if it came down to it, but for now, he was able to keep his grasp on the power and to use it.

He searched the ground, scanning it, and wasn't surprised to find the iron dragon down there, standing between the maroon dragon and the black one. What surprised him was the fact that the iron dragon didn't glow with the same heat as he normally did.

It was almost as if the dragon wasn't afraid.

Could the Dragon Souls have gotten to him?

It was possible they had. They were powerful, and they

were drawing on significant energy, and if they had, then it would explain why the iron dragon wouldn't be concerned, and it would explain why it wasn't blowing with the same heat and intensity as it had been before.

They circled and Jason focused, listening to the bell tolling.

It didn't give him any insight, and yet as he held on to that anger, power bubbled up within him.

It was a strange thing to be able to detect, and yet as he focused on that energy, he was able to borrow from it. As Jason drew through the dragon pearl, the iron dragon glowed a bit more brightly with each attempt to pull on his power.

Strange.

Would the iron dragon know what Jason was doing?

The better question would be whether or not the iron dragon even cared.

It was possible he didn't care that Jason was trying to draw upon his power, and it was possible the iron dragon wouldn't do anything. Jason and the ice dragon had done everything they could to protect the iron dragon, and it was possible that they had succeeded, keeping anyone else from influencing him.

They circled high overhead, and he focused on the Dragon Souls below.

Something that David had said occurred to him.

There were three dragons that came. One had been sent away. Two remained.

These were the two that remained.

How many Dragon Souls were down there? He remembered three on one dragon and two on the other, and with David down there, it was possible that the different dragons would also be enough to overwhelm all three dragons on the ground.

Two Dragon Souls per dragon.

Would the numbers matter?

He borrowed from the iron dragon, and he focused on what he could detect of the other two dragons, and he pushed, borrowing power through the dragon pearl, washing it over the black dragon and the maroon dragon. When the power struck, there was no sense of resistance as there had been before.

Either the dragons were unharmed, or whatever power he was able to summon through the iron dragon was different.

"We need to land," Jason said.

"Are you prepared for what must be done?"

"I don't know what must be done, but I don't know if the iron dragon is injured."

Whatever had happened to him had left the iron dragon changed, though how much had he altered?

It was part of the question that Jason couldn't answer, something he would need to better understand, and yet, he worried that the Dragon Souls would continue to attack.

They streaked downward, the ice dragon shooting forward, the air around them solidifying, becoming colder, icicles forming on the dragon's side. This was a different approach, and as they did so, wind whistled around them, the air took on sharp notes, and it seemed almost as if snow began to fall around the dragon.

As it swirled, something awoke within Jason.

It was a familiar scent, one that he remembered from his homeland. He was able to use that. That cold washed through him, and it seemed to help awaken him.

He took a deep breath and, when they landed, he hopped off the dragon's back and darted forward.

Three of the Dragon Souls turned toward him and he focused, using both the power of the iron dragon and that of the ice dragon, fire and ice, and he connected them, allowing that combined force to explode outward from him. He had done something similar before, but this had only been a part of it. When he had freed the iron dragon, he had needed to use that combined power, and now he thought that he could do even more with it.

And if he could, then he might be able to attack the way that he needed to.

Power flowed through him. He struck, using the power of the combined dragon pearl, again and again. Each time that he did, power exploded out from him, and it connected with the Dragon Souls.

He was able to throw them back, and with the doubled power, they didn't get back up. He turned toward the other two Dragon Souls. He stormed forward, holding power in his hand, and he struck. He didn't give them a chance to attack, sending his surge toward them, uncaring.

It left only David.

He turned toward the man.

"You would have betrayed us?"

"I spoke the words of—"

"I know you spoke the words, but apparently the words mean nothing to you."

"You don't understand."

"I obviously don't." He held up the dragon pearls, gripping them tightly, and he sent power exploding away from him. He diverted it at the last moment, not wanting to strike David, but wanting him to be aware of the fact that he could. David had betrayed them, and though he had said the words of the flame, and though Jason had no idea what that meant or whether it was anything significant, he still wondered if perhaps he should relent.

"What were you trying to do?"

"I was trying to show them they didn't need to harm the dragon," David said.

"That wouldn't work."

"You don't know the Dragon Souls the way I do."

"I understand the Dragon Souls used the dragons. I understand that if it were up to you, you would try to harm them, destroy them, and you would use them. I understand enough," he said.

David took a deep breath and met Jason's eyes. "You know nothing about the Dragon Souls, but I could help you. If you would listen, I could show you. You have potential."

"You don't see me as somebody with potential. You see me as a slave."

There was a hesitation, and with it, he frowned, wondering whether or not David would admit to that, but he shook his head. "Perhaps I would once have considered you a slave, but I have seen what you have done. I understand the nature of your power, and that you have uncovered something we have not."

Jason looked at the fallen Dragon Souls. He had no desire to continue attacking, and yet he thought he would need to, if only to better understand what had taken place here, to see if there was any way to stop these others.

He needed to protect the dragons.

"I'm not going to leave you behind," Jason said.

He turned to the fallen Dragon Souls, and he debated what to do with them. There was one thing he thought he could do, but he wasn't sure if he wanted to unclothe them. Then again, taking the dragonskin cloaks seemed fitting.

He worked quickly, and as he did, he found that David was working alongside him, helping to pull the clothing off some of the Dragon Souls. Working together, they undressed the rest of the Dragon Souls and piled up the dragonskin.

"Why did you kick me off the dragon?"

"I was trying to grab you," he said.

"You didn't. You pushed."

"You were starting to fall and I reached for you."

Jason thought about what happened, and he couldn't

remember the exact details of it, only that he had felt as if he had been pushed off. Possibly even kicked off.

And from there, he was falling.

Had it not been for the ice dragon, Jason wouldn't have survived.

By the time they had the Dragon Souls all undressed, he wondered what to do with them. It was time for them to get moving, and yet, he didn't know how to awaken them.

If his next task involved going back after the forest dragon, then he would, but he didn't know if the dragon in the forest wanted them to pursue it. It was possible that the dragon was content, able to hide itself, and it was possible that anything they might do would only reveal its presence and make things worse for it.

"How long do we have?" he asked David.

"How long we have for what?"

"Before the rest of the Dragon Souls come? How long do we have?"

"Not long," David said.

"How many will come?"

"I suspect they would have sent word, so there will be many."

Jason clutched his jaw. Many. And then they would have to deal with the Dragon Souls searching and terrorizing this place, and worse than that was the thought of how to deal with any attempts to harm the forest dragon, let alone the others.

How many other hatch mates would they need to protect?

Jason didn't know.

All he knew was that they had to protect the three he knew about.

Family first, then village...

There was only one thing to do. It was the one thing he had avoided, and yet now it was time to stop avoiding it. There was no reason not to return to Dragon Haven other than the fact that he if he brought David with him, there was a real risk to the others.

He could leave him.

He didn't necessarily trust David, but he also didn't know if he needed to harm him. He didn't really want to hurt the man, and he couldn't shake the sense that David knew something he wasn't sharing yet.

"You can go," he said to the dragons. He turned to the maroon dragon, the black dragon, and he wondered how much they would understand and whether they would even respond. It was possible that they wouldn't, that they wouldn't be able to do anything, and yet, he looked at them, feeling a connection to them. "Unless you intend to return to Lorach, you are free."

The maroon dragon turned toward him, and power emanated from the creature. It was heat, and it flowed, rolling over Jason. He had felt something similar from the other dragons before, and yet this time it felt different. It was a power that washed over him, leaving him uncertain.

That heat passed, leaving Jason unharmed.

"You are the one who freed me."

"I didn't do it alone. I had help from the dragons."

"Who are you?"

"My name is Jason Dreshen."

"Who are you?"

Hadn't he just answered that? Perhaps it was a different question, the same question he asked himself. Who was he?

There was a time when he'd thought he was a hunter, and that he would stay in the village, and yet now that he had been here, now that he had spent the time with the dragons, he could no longer feel as if he were a hunter. He was something else, more than what he had been before, and yet, Jason didn't know exactly what that was, only that he was no longer the same as what he had believed.

"I don't know, but I'm trying to understand."

The dragon rumbled and let out a streamer of fire.

He turned to the other dragon. The black dragon was powerful, and he suspected if he could, he needed to get some message to that dragon as well, and perhaps he could help the black dragon understand. When they had been attacked, there had been some way that the black dragon had disappeared. It was probably tied to the power the dragons possessed, or perhaps even whatever the Dragon Souls had done, using their magic, and yet, he didn't care. All he cared about was checking to see if the black dragon was unharmed.

The dragon watched him, and there was power radiating from him.

"You would be free as well," Jason said.

The dragon said nothing and launched into the air.

He spiraled up, circling the same way the dragons had when Jason had been near Henry. The maroon dragon watched them for a moment before following, taking off and heading off to the west.

When they were gone, David stared up at the sky. "I wonder what will become of that."

"Why?"

"Because they didn't head back to Lorach. I don't know where they're going, but it is somewhere else."

Jason sighed. If the dragons returned to Lorach, there would be nothing he could do to help protect them, and it was possible that the Dragon Souls would once again control them. And yet, that was their choice, wasn't it? Was not the entire point of all this that he didn't get to choose for the dragons?

He had done what he thought he could, trying to rescue them, to free their minds, but beyond that, he didn't know if there was anything else he would be able to accomplish.

As he stood there, he couldn't help but feel as if there were answers, and yet, he needed to move.

"What do you plan to do?" David asked.

"I plan to get help," he said.

"What kind of help?"

"The kind of help that will ensure the forest dragon"— and the other hatch mates, he didn't add—"is unharmed."

15

There was a part of Jason that wondered if he would remember how to find Dragon Haven. As they soared overhead, he focused on the token Henry had given him and was able to use that to guide him. More than just directing him, it helped guide the ice dragon. It was almost as if the ice dragon knew how to find where they were heading.

But then, the ice dragon had claimed he was able to use knowledge Jason possessed, and by doing so, he was able to know much the same things that Jason knew.

He wished there would be something else they could do, and yet, as they flew, he couldn't help but feel as if he were doing what was necessary. In order to help the dragons, he was going to have to secure the protection of Dragon Haven.

When he did, what was going to happen?

Jason worried it was going to require an all-out battle,

and yet, perhaps that was what was necessary. In order to protect these misfits, the dragons that had taken on characteristics of their land, he thought it might be.

"How much farther do we have to fly?" David asked.

"I don't really know. I can feel the effect of where we're heading, but I don't know how long it will take us to reach it."

"You've been here before?"

When Jason had shared with him where they were going, David had seemed almost excited. It was enough for Jason to consider not allowing David to come with him, and yet, he needed help, and he thought David would be able to offer either assistance or information.

More than anything, they needed that information. They needed to have some leverage over the Dragon Souls. But there was another reason he'd agreed to allow David to come.

"I've been here once, but it wasn't by my doing."

"How did you end up here, then?"

Jason said nothing. In the distance, there was a sense of change. It was a shifting on the air, that of warmth, and he allowed himself to breathe it in, feeling the way it changed the air, the nature of the power as it flowed through him.

It was strange, unique, and strong.

The more he pulled on that sense, the more he was aware of it, and the easier it was to know he was traveling in the right direction.

But that wasn't all. There was something else in the air,

some other sense, and the longer they flew, the more certain he was he detected it.

It had something to do with the dragons, but what?

He could feel it. It was a sense of power that flowed through him and energy that radiated around them.

And then it faded.

A barrier. That was what it was.

Dragon Haven was a large city, though not as populated as what the area could contain. There were hundreds of structures, all of them blending into the forest, the curves so different than what was found in his village. Black obsidian sculptures were scattered around the city, many of them of dragons. Those sculptures drew his attention even from the sky. One of the structures was larger than the rest, situated near the center of the city. It was where he had met Sarah.

Coming back to Dragon Haven left him feeling guilt. Mostly it was because he felt as if he had betrayed Sarah and Henry and even William. He had denied the existence of the ice dragon. He had denied the presence of that dragon, and he had withheld knowledge of it from them.

Would they forgive him?

He didn't have any idea what they were going to find, or what sort of greeting they would get, and as they approached, Jason realized he didn't even know how to find anyone.

But then, it didn't matter.

Five dragons suddenly leapt into the air. They came in formation, a massive golden-scaled dragon leading the way. The others all had similarly bright colors, red and yellow and green and orange, and they streaked toward them.

Jason glanced over at the iron dragon. He was still with them, and yet he had been silent during their travels. They had not needed to rest, and though he didn't expect the iron dragon to need rest, the moment that the other dragons approached, he worried what would happen.

On a whim, Jason reached for the ice dragon pearl. He pulled on power through it, and he sent it surging out from him, toward the dragons, sweeping into the nearest of them. There was no resistance.

He worked his way over the dragons, one by one, and he found no resistance as he had with the other dragons, telling him that they were all untouched. None of them had been tormented, tainted the same way that the Dragon Soul dragons had been.

As the dragons approached, Jason sat upright. He stared, worrying about what they might uncover.

He needn't.

Sarah rode the lead dragon.

She looked as he remembered. She had bright blue eyes, high cheekbones, and golden hair that hung down her shoulders, fluttering in the breeze. She was beautiful. A band of silver ringed her head, catching the sunlight. He smiled at her, but she seemed not to notice.

"Jason?" she breathed out as they approached. Her gaze swept over the dragons, lingering on David, before looking back at him.

"Hey there," he said.

"What are you doing?"

"I found a pair of dragons."

She stared at the ice dragon. "I thought you said you didn't find a dragon."

He said nothing. She whistled and the dragons turned, banking, heading toward the ground. The ice dragon and the iron dragon followed, and he had a sense that even if he were to want to, he wouldn't be able to guide them any other way. They would have to follow the course of the other dragons, and if they didn't, he worried they would be attacked. He stayed with them, landing alongside the others.

When he was down, he slid down the ice dragon's side. "You need to take to the air."

"This place does not cause any discomfort," the ice dragon said.

"It doesn't?"

"I feel pressure, but I am free to draw upon the cold."

"If you need to fly higher in the sky, go ahead. I can summon you if I need you."

The dragon rumbled and Jason turned toward Sarah. She was dressed in a deep green cloak, and her hair hung in a braid. She was lovely, as lovely as she had been when he'd seen her before.

"What happened?" she snapped, watching him before taking in the dragonskin clothing for the first time. "A Dragon Soul? You're dressed like a Dragon Soul. And not just a Dragon Soul, but one of their Aurans?"

262 | D.K. HOLMBERG

Jason frowned at that and shook his head. "I don't know what that is."

She reached forward, grabbing his cloak, and twisted the pin on it. "This. It marks one of the Aurans..." She paused, studying David. She grabbed for the bearskin, touching it a moment before shaking her head. "I see. You brought one to us."

"He has information we could use," Jason said.

"I'm sure he does, but do you know what he might do to us when he gets the chance?"

"I have spoken the words of the flame," David said.

Jason shook his head, turning toward him. "Would you stop saying that? That doesn't mean anything to them any more than it does to me." He glanced over at Sarah, but her face had gone pale. "What is it?"

"The words of the flame. It's a vow. What exactly did he say?"

"Something about not hurting me. Not hurting the dragons. Not betraying me. I don't really remember. It was in the middle of me threatening to kill him."

That wasn't entirely what he'd done, though it was near enough. He wasn't really going to kill David, though he would have left him behind with a broken leg. He had no interest in harming the Dragon Souls, but he did want to ensure that the Dragon Souls didn't harm the dragons. If it came down to either him or the Souls, then he was more than willing to do what was needed.

"You managed to get an Auran to speak the words of the flame?"

"He wanted to study the dragons," Jason said.

She frowned again. "About that. What kind of dragons are these?"

Jason turned to the ice dragon, patting his side. "This is the ice dragon. I'm sorry I wasn't truthful with you when we were back in the mountains, but I had the sense from him that he didn't want to be discovered. And he saved me, so I kind of owed him."

"You hid a dragon from us. Do you know what might've happened?"

"What might've happened?"

"She fears that the Dragon Souls would have found him and claimed him," David said.

Jason shot him a hard look. "You're not helping your situation."

"I am speaking the truth. How is that not helping?"

"Your truth is going to end up getting them angry with you."

"Be that as it may, that is what she feared."

"I was there, and I was watching for any signs of the Dragon Souls," he said. "Therin didn't return."

"Just because he didn't return didn't mean he wasn't going to send people to search for that dragon. As far as you know, this Auran was sent to investigate."

Jason turned to David. "Is that what it was? Were you sent to investigate?"

"I was sent for a different purpose."

"And what purpose was that?"

"To find the missing eggs."

"What about the missing eggs?"

"Therin has been hiding from the Dragon Souls. He took them from us, and he has been using them for his own plans. I don't think any of us would've expected anything like this, and yet, with Therin involved, it's not altogether surprising."

"What do you mean by that?"

"I imagine Therin had you believe he was acting under our orders."

Jason shrugged. "He told me that he was working on behalf of Lorach. Isn't that the same?"

"Perhaps to him. And perhaps he was. Therin did sit above even the Aurans, given a place of authority beyond what most have. Because of that, he had less account-ability than he should have had. Therin abused his place and tainted the work we do."

"I'm not so sure you should be proud of the work you do."

"You don't understand."

"You keep telling me that, but I think I understand more than you believe, and I understand the nature of what you've done, the difference in the way you and I believe the dragons deserve to be treated. I understand far more than you do." He looked around. "How can you be in a place like this and not comprehend that?"

"Dragon Haven," David said, disdain dripping from his words. "A place where the dragons have been stolen, preventing us from training them. A place of the rebels and the rebellion."

"You're going to have to be careful. You're in a place where they don't view the dragons the same way as you."

"The rebels have never viewed the dragon the same. They have thought they could overcome us for ages, and where has that gotten them?" David looked around, his brow narrowing. "It has gotten them to Dragon Haven. Isolated. Separated from the rest of the world. Cut off from power."

"It has given the dragons the chance for freedom," Sarah said. She glared at David for a long moment before looking at the iron dragon. "I understand what happened with the ice dragon, and I can even understand your reasoning, but what about that one? I don't even know that I recognize what kind of dragon that is."

"I call him an iron dragon. The ice dragon said he detected his hatch mate, and he wanted me to help find them. We went looking, and we came across him."

"How?"

"He was held captive, and I think he has an affinity for iron. You should see the way his scales change when he's using fire. It's almost as if he becomes molten metal."

Sarah's eyes widened briefly. "You said hatch *mates?*"

Jason glanced over at David. "According to the dragon, there will be others."

She breathed out heavily. "We need to discuss this."

"I'm sorry I didn't bring it to you sooner. I was trying to help the dragon, and..."

"Why did you come now?"

"Because the Dragon Souls know."

"What do they know?"

"That there's another dragon." He glanced over at David. He hadn't shared much with him, either, and he didn't necessarily want to share, but he thought that Sarah of all people needed to know, to understand what he was concerned about and why he wanted to offer protection. There had to be some way to do so, and if it came down to it, he was willing to return. He would do it with or without the people of Dragon Haven, even though he understood that it involved danger.

"Let me guess, a water dragon?"

"No, though it wouldn't be surprising if we found one. This one was in the trees. He—or she; I didn't really know —had deep green eyes and wings that looked like the canopy of the trees. I could barely see her even when I was up close to her."

"You do realize what you're saying," Sarah said.

"I understand and I know how it might sound, but I'm telling the truth."

She frowned at him. "Considering how you appear to have a very different view of the truth, I'm not sure how much we can believe you. But I suppose that as you did bring the ice dragon and the iron dragon with you, we need to put some stock in what you're saying."

Jason sighed. He looked around the clearing. There were three smaller dragons off to the side, and they sat rigid, watching the ice and iron dragons, but the two misfit dragons were completely ignoring them. They were focused on the other dragons, the five that had arrived to greet them.

"What now?" he asked.

"Now we need to go to the others. If this is as critical as you say, we don't have much time."

"I'm sorry," he said.

"Don't tell me that you're sorry. Tell the dragon if we don't manage to get to it."

Sarah motioned to David, and he was forced in front of her. She glanced at Jason before following along the path that wound beside the forest, and every so often, she would look over, irritation glimmering in her eyes. He had worried about telling Henry what he'd done, but he hadn't given much thought to telling Sarah. And yet, perhaps he should have. Sarah had been there, fighting alongside him, helping him, and now that he was here, now that he realized what he had done, he thought that he had betrayed her.

Perhaps by hiding the ice dragon, he'd betrayed all of them.

"What has William been doing since he's been here?"

"He's worked on training dragons."

At the mention of training, David's head perked up.

Sarah pushed him. "Nothing like how you would train them. We train them differently. We train them on patterns, coordination, and we work with them to better understand how we use their power. It's almost as much training ourselves as we are the dragons."

"I didn't realize that William had any ability to reach the dragons," he said.

"He doesn't. At least, so far he hasn't shown that he does, but he wants to work, and in Dragon Haven, we don't exclude anyone who shows an interest in working."

David laughed softly. "It's a waste of time. If someone doesn't demonstrate a talent with the dragons, then they will not develop one. You waste not only your time, but the dragons.'"

"We don't decide for the dragons," Sarah said.

She shoved David forward again.

As she did, she shot Jason a look. It was filled with annoyance, and he worried that he'd made a mistake by bringing David here. Perhaps he would have been better served by leaving him behind with the other Dragon Souls. At least then, he would not have to worry about what Sarah might do or how she might react; and yet, there were things David knew, information he thought he could glean from the man.

They reached the building Jason remembered from before. It was all strange curves, made of stone, and blended in with the forest. The air here hung with the fragrance of flowers, mixing with that of the forest, and having been to various towns recently, he no longer found the smells to be quite as strange as he had before. In his village, there were no scents like that. The smells that he was familiar with were those of the burning of dung, the coppery scent of blood from a kill, the crisp cleanness of snow, and the smoky sweetness of tellum. That was it.

Sarah paused at the door and went over to David. She studied him for a long moment before shaking her head. "I can't believe we're going to do this," she muttered.

"You can't believe that we're going to do what?"

"Allowing an Auran in here. We've been safe for all these years, Jason. And now you bring somebody like this here, and yet, as strange as it is, I can't help but feel as if we need to do this," he said.

"I'm sorry," he said.

"You don't have to apologize to me. You have to apologize to the dragons if something happens to them."

Jason glanced toward the field in the back, and even though he couldn't see the dragons, he could practically feel them. With his connection to the ice dragon—and even to the iron dragon—he thought he could draw upon that power, and if he could, he thought he could summon them if he needed to. He didn't feel like he was going into any danger here, but at the same time, he didn't necessarily know for certain.

They stepped into the building and dim light greeted him. It took a moment for his eyes to adjust. Even with the dragon sight, it was a jarring change. As his eyes began to gradually adjust, he was able to make out shapes in the distance. Sarah reached a wide stairway.

When she motioned for David to start down it, Jason hesitated. "This isn't where we went the last time," he said.

"It isn't. We went a different way."

"Why this way?"

"Because of what we need to do."

"What do we need to do?"

Sarah shook her head. "Just get moving."

"Sarah?"

"Jason, don't challenge this."

They headed down the stairs. Lanterns glowed softly, illuminating the stairs. The deeper they went, the more the air began to change, taking on a faintly moldy scent. There was moisture somewhere nearby and the air was cool, though not unpleasantly so. Then again, he doubted he would find a place where the temperature was unpleasant to him.

They reached a lower level. The stairs didn't continue, but there was another door there. Sarah motioned for David to approach. Something about his bearing seemed to change; it was almost as if he stiffened. Sarah pulled keys from her pocket, unlocking the door, and when she pushed it open, it occurred to Jason just were they were.

"What is this?"

"You brought an Auran here," she said.

"You're going to put him into a cell?"

"You don't understand what an Auran is, Jason, but trust me when I tell you that I do. We have enough experience with them and the things they've done to know he will use any opportunity to harm us."

"Even though he said he spoke the words of the flame?"

"Seeing as how I wasn't there when he spoke them, there's no way for us to know what words they were and what they meant to him. And an Auran would likely have some way of maneuvering out of his oath."

Jason glanced over at David. All of this had been to try to find help, but he hadn't wanted to end up with David in jail. David had facilitated their discovery of the forest dragon, and now this would be his reward? It felt wrong, but more than that, he couldn't help but think that Sarah was acting without thinking.

They made their way along a narrow hallway lined by doors. Each of them had metal locks, and each was made of iron or steel. When she reached one, she unlocked it, and she motioned for David to step inside.

He looked over at Jason for a long moment before turning and heading into the cell.

"I spoke the words. What words will you speak?" he asked.

"I speak the words that protect the dragons."

"You don't have any idea—"

David didn't get the opportunity to say anything more. Sarah pulled the door closed, silencing him. On the other side, Jason could feel the energy, almost as if David were calling upon power, unless that wasn't what it was. It was possible the power he detected came from this cell.

Sarah started back toward the main door and paused at another cell, opening the door. She stood there for a moment, looking inside, staring, and then she shook her head. "Go," she said.

"Go where?" Jason asked, looking toward the stairs.

Sarah inhaled deeply. "Go into the cell, Jason."

"What?"

"You brought an Auran here," she said.

"I brought two dragons here as well."

"And one of them was one you tried to hide from us. Please. Don't make this harder than it needs to be."

"Or what?"

"We don't need to go into that."

"You don't need to do this," he said. "I am working on behalf of the dragons. I've been helping the ice dragon find the other hatch mates. I'm—"

Something grabbed him. He was too startled to process what was, but a band of power wrapped around him, thrusting him into the cell. He staggered forward and spun around, but not before the door closed on him. As it sealed shut, there came a sense of pressure all around him.

Jason didn't know what to say. He didn't know what to do. The only thing he could think of was that he had been betrayed. The worst part was that he didn't know whether he had been betrayed, or whether he was the one who had done the betraying.

He *had* kept information about the ice dragon from them, and because of that, the ice dragon had very nearly been captured. It was more than that, though. There was the danger of what he had done, the way he had almost betrayed the iron dragon. How much of this would've been better had he just brought news of the dragons to them here?

Jason stared at the door. He couldn't help but think that Sarah would open it, would release him, and that he would be free again, and yet now that he was here, he didn't know if that were the case or not.

The ice dragon would have to know. He didn't want the dragon to worry, didn't want the dragon to do anything. In this place, it was possible they would celebrate him and that they would protect both dragons, and yet, Jason didn't really know.

Breathing out, he pulled out the dragon pearls. Sarah hadn't even tried to take them from him. It was almost as if she didn't care—or she wasn't worried about them.

He held the ice dragon pearl, focusing on the cold. Though he was able to feel it, though there was a sense of cold flowing through here, he wasn't able to call upon its power.

What about heat? He held the dragon pearl that he'd taken from David. It might alert the others to him.

He wasn't going to do that. Regardless of the fact that they had held him here, and that they had decided to capture him, he wasn't going to be the reason Dragon Haven was identified by the Dragon Souls and Lorach. If nothing else, he would hold off.

There was another option.

The iron dragon pearl.

The only problem was that in order to use that power, he had to summon something. He didn't know if he could. He would have to find anger.

Was he angry?

Jason didn't necessarily feel angry. What was happening now was partly his fault. He had been the one who had withheld information that the others needed. Had he spoken up sooner, perhaps the dragons wouldn't be in danger.

If he didn't get free, then more than just the ice and iron dragon were going to be in danger. The forest dragon would be in danger too. If there were others, perhaps a water dragon as Sarah had said, they would be in danger. The Dragon Souls would go for them, and without his help, the people of Dragon Haven, anyone who might want to assist, wouldn't know where—or how.

That was the anger that filled him.

It did so slowly, building gradually, boiling up within him. It was the rage of the fact that they held him here, that they were going to keep him isolated. Regardless of any powers they might need to separate him from, severing any ties to the others, he didn't think they would have the ability to disconnect him from the iron dragon. The magic of that dragon was so different than any they knew.

Jason let that power flow through him, letting the anger and rage fill him, thinking about what the iron dragon had felt like what he'd been caged.

Images came to him.

They rolled through his mind, one after another, images of men on the other side of the bars, taunting the dragon, throwing things at him, jabbing him with sticks. They had offered food, but it had been rotten. Somehow the iron dragon had survived all of that, and despite all of that, he had still thrived.

And yet, he deserved better.

Rage began to build, flowing through him, the anger of the dragon, the anger that matched his own, and as it grew, he let it pour out into the dragon pearl.

He sent power toward the doorway. It slammed into it and then bounced back toward him. Jason was struck by his own magic and was thrown against the wall, striking his head, and he blacked out.

16

J ason came around slowly, his head throbbing. It took a moment to realize what had happened, and when he did, he remembered the way he'd drawn upon the anger, letting it fill him, and the way that he'd thrown it at the door. It had been useless. Whatever protections they had upon the cell were solid even against the iron dragon's magic.

Jason sat in place, crossing his arms over his legs, staring, completely trapped.

He didn't know if he could even figure out a way to escape. They had neutralized any connection he might have to the dragons. He focused, thinking about the strength he wanted, thinking about the power of the ice dragon, that of the iron dragon, and wondered if he could mix them. They had been joined when he had tried to heal one, and he wondered if perhaps he could join that power again.

Nothing happened.

The only other option was to draw upon the heat of one of the remaining dragon pearls, but he didn't want to do so and draw attention to this place.

He pulled out the dragon pearls he'd claimed from the Dragon Souls.

He now had nearly a dozen, and as he sorted through them, he was surprised to find that they were grouped by color.

Jason had not made that connection before, and when he'd been taking the dragon pearls, he hadn't paid any attention to their colors, only that he was claiming them. There was power within them, and a part of him knew he could use them, and yet, now that he had them, he didn't know if he truly could.

One of the dragon pearls was a deep maroon. He didn't see a black pearl, though he had to wonder if the blue dragon pearl with the black lines through it was the black dragon's pearl.

The maroon dragon. He had freed her. He had felt that freedom as he had done it. And regardless of where she had flown off to, he thought he could use her power. The more that he thought about it, the more certain he was she wouldn't even mind if he did. She'd been freed by him and he had done nothing to harm her afterward.

It was a gamble. If he was wrong and if this wasn't the maroon dragon's pearl, then there was a chance he'd be calling to the Dragon Souls, revealing the location of

Dragon Haven. Regardless of why they were holding him here, he didn't want to expose that.

Calling upon the heat, he felt it fill himself, and he poured that heat into the maroon dragon pearl, then added to the sense of cold, mixing hot and cold, ice and fire, and he fed them into the dragon pearls.

He let it out, exploding it against the door. This time, Jason stood off to the side, prepared for the possibility the power would bounce back on him. When it did, he was ready.

The door held.

He staggered toward the back of the cell.

Jason tried again, focusing on the two different powers. As he did, he could only draw upon an explosion. He didn't have any finesse. He let that power flow through him, holding the fire in his left hand, drawing cold through his right, and he combined them, blasting the doorway.

As before, the power rebounded, exploding back into the room. A streamer of dust trailed down from the ceiling, but nothing else changed.

What if he targeted one of the walls?

Jason focused on the stone next to him. He took a step back, and using a combination of fire and ice, he blasted it.

There came the explosion. The stone shattered, and yet it only created a small hole.

He tried again, sending power through it, and as

before, there was another hole, though this one seemed to go deeper.

The power plunged into the opening, and as he used that, he couldn't help but think that he could go from place to place before finally finding some way out.

And if he did, where was he going to go?

He was trapped here, and the moment that Sarah—or any of the others—found him, what would they do to him?

Jason ignored those thoughts, focusing instead on the hole. He would blast it open, get himself to freedom, find a way to get to the dragons.

He wasn't about to wait behind while the Dragon Souls reached the forest dragon.

Coming here had been his idea, and in doing so, he'd taken time away from the ice dragon and the iron dragon, separating them from one of their hatch mates and potentially putting that hatch mate in danger because of the Dragon Souls. He was going to do anything in his power, regardless of what it would take, to get to the hatch mates and free them.

Focusing on the heat and the cold, he built power, and exploded it one more time.

He leaned his head down, looking at the hole.

It led into the next cell.

"Stop," a voice said.

"David?"

Had he blasted his way into David's cell?

"Just stop," David said.

"I'm trying to get out of here," he said.

"I can tell." David's face appeared at the opening of the hole. It wasn't wide enough for one of them to crawl through, but David was able to stare through at him. "I thought these were your people."

"They aren't very happy that I didn't reveal the presence of the ice dragon to them."

"Why would you hide it from them?"

"Because I didn't know what they might do to it."

"You heard her mention training."

"Their training is different than yours."

"And yet here you are. Trained." It seemed almost as if David smirked at him, though in the darkness it was difficult to tell.

"Do you have any ideas on how to escape?"

"I imagine you have found that your magic is ineffective."

"It bounces off the door."

"And not the stone?"

Jason shook his head.

"Interesting. I would have expected their protections would have enveloped even that."

"I've used both fire and ice. The combination is how I freed the iron dragon. I tried the connection to the iron dragon, but..."

David leaned forward and stared at Jason. "You can use the power of the iron dragon?"

"I've begun to be able to use it."

"What's the key?"

Jason shook his head. "I'm not going to tell you how to use it. I don't want you to torment another dragon."

"Have I tormented the ice dragon?"

"No."

"Your friend doesn't trust the Aurans."

"I see that. What *are* the Aurans?"

"We're Dragon Souls, but we search for knowledge and understanding. Aurans have a unique role within Lachen. We sit outside of the Dragon Souls. We study, seeking to understand the history of the dragons and their relationship with our people."

"With the people of Lachen?"

David regarded him for a moment. "With the people of Lachen. With others. There are other lands that have known the dragons over the years, and the Aurans search for understanding. Knowledge."

"So that you can better control the dragons."

"Not control. Train."

Jason thought that he had a better understanding as to the role of the Aurans. He also thought he better understood why Sarah had been offended that he had dared bring one to Dragon Haven. They were the scholars, but they were the ones responsible for instructing the Dragon Souls on how better to control the dragons.

"If you really search for knowledge and understanding, then you would understand the dragons aren't what you believe them to be."

"It is precisely for that reason the Aurans exist. We understand exactly what dragons are, we understand the power they possess, and we understand the dragons' lack of control. Because of Dragon Souls, because of the Aurans and the way we've trained the dragons, we've kept that power in check. We have prevented others from being harmed by significant power."

"You've been around the ice dragon. Have you seen significant harm?"

"You have only minimal experience with the ice dragon. What do you think would happen if that dragon were free in a city?"

"You mean a city like this?"

"A city where other dragons exist? A city where they train dragons, regardless of what they claim? No. I'm talking about what would happen if they were to escape in your village. How do you think the dragon would be received?"

"I know how the dragons would be received," Jason said.

"They're feared, are they not?"

"Because people don't understand."

"And you think you could help them understand the dragons are peaceful creatures? Do you think you can help your people believe the dragons want nothing more than to live peacefully among you? Do you think you can convince your people the dragons are safe?"

Jason took a deep breath. He knew better. He'd lived his entire life believing the dragons were dangerous and deadly. He knew the way his people would react if they encountered a dragon. Even though the ballistae hadn't been fired in years, the people of the village would try.

"You believe training the dragons gives people less reason to fear?"

"I believe giving people the perception of training allows them to not fear the dragons."

"How is that different?"

"When you have trained dragons, and the people believe the dragon is trained, do you think they fear the dragon or the handler?"

"Probably both," he said.

"Perhaps, and yet, my experience in Lorach is such that they fear the handler. They recognize the power of the Dragon Souls, and they would do nothing to attack us."

"You want your people to fear you?"

"I want our people to know the dragons are trained. I want our people to know the dragons will be fighting on our side. I want our people to know the Dragon Souls provide defense of the kingdom."

"And what do you know about the dragons?" Jason asked.

"I know what the Aurans have known for centuries," he said.

"And what is that?"

"Where you see intelligence, I see a need for training. They long for that, and though you might disagree, I have seen it in every dragon I have encountered. All of them need the training."

"That wasn't my sense from the two dragons I freed."

"And what do you think those dragons will do?"

"I don't know what dragons will do, and I don't even know where the dragons will go. They're free, so they get to choose."

David stared at him, and a hint of a smile began to spread on his face. "Have you ever seen a dragon hunt?"

"What does that have to do with anything?"

"Have you seen it?"

"I've been with the ice dragon when he's hunted. Why?"

"What do you think would happen to people in your village if the dragon decided to hunt there?"

"I don't think dragons hunt people," Jason said.

"You don't think. I've seen it. I've witnessed the violence of dragons, and I know the way they would torment others."

"You aren't going to convince me the dragons need to be trained."

"I don't care to convince you of anything. I'm telling you what I know." David stepped closer to the opening. "There is one thing. You have convinced me that I was wrong." Jason arched a brow, and David stepped closer to the opening. "About your kind. Seeing the power you wield has opened my eyes. When I return to Lorach, I intend to test your kind to see what more they might be able to do."

Jason leaned back, unable to know what to do. Here he had thought he might be able to get through to David, that he might convince him to do something else, but it seemed as if he were determined to return, to continue his attacks on people like him.

What did that mean? What was he going to do?

At this point, probably nothing. Jason had wanted to try to help, to offer anything he could, and yet, it didn't seem as if there would be any way to influence someone like David.

He stared at David, looking through the opening, and wondered if perhaps he should leave him behind. Maybe it was best that he was trapped here. But Jason was determined to escape. It was going to be difficult, and he didn't know how much it would take to fight his way to freedom, but he would try.

Jason pointed the dragon pearls at the opening again. As he did, David backed up, looking away.

"You won't be able to do anything," David said.

"I'm going to get out of here. I'm going to reach the ice dragon and the iron dragon and I'm going to do anything I can to help them."

He let the energy that he was pulling explode out from him. As it did, it hit the wall between the two cells again, cracking it as before. The opening became wider, and David backed up. Jason attempted to pull on power again, letting it flow through him, and as before, he poured it out into the wall.

Each time he did so, he let that energy explode from him.

David merely watched.

Jason had the sense that David would be able to help if

he wanted to, and yet David stood back, letting Jason expend himself. Was he going to try to take the dragon pearls from him when he entered the cell? David had proven he had some connection to the ice dragon, and it wouldn't surprise Jason to learn he had some way of using the heat from the maroon dragon, but he wasn't about to abandon what he was doing. He needed to continue his assault and find some way to break through the walls.

And once he was in the same cell as David, he was going to keep going. Eventually he would have to find some way out. Then he could escape. The power flowed from him, slamming into the wall, again and again.

"Are you going to stand there and watch?" Jason asked.

"Do you think I should do something else? You're the one who's using this power. Do you even understand what you're doing?"

"I'm drawing from the dragons."

"Is that what you believe?"

"That's what Therin told me."

"If that's what he told you, then he was misleading you."

"What am I doing, then?"

David stepped forward, crossing his arms in front of him. It was a strange thing to look at the man dressed in Jason's bearskin, appearing as if he were like anybody from the village. "You're summoning power from yourself."

"From myself?"

"Some among the Dragon Souls have innate power.

That's what we use to call upon the power we borrow from the dragon."

Jason smiled at him. "I don't have any power."

"And yet here you are, holding on to dragon pearls and blasting a hole between cells. What do you think that is other than power?"

Jason took a step back, clutching the dragon pearls, looking at the opening that he had formed between the two cells. He did have some power, but he didn't really know what it meant or what he was supposed to do with it. He'd created the openings between the two cells, and now that he was here, now that he had done so, he didn't know what he would need to do next.

He looked back toward the doorway. That was where he had to focus his energy. Even if he couldn't blast his way free, he had to find some way of opening the door. If he went cell to cell, he wasn't going to be able to escape.

And he needed to focus his energy, his anger, on what had happened, why he was here. Sarah blamed him, and yet by holding him here, by confining him, wasn't she to blame as well?

Could he draw upon both hot and cold and the iron dragon?

He didn't know if he was able to summon that much power. He leaned against the wall, holding the different dragon pearls in his hand, staring at them, focusing. It would be a different technique. He could reach the ice dragon and the maroon dragon at the same time, but reaching for the power within the iron dragon took a different type of focus. He strained, trying to come up with what he could in order to find that focus, and struggled to do so. The energy might be there, but he was unable to reach it. The longer he stood there, the more uncertain he was that he could even do anything. He debated releasing the hot and the cold at the doorway again, but he'd done that twice before and failed.

He wasn't going to be able to do anything. He wasn't going to be able to get out of here. He was going to remain trapped, no different than David.

"You begin to see the dilemma," David said.

"I don't deserve to be trapped like this," he muttered.

"And I do?"

"You're an Auran."

"You say that as if you suddenly understand what that means. You know what it means no better than they do."

"I know what you are doing to the dragons."

"You know what they tell you was done to the dragons. We can go around and around with this, and I can continue to share with you what I know, but it won't change your mind."

Jason took a seat on the floor and stared at the door to the cell.

He couldn't shake the sense the dragons needed him. It was more than just the dragons outside; it was the dragons in the other part of the world, the misfits, the dragons that the Dragon Souls would go for. If only he had some way of finding them, of chasing them down, and yet he didn't even know how to get out of the cell and help them.

He rested his head on the wall. As he did, he held on to the dragon pearls, rolling them in his hands. Regardless of what David said, he didn't have the power within himself. He might have the ability to draw upon the dragons, and that was a specific type of power, but he didn't possess anything more than that. It was a wonder he had the magic he did.

"You should get up," David said.

"And do what?"

"Someone is coming," he said.

Jason grunted. "How can you tell?"

"Do you think I need a dragon pearl to use my ability?" Jason glanced over at him. David stood rigidly in the opening between the cells. "You saw me in the forest when you were trying to help that dragon. Did I require a dragon pearl?"

"We'd taken the pearls from you," Jason said.

"You had, but you didn't eliminate my ability to use power. You might have believed you did, but I'm not completely helpless."

"If you're not helpless, then get yourself free."

"As you have seen, they have protections that prevent that. I can use my own abilities to recognize when some-thing is coming. And as I said, something *is* coming."

Jason stared at the door and didn't want to move. He didn't want to say anything, and he didn't want to even look up. Regardless of what David told him, he didn't have that power, and perhaps he didn't even care. The longer he was here, the more he was doing, the more uncertain he became.

This was beyond him. All of this was beyond what he could do. He had come thinking he could help the dragons, and though he might have aided the iron dragon, and though he had discovered the forest dragon, he didn't know enough to be of much use.

"You *do* need to get up," David said.

"I'm comfortable here," Jason said.

"I didn't take you for the type to abandon hope so easily."

"I'm not abandoning hope. I'm merely waiting."

"I've seen men like you before. This is abandoning hope."

"Do you think I should do something different?"

"I think you should be ready. The moment your door opens, you can attack. When you do, then you can find your way to freedom."

Jason sighed. He doubted he would be able to get to freedom, but then, it was possible he could attack when the door was opened. He thought about using the combination of the powers, drawing upon both the fire and the ice. If he put them together, it was unlikely that anyone would be able to overwhelm that.

Getting to his feet, he watched the two dragon pearls, and then he changed his mind.

The iron dragon pearl instead.

He let his irritation, his anger, the fact that he wasn't

able to help his family, his sister, his mother, and his village, fill him.

Those emotions rolled through him, the boiling rage that began to bubble up within him. It matched the anger within the iron dragon, and he held on to that simmering sort of heat. It flowed into the dragon pearl, leaving the pearl to glow with the heat that he didn't feel. It was almost as if he were immune to it.

The door opened.

Jason unleashed that anger, the nature of the heat, and it exploded.

It struck the opening and he ran toward the door, prying it open.

On the other side of the door, Henry lay unmoving.

J ason hesitated. Now that the door was open, he should escape. He looked along the length of the tunnel, debating what to do, and yet this was Henry. This was someone who had helped him, who had explained to him all that he knew about the dragons, and though Henry was a strange man, he had been responsible for supporting Jason.

He wore his black furs, but the heavy beard covering his jawline seemed to be trimmer than the last time Jason had seen him. The wrinkles along the corners of his eyes appeared more etched than before. He didn't move.

What had Jason done?

He glanced back. David was trying to crawl into the room.

Holding on to the ice dragon pearl, Jason pushed power outward, letting it flow and slamming into the wall where David crawled through. He yelped and backed up.

Taking a deep breath, Jason turned his focus to the fallen man in front of him. He held on to the dragon pearl and debated. Which dragon pearl should he use? He wanted to help Henry. He wasn't about to leave the man to suffer. Who knew how long he could lie here until someone found him.

He used the power of the ice dragon. He let it flow through him, and having gone through the motions several times, he understood the way the ice dragon magic could be used to heal. It flowed out from him, washing into Henry. This time, there was no guidance, no sense of the ice dragon helping him, and yet Jason thought he understood how to use it. He used the energy while searching for injury. When he encountered it, he continued to push, letting that power overwhelm Henry.

With a gasp, Henry opened his eyes.

He rolled over, and power began to build from him.

Jason backed up, gripping a pair of dragon pearls, ready to protect himself, though he wasn't sure how.

"What was that?" Henry asked.

"That was my fault."

"You?" He flicked his gaze into the room before looking back at Jason. "You've grown since the time I saw you last."

"What do you mean?"

"In skill." Henry sat up, flicked his gaze once more into the room, and frowned. "Stay in your cell."

Jason turned to see David trying to crawl through

again. When Henry said it, David crawled back, muttering something.

"If you knew I was here, why would you let them keep me trapped?"

"I only learned you were here now. Sarah did what she thought was necessary."

"By trapping me here?"

Henry nodded to the back of the cell. "You brought an Auran."

"I brought him here because I needed answers. There are other dragons out there we need to help."

"I know. That's why I'm here."

"You know?"

"I don't believe I would've known otherwise, but your dragons made it clear."

"What do you mean by my dragons?"

"The dragons you brought with you."

"You were talking with them?"

"No one has been talking with them. Once you were brought away, they became unsettled. They are quite powerful."

"I'm sorry about that."

"No you're not. And you shouldn't be. You didn't control the dragons. You connected to them. That's the ideal of the Dragon Haven. And yet, we need to do something so they don't harm anyone else."

"How many people have they harmed?"

"Come with me, and I will show you."

"No." Jason went back to David. "I'm not sure who I

should go with. I'm not even sure who I can trust anymore."

"It's about time," Henry said.

"What do you mean by that?"

"I mean you should have been questioning all along. Dragon Haven is safe for the dragons. I've shown you that, but you need to come to your own understanding. I thought you had when you decided to remain in your village."

Jason turned away. "I remained because I didn't know what to do with the dragon. And I needed to help my family."

Henry studied him. "That's the only reason you remained?"

"Mostly. I did what I needed to in order to protect those I care for."

"Interesting. What brought you out of your village in pursuit of the other dragons?"

Family first...

"The ice dragon." Jason looked up, meeting Henry's eyes. He had two deep silver eyes, unlike Jason, who had only one. There was a sense that radiated from Henry, the same sort of power he'd picked up on when he first met the man. "He recognized his hatch mates were in need of help. We went looking, and..."

"You found the iron dragon."

"I did."

"Where?"

"Why does that matter?"

"Because I've been searching for evidence of other dragons. Ever since we left you, I have been hunting for that information, knowing Therin wouldn't have left only one egg. There would've been more, and if he was successful anywhere, I thought I would hear."

"Varmin."

Henry scratched his chin. "Interesting. That would make sense with it being an iron dragon, but I didn't hear anything in Varmin about the presence of a dragon."

"They had it held captive in one of the iron mines."

"How were you able to find it?"

Jason shook his head. "I don't really know. I followed the sense of rumbling, almost as if I were hearing the dragon, but honestly, I think it was chance more than anything else."

"It is unlikely that it was chance."

"Why would you say that?"

Henry flicked his gaze past Jason and held David's eyes for a long moment. "You have an Auran with you. And not just any Auran, but one who sits high within Lorach. He serves at the right hand of the throne. Unfortunately, I suspect he hasn't been completely truthful with you."

"I don't know. I think David has been the only one who has been truthful with me."

"David? Is that what he's calling himself?"

"It is my name," David said.

"Is it? When I was in Lorach, you went by another moniker. Do you want me to share that with Jason, or would you care to do so?"

David turned away. He retreated from the opening in the cell, leaving Jason watching that emptiness.

"What was he called?"

"He was known as Dragon's Bane. A powerful Auran, perhaps one of the strongest. And he has a very particular understanding of the nature of the dragons and views his role with them in a very specific way."

Why would David have lied to him?

Then again, why wouldn't he have lied to him? He was an Auran, he was a Dragon Soul, and he'd been hunting the dragons. He wanted to learn everything Jason might know about finding the other dragons, and it wouldn't surprise Jason that he would be willing to lie in order to uncover anything he could.

"What now?"

"Now you need to come with me, no differently than I said before."

"What about him?"

"He will remain here."

"In this cell?"

"Do you think there should be another place?"

"Are you sure the cell can hold him?"

Henry studied the inside of the cell. "I would have said yes, but then again, I've never seen anyone able to blast a hole between cells. We've held other Dragon Souls here over the years, and none have managed to do anything like that. This place is meant to protect from it. The power of it is too overwhelming, and yet..." He leveled his gaze on Jason, a hint of a smile curling his lips. "You managed to do so."

"I didn't do it alone. I had help."

"I imagine you did. And considering the type of dragons you've been working with, I suspect that help has been considerable."

Henry held out a dragon pearl, and he pushed power into it. It flowed into the room, something Jason could almost see, and it washed along the walls. When it was done, whatever Henry was doing retreated, but the power remained. He frowned for a moment before nodding. Closing the door, he locked it again and motioned for Jason to follow him.

"What are the words of the flame?"

Henry froze. "What did he say?" Jason told him, and Henry looked toward the cells. "The words of the flame are dangerous. It is where you make a promise to the fire within yourself, and use that energy. If you betray the vow, that energy will burn off you."

"What does that mean? You won't be able to use your magic?"

"I'm afraid it's a bit more than that. I've only seen the words of the flame spoken a few times, and I've only seen them violated once. It is a brutal thing. When someone speaks the words and then they violate that vow, the words and the vow tear through them, as if fire is burning from the inside out." Henry's voice trailed off toward the end and became much softer. "You claim he spoke the words of the flame?"

"He did speak them," Jason said.

"And my suspicion is that he spoke them with the intention of finding a way beyond them. I don't know what he planned, or how he thought he would be able to maneuver around the words, but it's unlikely that he spoke them intending to comply by them." He glanced toward the door. "Knowing him as vaguely as I do, I have a feeling he spoke them thinking that he would convince you. Most people from Lorach are at least familiar with the words of the flame, and they understand that if a Dragon Soul speaks them, there would be no way for them to violate that."

"But I didn't know what it meant."

That was the part of all of this that troubled Jason the most. David had spoken words, even though Jason had not really understood what they meant. David had said it anyway. He could have said anything. He could've claimed any vow. Why did it have to be words of the flame?

He looked back toward the doors.

"I know you don't believe him, and I'm not sure I can believe him, either, but…" The more Jason thought about it, the more certain he was that there was something more taking place. He couldn't help but feel as if, regardless of Henry's feelings about David and about Aurans in general, there was something more he was missing. It was the same thing he felt about Sarah and her abrupt decision to imprison him.

There was more taking place here.

Jason spun, facing the cell, and he headed back toward

David's cell, stopping in front of the door. "We need to understand what he's doing, and he has no power with him. I've taken his dragon pearls. I've even taken his clothing," he said, motioning to himself and the dragonskin he was wearing. "I made sure the dragons accepted me wearing it, but he doesn't have anything. No marker of his office. No power."

"You asked the dragon if you could wear the dragonskin?"

"I thought it was appropriate. I didn't want the dragons to be angry if I suddenly was wearing a dragonskin cloak and jacket."

Henry smiled. "How did that go?"

"The ice dragon was fine with it." He hadn't really asked the iron dragon, but the iron dragon was different. The more he understood that dragon, the more certain he was of that fact.

Henry chuckled softly, shaking his head. "Interesting. Regardless, the Aurans don't need dragon pearls in order to use their power. It will certainly augment it, but without a dragon pearl, they still have some power within them."

That was the same thing that David had admitted. It was even more reason to question how much David had been lying to him. It might not be nearly as much as what Henry believed. And if he wasn't lying, and if at least part of what he said was the truth, then they needed to include him. It might be difficult for Henry and the others in

Dragon Haven to believe, but the more he thought about it, the more certain he was.

"He's going to have to come with us," Jason said.

"I can't allow that."

"You can't, but I can."

"He knows how to find Dragon Haven."

"Then find some way to prevent him from remembering."

Henry shook his head. "It doesn't quite work like that. We don't have any way of restricting memory. That's not how the dragon pearls work."

"Make him say the words of the flame that he won't share the location."

Henry stared at him, and there was a debate waging behind his eyes, flickering there. Jason didn't know all that Henry had gone through when he served the Dragon Souls, but he did know that Henry had changed, and that because of that, he viewed those commitments very differently. He viewed those who still served the Dragon Souls differently as well. If anyone would understand wanting something different, wanting to be someone different, it would be Henry.

Jason wasn't completely convinced that David wanted to be anything different. He still had mentioned returning to Lorach, and being here hadn't changed David's belief that he would be able to return. If he did so, there was little doubt in Jason's mind that David would try to use the knowledge he had gleaned to somehow harm dragons here.

Then again, if he made a commitment, if he spoke the words of the flame, then perhaps Henry and others here would believe him.

"Have him do it publicly," Jason said.

"Publicly?"

"In front of the dragons."

Henry frowned, taking a deep breath and letting it out slowly. "You don't know what you're asking," he said.

"I don't, but I think you need to risk it."

"Why?"

"Because we might need him for this."

"We can't trust him."

"Did the people of Dragon Haven say the same about you?"

Henry held his gaze for a long moment. "Yes."

"Then it's even more reason for you to do this. You know what it's like. You know how hard it is to gain the trust of someone who believes you have no interest in what is important to them. I'm not saying David is reformed and I'm not saying that he's going to work on behalf of the dragons, but I do think he can be useful. And he was helping me."

More than anything, that thought stuck with Jason.

Henry let out a loud sigh and turned toward the door, twisting the keys in it and unlocking it. When he pulled it open, David stood on the other side.

"I know you," David said.

"If you know me, then you know what I'm willing to do."

David glanced beyond Henry to Jason, locking eyes with him. There was a question there, though Jason wasn't sure what David was thinking. Was he upset he'd freed him from the cell?

"I know how you betrayed our people," David said to Henry.

"Not my people. Not anymore."

"And yet you still betrayed them."

"Did I? What if those people betrayed me?"

"You were trained. You were given power. And you betrayed it."

"I was betrayed. The lessons taught to me were wrong. And everything we believed was wrong."

"Is that what you think to teach him?" David nodded to Jason. "And yet you don't give him the other side. You don't allow him to know what his power can do."

"I haven't done anything to his power."

Henry grabbed David and jerked on his back, thrusting him in front of him. Henry was considerably larger than David, larger than Jason, and he forced David forward. "Get moving."

"Is this how it's going to be? Are you going to bring me out here and destroy me?"

"I'm not going to bring you out and do anything. And you have Jason to thank for this."

"For what?" David asked, studying Jason. He crossed his hands over his arms, watching him.

"For your new vow."

"What new vow?"

"You're going to make a vow in front of the dragons. You are going to speak the words of the flame. And you are going to commit to protecting them."

"You know I can't do that."

"I know you think you can't, but you will. And if you don't, you'll be returned to the cell and that will be the end of it."

David laughed bitterly. "Is this how you treat all of us? Do you force all of us to make a vow in front of the dragons? Do you think such a thing will change anything?"

Henry shook his head. "We haven't made anyone do this before. This will be the first time."

"Will it? Then why me?"

"Ask Jason."

Henry started off and David regarded Jason for a long moment, saying nothing. There was heat in his gaze, and something burned within his eyes, but he remained silent.

Jason followed Henry to the end of the hall, to the stairs, and back up to the main level. Once there, Henry guided them outside. Jason focused on his connection to the dragons, the power within him, and found no resistance to it.

There was more activity out here today than he remembered from the other time he had been here. He caught sight of movement along the street, and though it was distant, he could tell there were a dozen people marching. All of them were dressed in dragonskin, and all were heading toward the field where he had left the dragons.

Jason looked up at Henry. "What's going on?"

"You are what's going on," Henry said.

"Me?"

Henry smiled. "When you brought the dragons here. By bringing something we've never seen before to Dragon Haven."

They wound along the street, where more and more people were gathering. Jason counted dozens upon dozens of people, though not all of them headed in the same direction. He glanced over at Henry, watching to see what Henry might do or say, but he showed no reaction.

As they reached the edge of the city, Jason looked around, focusing on the energy coming from the dragons. He could practically feel that energy, and as he did, he looked for the ice dragon. Where was he?

There was no sign of the ice dragon. Had they done something to him?

The iron dragon was here. There was heat radiating from the center of the clearing, an incredible amount of heat. It wasn't just the heat, but the way the iron dragon glowed, the metal pulsing along his sides, the undulating, molten nature of his scales.

"What did you do to the ice dragon?" Jason asked.

"When you didn't return, he disappeared," Henry said.

"Disappeared?"

Henry glanced toward the sky. "Disappeared. We haven't been able to track him."

"Is that unusual?"

"We are familiar with dragons, and we should be able to track all of them, and yet... he has evaded us."

"You realize how you sound," David said.

"How do we sound, Dragon's Bane?"

David ignored the barb and looked toward the sky. "You blame the Dragon Souls for behavior you carry out. Do you really think you are so different?"

"I know we're different," Henry said.

He continued into the clearing, heat rising all around, and Jason approached the iron dragon. He realized that a circle of people surrounded the dragon, though none of them got too close.

Even David slowed as they neared, turning away.

Jason cautiously approached. He held his hand out, looking into the iron dragon's orange eyes. "Did they hurt you?"

"Where were you?"

"They decided I was a danger."

"You are no danger to the dragons," the iron dragon said.

"I know that. I think you know that. But they..."

He looked behind him. The faces were watching him, but there was only one among them that he had any eyes for. Sarah stood among the circle of people, slightly forward, and she frowned as she watched Jason near the iron dragon.

"How come they aren't able to approach you?"

"I choose not to let them," the iron dragon said.

"And me?"

"I choose to let you."

"Why?"

"You helped when you did not need to."

"You needed my help," Jason said. He looked behind him again. "Now it's time for you to relax. I don't know if they intend to do anything. I think they're more curious about you than anything."

"Why?"

"Because you aren't anything like the other dragons."

"That isn't a reason for them to watch me," the iron dragon said.

"Perhaps not." Jason sighed. "We still need to go back and stop the Dragon Souls from reaching your hatch mates."

"You came here for help."

"I came for help, but I'm no longer certain there is anything here that will help us with what we need to do. At this point, I think we need to get back to the forest, to ensure the forest dragon isn't harmed."

"She is able to hide better than any others."

"She?"

"You didn't know?"

"No. She was amazing, but I've never seen anything like it before. I worry if the Dragon Souls reach her, they will be able to control her, the same way they attempted to control you."

"They won't be able to control me any longer," the iron dragon said.

"Is it because of the ice dragon's healing?"

"What you did has prevented them from reaching me."

"Did they try?"

"They did, but there is no way for them to reach me. The other decided to test whether they could."

"The other..." Jason glanced over at David. Had he wanted to test whether or not the healing was enough to protect the dragons?

It was almost too much to believe, and yet, there had been no evidence that the dragon had been harmed by going with David.

"He asked if we could test it," the iron dragon said.

"And you went along with it?"

"I thought it was appropriate."

Jason smiled to himself. "The forest dragon seems to have some natural resistance, though I don't really understand how."

"Did you free her as well?"

"I didn't do anything with her. Any resistance she might have is within herself. I didn't notice any influence on her at all."

It wasn't for a lack of testing. Jason had tried to determine if there was anything there, but when he had reached for her mind, he hadn't come across anything. For now, she remained free, though he wondered how much longer that would be the case. It was possible that something would happen and she would end up captured, and given her ability to camouflage, it would be an even greater challenge if she were.

"Jason?"

He turned and saw Sarah approaching slowly. Her jaw was clenched and sweat shimmered on her brow.

"What?"

"How is it that you can approach the dragon?"

"What do you mean?"

"The rest of us can't get any closer than this. And yet you're standing right near him."

"Because he allows me to."

"He allows it?"

Jason nodded. "The dragon chooses who gets to approach."

"That's not how it works," Sarah said.

"Maybe not with your dragons, but with him, it is."

And with the ice dragon, there was a very different sort of protection. Considering the way the ice dragon could form ice spikes and shoot them, he had a different sort of defense mechanism. It didn't take much for the dragons to use that power, to ensure their safety.

"I'm going to go and prevent the Dragon Souls from capturing the other misfits."

Family first.

Did it mean he viewed the dragons as family?

They had changed him. Were still changing him. Perhaps they *were* family now, in a way.

"Misfits?"

Jason smiled at the iron dragon. "That's what David called them. I think it fits. They *are* different. They are what they are."

"You came here for a reason."

"I thought I did, but it doesn't seem as if anyone here wants to help. I'm not about to leave the dragons to their fate. I'm going to see if there's anything I can do to ensure their safety. Whether or not anyone comes with me is a different matter."

He reached for the iron dragon and climbed on his back. "Will you allow David to come with us?"

"He may come."

Jason locked eyes with David and nodded.

David approached, making it through the heat to stand near Jason.

Sarah stared for a moment before letting out a frustrated sigh. "Let me help," she said.

"Are you sure? That means attacking the Dragon Souls."

"I wouldn't be able to bring any of the dragons with me. It would just be me. Maybe Henry," she said, glancing at him. "There might be a few others."

"That's not going to be enough," Jason said. He had no idea how many dragons the Dragon Souls might bring, but he had a feeling that however many the people of Dragon Haven brought wouldn't be enough. With their connection to not only dragons, but the dragon pearls, the Dragon Souls would be formidable.

"We don't dare risk them. We've managed to rescue them from the Dragon Souls, and many of them have been born free, but they won't stay free if we bring them too near the Souls."

"I can help with that," Jason said.

"What do you mean?"

"There's a way of protecting the dragons."

"You can't protect them. We've tried."

"As a matter of fact, he can," David said. He nodded to the iron dragon. "I went so far as to test whether such a thing were possible, and whatever he has done has protected the dragons. I am unable to influence the dragon."

"I don't know that I can believe you."

David smiled. "You are a Dragon Soul," he said, looking past Sarah and to Henry. "Or were. Try it."

"That's not how we do things here," Henry said.

"Do you fear that you're unable to do so?"

"I fear the dragons would be unhappy with me if I tried," Henry said.

"And yet, Jason has told you he has protected the dragons."

"I'm sorry, but Jason doesn't know anything about his abilities. Anything he's learned has been from—"

"The dragon," Jason said, glancing from David to Henry. "That's where I learned it. I might not really understand the nature of using the dragon pearl magic the same way as you do, but I learned from working with the ice dragon. And now from the iron dragon. They helped me understand how to use this power, and I'm able to do so in a way that protects the dragons."

"Jason—"

"Try it," he said, looking at Henry.

Henry took a deep breath and focused on the iron

dragon. There was a sense of energy radiating from him, and it built steadily, rising in intensity, and the more that it rose, the more intense that pressure became, the more heat he felt radiating from the iron dragon. It was as if the iron dragon were beginning to use his own power, summoning it in order to fight.

Jason touched upon that power, using his connection to the iron pearl, letting his anger and rage flow through him, filling it with his experience. He had been trapped, captured the same way that the iron dragon had been, and he would use that knowledge, and he would ensure that he was able to detect what the iron dragon was experiencing.

Henry continued to target the iron dragon, and power poured out from him. He focused it on the dragon and yet, nothing changed.

Jason waited, watching.

Henry said nothing. He shifted his stance, positioning himself so he could face the iron dragon. Sweat streamed off his brow, mixing into his beard, and Henry ignored it. He continued to focus on the iron dragon, locking eyes with it.

"Am I supposed to feel something?" the dragon asked.

Jason laughed. "I think he wanted you to."

"There is nothing."

Henry stood and let out a shaky breath. "How?"

"I used what the ice dragon showed me," Jason said.

"How?" he asked again.

Jason shrugged. "I don't know that I could demonstrate it, only that I know how to protect the dragons."

"We have tried for ages. Some have tried for centuries.
In all that time, we haven't found any way of protecting
the dragons from the influence of the Dragon Souls." He
looked over at Sarah. "Do you know what this means?"

"It means we can go ensure the safety of the misfits."

"It's more than that, Jason. It means we can rescue the
dragons the Dragon Souls have captive. It means we can
take the fight to them for the first time." He fixed David
with a hard glare.

"And how do you intend to fight?" David asked.

"Why do you care?"

"I just want you to share with your friend how you
intend to fight."

"It wouldn't be just us. We would be going with the
dragons."

Jason took in a deep breath, looking around. That was
the point David was trying to make about training the
dragons, and the Dragon Souls. They existed for a purpose,
and though Jason didn't necessarily like the purpose, and
though he didn't agree with the training methods, the
purpose of the Dragon Souls was to ensure that the people
of Lorach recognized the dragons were under control.

"You can't use the dragons to attack," he said.

"We need to remove the threat of the Dragon Souls,"
Henry said.

"At what cost?" Jason glanced from Henry to Sarah

before looking at David. "The people in my village are terrified of dragons, and they haven't even seen a dragon for a generation. Long enough that there should be no fear of them, and yet, the people are terrified of the possibility they might come and attack. What would happen if you did the same thing in Lorach? What do you think the people there might feel?"

"As long as the dragons are freed, it doesn't matter," Henry said.

"It does matter. I think it matters even more than you realize. If we free the dragons but end up with them viewed as dangerous, we've failed."

That might be the part he needed to focus on the most. Regardless of anything else, he needed to try to protect the dragons, to allow them to be freed, but he needed to do so in a way that wouldn't motivate others to destroy them. Not the same way he had been motivated.

He took a deep breath. "I am going to go do what I can to protect the dragons, and then from there, I will…" Jason didn't know what he would do, only that he would have to do something. The more that he thought about it, the more he had to wonder if there was anything he could do. He might not have the necessary strength.

And because of that, he needed help, but he no longer knew who to seek help from. The people of Dragon Haven left him uncertain.

What Jason thought necessary was for there to be a balance. He wasn't sure whether he was the person to help achieve that balance, but he did agree with David that if the dragons hunted openly, they would only be perpetuating the challenges for themselves.

"Let us help," Sarah said. "If you have some way of protecting the dragons, let us help."

Jason looked around. There were several other larger dragons in the clearing, though they remained near the edge of the forest, near the trees. They were hiding, though Jason didn't know if they were hiding from the people or from the iron dragon.

The heat from the iron dragon persisted, like a furnace radiating heat, and his entire body glowed, though Jason wasn't pushed back by it the same way the others were.

"I will do what I can," Jason said.

"And then we will stop the Dragon Souls. And then..." Sarah started.

Jason locked eyes with Henry. "And then you can decide what you will do next."

"Just us?" Sarah asked.

Jason inhaled deeply. He had come here, thinking he would offer some protection to the dragons, and yet, now that he was here, he no longer knew what he needed to do.

"You get to decide," he said.

Sarah watched him a moment, and then she nodded.

F ive dragons surrounded Jason, all of different colors, though they seemed to be the same five that had joined them in the sky when he had first arrived in Dragon Haven. He had pushed through each of them, using the power of the ice dragon and letting it guide him as he tried to layer a protection on each of the dragons. He thought he was successful but wasn't sure.

"Is it done?" Henry asked.

Jason looked around the clearing. The crowd had thinned a little bit. At first, Jason worried it was because they didn't want to know what he was doing, but the more that he thought about it, the more certain he was that they weren't sure whether he was going to be successful.

When he had first approached the dragons, letting them know what he was going to do, they had been hesitant, but then the iron dragon had done something—or said something—that had changed their minds.

"It's done."

"How will we know?"

David shook his head and strode forward. He held his hands up and muttered something under his breath. Henry dove toward him and David flicked his wrist. Henry went flying.

Jason stood frozen, unable to even react.

Power washed away from David.

It struck the yellow dragon in front of him. The creature lowered his head, blinking pale golden eyes, and breathed out a streamer of steam.

"Have I influenced you?" David asked the dragon.

"No," came a deep voice.

Henry pulled himself off the ground, dusting himself off, and approached. "Don't try that again."

"If you aren't willing to test it, I am. And I am unable to do anything." He turned to Jason. "And you see, I don't need a dragon pearl in order to summon power."

"How did you do that?"

"There is much you could learn, if only you believed."

"I believe you have power, but I don't know what it was that you were doing."

"I was using what I learned as an Auran on them."

"That's what it means to be an Auran?"

"It means we're willing to explore a different side of power. We're willing to work with what we have within us. I have seen something similar in you."

Henry regarded Jason for a moment before turning his attention back to the dragons. He squeezed on something in his hand, and a sense of energy radiated from him, washing over the nearest dragon. The pale yellow dragon lowered his head and looked into Henry's eyes, studying him.

"You did it," Henry said.

"I told you I did."

"Can you repeat it?"

Jason thought the question was for him, but it seemed that he was directing it at the dragon.

"We cannot. We don't have the same type of power."

"Is it him, then?"

"I don't know," the dragon said.

Jason didn't think it was him. The power had come from the ice dragon, not from him. And yet, if it was not from the ice dragon, if it was from him, then why would he be different?

He looked over at David, but David said nothing.

Something about all of this troubled him. The Auran was hiding something, and the more that Jason learned, the more certain he was that David wasn't quite who he wanted others to believe he was.

Why would he conceal that?

If he had no interest in harming the dragons, and Jason felt increasingly certain that was the case, then why not come out and say it?

Henry went from dragon to dragon, testing each of them. When he was done, he turned back to Sarah. "I can't influence any of them. Whatever he did seems to work. We won't know for certain until we encounter Dragon Souls, but..."

"You think it worked," she said.

"I think it worked," he said.

Jason turned away. He wasn't going to remain here, not now that the dragons had been protected. Which meant it was time to go and do what he had intended to do all along. It was time to return and protect the dragons.

He stopped in front of the iron dragon. He nodded to the creature, who lowered his head, allowing Jason to climb on. David followed him, but waited before mounting.

"You can come as well," Jason said.

"That's it?"

"For now."

"What about them?"

Jason looked over at Henry and Sarah. "If they're going to come with us, they will make that decision. Now, I can't wait any longer. I need to get to the forest dragon."

He didn't know what Henry and Sarah were going to do, and, as far as he was concerned, it didn't matter. They could choose for themselves, and if it involved coming with him, working to help protect the misfits, then he was glad of the help.

"Jason," Sarah said, approaching carefully.

"What is it?"

"We aren't ready to go. The others need more time."

"There is danger."

It came from the ice dragon, as if he were speaking within Jason's mind. The dragon was high overhead, circling and waiting for them.

"What danger?"

"They come."

Immediately, he knew the danger. Dragon Souls.

If they waited, the forest dragon would suffer.

He turned to Sarah. "I can't wait any longer."

"You don't know that."

"The ice dragon does, and we have to go. Please help."

She frowned at him, and he hoped that she'd come, but she backed away.

Shaking his head, he tapped the iron dragon on the side. With a surge of heat, the dragon blasted into the air.

They circled for a moment, parting the clouds, and as they did, he looked up to see the ice dragon high overhead. Spikes protruded from his body, and it seemed as if snow drifted around him, swirling in a cloud.

It was enough to make Jason smile.

"You are an interesting man," David said.

"Why?"

"Because you really *do* care about them."

"I didn't," he said. He turned so that he could meet David's eyes. "I feared dragons. My entire life, I was taught to hate them, to be afraid of them, to know they could destroy my village. And then I met a dragon. And then I met another. I came to understand they aren't at all what I believed."

They were something so much more than what he'd ever imagined.

"If you learned from Dragon Haven, then why aren't you staying with them?"

"Because they revere the dragons, almost to the point where they feel as if they need to serve the dragons, but that's not been my sense at all."

"What is your sense?"

"That we're equals in a way. Different, and yet, I think the dragons need us as much as we need them."

He turned, wrapping his arms around the dragon, and held on tightly as they surged forward.

"Others are coming," David said.

"How do you know?"

"Because I can feel them."

Jason slipped off to the side. "You said that before. How do you feel them? How are you so connected?"

David shrugged. "You believe you are only connected to the dragons. And yet, your power is different. I see it within you. I know you may not believe it, but I understand the nature of what it takes to be an Auran, and I understand just how similar you are to us."

"I don't even know what an Auran does."

"No, but you could."

"I don't want to."

"Why not?"

"I want to return to my village. I want to help my mother. I want to save my sister." He trailed off at the end and inhaled deeply, looking back behind him. As David had said, there were dragons now following them, but it wasn't the dragons he expected. The five dragons he'd helped weren't there. The maroon and the black dragon were instead.

"Did you know they were here?" Jason asked David.

David stared into the distance. "I did not. When you healed them, what did you do?"

"I tried to free them from what had been done to them, but I don't know that I did anything else."

"Interesting."

"Why?"

"We've always believed that once freed, the dragons would roam, and they would hunt and potentially harm others. That's part of the reason we have felt they needed to be protected. They needed it as much as we do. But if they are free"—he studied Jason for a long moment, almost as if uncertain—"and if what you did has ensured they can't be controlled, then there should be no reason for them to come after us."

Jason glanced over as the two dragons took up positions on either side of them. The black dragon roared and the maroon dragon swished her tail. Somehow, Jason was aware that she was a female.

How would they have known?

"They felt me using the dragon pearl," he said.

"Possibly," David said.

"And if they felt it, they didn't have to come, but they chose to."

"I believe that is true," David said.

Jason smiled to himself. If he could free dragons, and if he could ensure that they were safe...

No. That wasn't his task.

He turned his attention back in front of him, and they flew, gliding toward the distant mountains.

As they went, every so often, Jason would look behind him, searching for any sign of those from Dragon Haven, but there were none.

Whatever was going to happen would have to be up to him. And perhaps it wouldn't even matter. If it was a matter of freeing the dragons, he could do that. He could ensure they were protected. He could take away any influence these others might have on them. And if he could manage that, he wouldn't have to worry about the dragons being used.

The only challenge would be in doing so in a way that wouldn't cause danger to the dragons. If they crashed from a height, they would die the same as he would.

The longer they flew, the more a sense of energy began to build around him. Jason thought that might come from their proximity to the dragons, but he wasn't sure. He started to scan the sky, looking for signs of anything, but there was nothing.

"I think we need to—"

He never got a chance to finish. A blast of fire exploded, catching the side of the dragon.

It did nothing to harm the dragon. Fire wouldn't hurt it, but it did startle him.

And there was something more.

He looked over to see that the ice dragon struggled.

Heat *was* a challenge for the ice dragon.

Other blasts struck, coming close, and surprisingly, the black dragon swooped in front of the ice dragon, blocking and protecting it. The heat rolled through the black dragon and then disappeared.

David pressed his lips together in a tight frown. "I have never seen anything like that."

"Like what?"

"They recognized his need."

"In that he can't tolerate the heat?"

"The ice dragon should return," David said.

"I don't know that he would."

"If Lorach brought power to bear, they would be able to tear through him."

"I thought they wanted to understand and train the dragons."

"They do, but if it is a matter of understanding and controlling versus losing the dragon altogether, they would lose the dragon if it came down to it. Have him go."

Jason looked over at the ice dragon. A thick layer of ice surrounded him, though it glistened. It was almost as if the heat of this place was too much, and Jason realized it seemed to be growing hotter.

He hadn't expected that.

"You need to go," he said to the ice dragon.

"I can be a part of this," the dragon said.

"You can, but I don't know if you should. Not like this. I'm going to need your help in order to save the rest of the dragons." He needed the ice dragon, and he needed that connection between them in order to do what he thought was necessary to save the other dragons.

"What would you propose?"

"How high can you fly?"

"Why?"

"It's colder up above. You can tolerate it. The other dragons might not."

Jason didn't know if it would work or not, but it seemed reasonable to at least attempt. The ice dragon rumbled, a roar splitting his mouth, and he breathed out a streamer of ice and then streaked straight up.

Movement on either side caught Jason's attention.

"They were waiting for him," he muttered.

He focused on the nearest of the dragons. He saw it as little more than a shadow, a smear of darkness, and he drew upon power through the ice dragon pearl, letting it flow from him, and he shot it toward that shadowy form.

It struck, and Jason felt resistance, and he pushed through it.

"You're going to kill the dragon," David said.

Jason held on to his connection, ignoring David.

"I thought your desire was to save them."

"I'm not going to let them destroy that dragon."

And there was another possibility, but it was one that he didn't know would work. If he could free the dragon while it was high enough, he had to believe something could change and the dragon would begin to regain control. If that happened, then it seemed to him the dragon should be able to prevent himself from crashing into the ground. Jason continued to push, sending more of the ice dragon's power through the other dragon, focusing on that energy, and when he met the resistance, he forced even more power through.

Something struck him.

It was a jolt, and Jason was thrown forward.

He almost lost the dragon pearl. He did lose his seat on top of the dragon.

He went flying forward.

Something grabbed him, and for a moment, he thought it was the iron dragon, but David held on to him. He pulled, forcing Jason back onto the dragon's back, and released him.

"You're not going to get out of this that easily," David said.

Jason redoubled his effort, focusing again on the dragon. As he did, power flowed out of him, and he held on to it while the iron dragon rotated, spiraling in place, twisting through the air. It was a strange feeling, but he held on. As he did, he could feel the heat intensifying. He had no idea what the iron dragon was doing, only that he was somehow using his connection to power in a way that would draw more heat, and from there, Jason knew that the iron dragon would unleash it.

He ignored that, thinking only of what he was trying to do, the way he was holding on to the power from the ice dragon, letting it flow through him and into the shadowed form of the other dragon. Jason continued to push, sending more and more power across, and he felt the resistance begin to fade. With another surge, it disappeared altogether.

There came a shriek. A royal blue dragon dropped from the sky and plummeted. Two figures were tossed free, flailing as they plunged to the ground.

Jason focused his energy on the falling dragon, wishing there was some way he could help the dragon, and yet, he believed that with enough time, the dragon would be able to correct course and free itself.

"I don't think it worked," David said.

They were spinning, and Jason fought the urge to vomit. The steady rotation was intense, far more than he had ever experienced before, and the dragon was spiraling in a way he thought should toss them off, but somehow the momentum of it held him to the dragon's neck. It practically pinned him down, allowing him no choice but to lie there.

"I thought—"

A loud roar erupted from far below.

Jason listened, worried the dragon had perished in the fall. He knew how hard it was for dragon eggs to hatch, and he hated the idea that he was responsible for a death. Maybe David was right that they had to bring the dragon closer to the ground, but if they were going to be attacked up here, he wasn't sure they would be able to do so.

Then with another roar, the dragon reappeared.

He turned his attention to Jason, deep blue eyes that

matched his scales surging, catching a glint of gold, and then roaring again.

"You freed him," David said.

"I think we were lucky that worked," Jason said.

"It worked, but there are others." He pointed, and in the distance, Jason noted another red-scaled dragon. This one was enormous, easily twice the size of the maroon one.

He focused on it. He would need to pick off the largest dragons first, and from up here, he thought there would be enough time to heal the dragon and give it time to recover before it crashed to the ground.

As he drew power from the ice dragon, sending it across the distance into the other dragon, he felt resistance. It was more than he had detected before. Jason focused, pulling on power from the ice dragon, sending it across that distance, into the other dragon. He strained against that resistance, trying to find some way to overwhelm it.

He had to pull on more power.

He needed the ice dragon to help.

Was there any way to signal to the ice dragon that he couldn't do this alone? The dragon seemed to know his mind, and in doing so, he should have some way of recognizing what Jason was doing, but how was he to bridge that distance?

Power exploded.

He was thrown back, and the iron dragon roared.

Another explosion struck the side of the dragon, this one ringing out like a bell.

"There are too many," David said. "A dozen. Possibly more. It seems the dragons brought a regiment."

"How many is in a regiment?"

"Two dozen."

"How many regiments are there?"

"Many," David said, staring into the distance. It might be Jason's imagination, but it seemed almost as if David were disappointed by this turn of events.

"They aren't going to claim these dragons."

"There's only so much that you can do against them," David said. "I hadn't expected them to bring such power out here."

"They would have if they knew there were other types of dragons."

"They didn't know. There was a suspicion, but no one knew what might be out here. We came thinking that we might find something, not knowing we would."

Jason looked across, seeing the massive red dragon as it approached.

A figure on the back caught his attention. There was something about it that was familiar.

Therin.

"Look," he said, pointing.

David leaned forward, and a strange sense radiated from him. "That is unfortunate. If Therin has decided to join this fight, there may be very little that you can do to prevent him from succeeding." David looked at him. "Therin commands the largest regiment of Dragon Souls."

"How many are in his regiment?"

"Many."

David leaned forward and closed his eyes. He began to mutter to himself, saying quiet words, but Jason couldn't hear them. The wind whistling around them carried the words away, and yet, he had a sense of them.

It was something of mourning.

19

J ason tapped David on the arm. "You need to come back around."

"I'm sorry, I really am. As much as I want to help, there isn't anything that can be done."

Jason didn't know whether David really wanted to help or not, but he did get the sense something bothered him.

"You never really wanted to harm the dragons."

"I've never wanted to harm the dragons. I've wanted to understand them, to work with them, but they do need to be protected, much like we need to be protected."

The wind whistled around them, and it carried a strange scent on it. It was that of ash, but it was something else as well.

Heat blasted them, one explosion after another, and with the way the iron dragon spun, they managed to avoid most of it, though Jason didn't know if they were avoiding it or the iron dragon was absorbing it.

The other two dragons that had joined them were twisting in the air, shooting flames from their mouths and roaring. The sound of it filled the air, that of explosions and dragon screams and thunder.

All of it was a torrent of power, a torment of explosions. All of it was more than Jason could stomach.

And all of it had come here because of him.

He could have done nothing. He could have sat back, hiding on the mountain, staying with the ice dragon, and if he had, then Therin would never have known about any of the other dragons. He would've known about the ice dragon, but that was it. Jason could have brought the ice dragon to Dragon Haven, and... then what?

The dragon wouldn't have been happy in Dragon Haven. He might've been able to tolerate it, but it wasn't his home.

Much like anyplace else wasn't home to the iron dragon. He deserved to go to Varmin, not anywhere else. And what about the forest dragon? What would happen to that one? He had no idea how many other misfit dragons there were, however many strange and powerful and wonderful dragons existed, but the ice dragon believed there were several more.

What would take place if the Dragon Souls managed to acquire them?

Jason knew what would happen. They would be controlled. They would be used.

He focused on the dragon Therin rode. He called upon power, sending it through him, through the dragon. The ice dragon seemed to recognize what he was doing, and he added to it, sending strength flowing through Jason, and it spilled outward, exploding into the red dragon.

It was getting closer. The twisting movements of the iron dragon were hard for Jason to follow, but it seemed almost as if the iron dragon recognized what he needed and understood where they needed to target. He focused on the red dragon, hurtling toward it. They were moving quickly, so quickly that Jason was struggling to track it all, and he focused power instead, letting it explode outward.

The other dragon roared.

Jason pushed with everything he could.

There was a surge of power, and it came from high overhead. Like a blast of lightning, only this was ice, and it arced through the dragon pearl, through him, and directed out toward the red dragon.

It slammed into the creature.

There was a brief sense of resistance, but it faded quickly. It was almost as if any resistance left was blasted by the lightning. Or ice lightning, however the case may be.

Jason sat for a moment, holding on to the iron dragon, feeling the intensity of the power the ice dragon had loaned him.

The red dragon roared.

Jason had done nothing.

He had been trying to heal the dragon, but was there nothing to heal?

"It didn't work," Jason said.

The red dragon was coming closer, moving with incredible speed.

"Let me help," David said.

"How can you help?"

"I need dragon pearls."

Jason hesitated. He didn't know if he could trust David, but David had been with him long enough that he had to trust him a little bit. If David betrayed him, what would it do other than lead to their failing that much sooner? With his help, there might be something that could be done, some way he could continue to overwhelm the dragons circling them, but...

Jason reached into his pocket, pulling out the dragon pearls for the maroon and black dragons. He handed them over, and David stared at them for a moment before cupping them and holding his fists out. Somehow, David managed to stay seated atop the dragon as it spun.

Power exploded from him.

When it struck the red dragon, it seemed to slow it.

"Work on it," David urged.

Jason focused his energy on the red dragon, holding on to the ice dragon pearl, sending power flowing through him and into it.

He summoned power from the ice dragon overhead, knowing the ice dragon was there, knowing the dragon understood what he needed. The connection between them was strong. It had to be for the ice dragon to be able to help him in the way that it had.

Once again, a bolt of ice lightning streaked toward him. It arced through the dragon pearl, flowing through it and then him, and slammed into the red dragon. This time, Jason paid attention to what was happening, and he tried to control the flow of the ice lightning, straining to guide the lightning. If he could manage to hold on to that control, he knew he could use it to help the dragon.

That was what he wanted most of all. The dragon wasn't his enemy. Therin was the problem, not the dragon. And in order to help, he was going to have to overwhelm the dragon. He was going to have to force the healing upon it. The dragon might not know it needed it, but it did. And Jason was determined to do everything in his power to help the dragon, to send what it needed, to find a way to heal it.

The dragon roared. It was almost as if it understood.

High overhead, there came a shriek.

The ice dragon added his power.

The flow of energy coming from overhead was enormous. When Jason had suggested the ice dragon go into the upper sky, he had known it was colder, but he hadn't expected the ice dragon to be able to draw upon such power. He understood that being in the sky overhead would allow him to reach for energy he hadn't been able to do otherwise. There was power. Now there was that which Jason couldn't fully grasp.

He unleashed it, letting it flow outward and into the red dragon.

Next to him, David struggled. He held his hands out, but they were trembling. Power flowed through him, though it was beginning to wane.

Jason continued to push, sending more and more through the red dragon.

The resistance was there, a barrier in the creature's mind.

As he recognized that, Jason understood what he needed to do.

It wasn't a matter of trying to heal, not quite the same way. What he needed to do was to separate that barrier.

The iron dragon rolled, jerking slightly.

Jason lost control. The ice lightning dissipated, streaking somewhere below him. Someone cried out, though it mingled with the other shrieks in the air.

They rolled off to the side and David slumped forward.

"He is too powerful," David said.

"I thought you were a powerful Auran."

"I have ability, but..." He shook his head, breathing heavily.

They weren't going to be able to keep fighting. The iron dragon rolled, and Jason tried to reorient himself, to position himself back on the dragon, but found it difficult. He was struggling with this, but then, the dragon was struggling as well. The longer they were here, the harder it was going to be for them to survive.

Perhaps the better solution was to join the ice dragon, to run.

Distantly, Jason was aware of the maroon and black dragon fighting alongside them. They had joined in the fray, and they were attacking the Dragon Souls, trying to tear them from the other dragons' backs. It was a mixture of tails and fire and wings flapping. It was a violent dance in the sky.

Jason hated it.

Dragons shouldn't be fighting other dragons.

He breathed out.

"I'm sorry," he said, tapping the iron dragon on the side.

"The fight is not over," the iron dragon said.

"We don't have enough power."

"You have all that you need."

"I've been trying, but…"

His attempt had not been enough. As much as he wanted to, he couldn't do what he needed in order to save the dragons. There was nothing he could do.

Suddenly, another shriek split the sky. He looked over, dreading how many more dragons would come. David had warned him that Therin had many dragons at his disposal, that his regimen involved dozens of dragons, and they had only faced a small number so far.

Even in that, they were surrounded. He worried about the ice dragon, wondering what was happening to him in the sky high overhead, but so far, the dragon remained aloft, as if untouched by what was coming.

Would it stay that way? How much longer would they have before even the ice dragon failed?

It was possible that from his position overhead, the ice dragon would be able to escape. He was able to fly higher —or so Jason thought—and hopefully could fly faster than the other dragons. If he were able to do that, then he should be able to get away.

And perhaps that was what Jason should have asked of the dragon. He didn't need the ice dragon to be caught up in this. He didn't need the dragon to experience this torment. He needed the dragon to have safety.

Another shriek came, and Jason looked around.

A faint yellow shape was surging toward them. Near it was an orange shape. Green. Pale blue.

The dragons from Dragon Haven.

They still wouldn't be enough.

It was a mistake. He needed to call out, to warn Henry and Sarah and whoever else might be on those dragons, but how could he?

He tried to turn the iron dragon, but he wasn't able to. The iron dragon was rolling, the movement keeping him from harm, power surging through him. That movement allowed the iron dragon to somehow absorb each fiery blast that struck. Each one that hit the iron dragon was deflected, or absorbed, but it didn't cause any pain or problems.

Jason tried to call out, to alert the others, but his voice wouldn't carry on the wind. He screamed out against it, but he couldn't get his voice out there.

He cried out again, shouting, but once more, his voice was lost.

The only thing he could do was focus on Therin. Focus on his dragon. And if he could do so, then he might be able to find some way of slowing this.

Even if he did, what would happen next?

With his massive size, Jason had to believe the red dragon would be able to help.

He breathed in, focusing on the dragon pearl. What he needed was power from the ice dragon, and he needed to call it down from overhead and let it flow through him.

Once again, ice lightning burst, streaking toward the ground, and it exploded through him, through the dragon pearl, and outward. He focused it on the red dragon, and this time, he shoved it beneath the influence he felt within the red dragon. That sense was deep within the red dragon's mind, and Jason was able to slide underneath, to force his way through it, and tear through the injury to the dragon.

He focused the lightning. And as he did, he could feel that influence shearing away.

The dragon roared, and Jason worried for a moment he'd done something that harmed it, but he could feel the necessity of what he was doing. He could tell tearing this influence away was going to help the dragon.

And then the dragon roared again.

Jason shoved, pushing with everything he could, separating the strange sensation from the dragon.

When it tore free, the dragon screamed.

Jason released his hold. The red dragon plummeted.

Therin remained on his back, and he watched as the other man dropped to the ground.

He tore his attention away, focusing on the nearest dragons. There were three near them, and he pushed power, drawing it from the ice dragon through its pearl and into the nearest dragons, tearing away the influence forced upon them. Now that he understood what it was and how to remove it, it wasn't so much a healing as it was a separation. He was able to rip through it. When he did so, he realized that it wasn't even ripping. He was burning through it, using the cold in order to seal it off.

The dragons fell, one by one, and he no longer worried they wouldn't catch themselves. He no longer worried about the Dragon Souls tossed free. He sat upright, perched on top of the iron dragon's back, using everything in his power in order to send the dragons scattering. He worked through them, tearing one injury after another away.

After going through a dozen dragons, the attack began to abate. He was tired. He didn't know how much longer he would be able to fight. The power he was drawing through the ice dragon was enormous. How would he be able to continue to fight when it came down to it?

Something shook the iron dragon.

Jason diverted his attention, looking over, and he felt for the dragon.

"What happened?"

"I am fine," the dragon said.

"But what happened?"

He didn't get a chance to answer.

Something else struck, and David was tossed free.

Jason's breath caught.

"Drop!" he shouted.

They plummeted.

They streaked toward the ground, moving with increasing speed, and he gripped the dragon with his legs, afraid of letting go, but at the same time, David was ahead of them. Somehow they had to get to him. David wasn't coming around, lying motionless in the air.

"We need to go faster," Jason said.

The iron dragon roared. Heat radiated from his back. It undulated, washing from his neck all the way down.

"You can use everything," he said.

The dragon roared again.

His head began to glow, and the heat rolled down his neck.

Jason was afraid of getting burned, but he didn't care. He was going to stay there, gripping the dragon's back, holding on until they reached David. When they neared, he tried to grab him but couldn't.

The iron dragon roared again.

With another surge, they shot past David. Jason twisted, grabbing David, and they jerked him back onto the dragon's back.

The ground loomed in front of them.

Jason cried out, but the iron dragon stretched his wings out, and they caught the air. He batted at it, but they weren't going to be fast enough. The ground continued to approach, and he braced himself.

The dragon slammed down.

Jason was tossed free, tearing David with him.

He rolled over, looking off to the side, and worried about where they were, what they might encounter, and yet he found he couldn't get up.

His leg was twisted.

He crawled, trying to get to David, but David wasn't moving.

He rolled off to the side, looking at the iron dragon, but even the iron dragon wasn't moving. He seemed to be breathing, but that was about it.

After all of that, they would fail here?

20

The dragon was breathing, so Jason focused on David first. David was lying motionless, so he crawled over, ignoring the pain that screamed through his body with every movement. Everything he did cried out, rebelling against him, and yet he needed to reach David, to see if there was anything he could do for him.

He got up to him and rolled him over. David's eyes were glazed, but when he checked the artery in his neck, working the way his mother had taught him, he found his pulse still beating. It was weak, but present.

Jason tried to call upon the power of the ice dragon, but didn't know if there was enough strength left in the dragon for him to do so. And at this point, it might be a mistake to try to keep drawing upon that power.

He needed to be careful, but he also owed it to David— and the iron dragon—to heal them. Healing would require him to do the actual work. He didn't know enough about that control, and didn't know if he would even have the necessary power to do what needed to be done, and yet, he was determined to try.

He gripped the ice dragon pearl, holding it tightly, and set it on David's chest. He pushed outward with power.

A surge of cold washed out from Jason into David. It was weaker than what he remembered, and he didn't know if that came from the distance between him and the ice dragon or if it was a matter of weakness for the ice dragon. Either way, Jason was concerned about trying to use too much more strength. At this point, it might be better to refrain.

Power surged from somewhere overhead.

The ice dragon recognized what was needed. And he gave his power willingly.

It washed out from Jason and into David. The power continued to roll through the man, and David sucked in a sharp breath.

Jason crawled away, reaching the iron dragon. He rested on his side, holding the ice dragon pearl up against it. Would it even work on a dragon like this?

The ice dragon didn't give him an opportunity to think about it too much. He sent power shooting through him in another sheet of ice lightning, and it arced from the sky and down into the dragon pearl and then outward into the iron dragon.

It flowed through him, melting into the dragon.

It was different than what the ice dragon had done for

David, but it was enough that the iron dragon began to rumble.

Jason sighed with relief. He was going to save the iron dragon. And David.

He rested on the iron dragon's side, barely able to move.

Laughter behind him caught his attention, and Jason lifted his weary head.

Therin strode toward him. He was dressed in dragon-skin, a pin on his cloak similar to the one Jason wore on his stolen dragonskin. The beard he'd sported when he had visited the village was shaved, giving him a sharp and angular jaw, and color rose within his high cheekbones.

"Look at you. Everything you've done, and now you dress like us? I could have brought you back to Lorach. Had you only wanted to, you could have been celebrated."

Jason didn't have the strength within him to argue.

"And now you've brought me this dragon." His gaze flicked high overhead. "And the ice dragon. You didn't think I would find him, but I knew. I was always going to return. He is quite a bit more than I ever would've imagined." He crouched down and looked Jason in the eye. "When word came to me of the dragon in Varmin, I didn't think it would be real, and yet more and more rumors continued to roll out of there. And then the Auran thought to get involved. It was a mistake, and it's one I will rectify now."

"What are you going to do?" Jason asked, his voice weak. He barely had the strength to keep his head up.

"Why do you even care?"

"Leave the dragons. They can't be used by you."

"All dragons can be trained."

Jason held his head up, sucking in a deep breath. He was tired. So tired. "Not these. I made it so that they can't. Try your red dragon. You can't train him anymore, either."

"The red dragon died," Therin said.

Jason's heart sunk. He was responsible for it. He was the one who had torn away whatever he'd detected. Because of him, the red dragon had plummeted to his death.

Wouldn't it have been better to allow the dragon to live, regardless of how Therin might have used it?

Perhaps it didn't matter. Not anymore. All that mattered was that he was here.

Maybe he could use whatever of his power was remaining to stop Therin. Perhaps he could remove him as a threat, and in doing so, he might be able to delay what was coming.

And he *had* freed some of the dragons. More than anything else, Jason understood that was beneficial. He had done something that others had not, had fixed a wrong.

Therin started toward David, unsheathing his sword.

Jason held out the dragon pearl, and he pushed power through himself.

When it struck Therin, he jerked upright. He turned toward Jason. "You would rather have me finish with you first? Fine. I will do that. But you should know I will not take pity on you. You have destroyed plans years in the making and very nearly disrupted everything that we have worked for."

"I'm going to keep disrupting it." He drew on more power, letting it out toward Therin.

It washed over him harmlessly.

Therin stood there, heat radiating from him. He was calling on the power of his own dragon pearl.

Jason wasn't going to be able to overwhelm him.

Therin had knowledge, and not only that, he had more power than Jason possessed. He was able to outmaneuver him, and he had far more experience than Jason.

Jason tried again, using the cold, drawing through the ice dragon pearl, but nothing happened. There was power, but it didn't do anything to Therin.

"You could have been useful," Therin said.

"I don't want to be useful to you."

"And now you're wasting your opportunity."

"I'm not wasting anything. I'm doing what needs to be done."

"By dying?"

Therin approached, and Jason shifted. Pain tore through him. His leg throbbed and he could not even move.

He had spent so much time and energy ensuring that the others were healed, he hadn't paid any attention to trying to restore himself. And that was a mistake. He should have tried to help himself, to use whatever power he could summon and find some way of healing his leg before it got to this point, but now there was nothing left.

And the worst part of it was that Therin seemed to know. He watched Jason, smiling, and power emanated from him, trickling away from him, but nothing more than that. It was almost as if he were playing with Jason. Toying with him.

"How do you want to suffer?"

"You won't be able to use the dragons. I've protected them."

"You might have thought you protected them, but you know so little. We have centuries of experience with dragons. Anything you think that you have done will fail. The dragons will be mine."

Anger filled Jason. "They aren't yours to claim."

Therin leaned close, laughing darkly. "If only that were true."

Power built from him. Jason reached into his pocket, fumbling for one of the dragon pearls, and came across the iron dragon pearl. The iron dragon was resting, healed, but would there be enough power within him?

The kind of power that came from the iron dragon was different than what came from the ice dragon, and yet, Jason didn't know how much energy the iron dragon had used for his evasive flight pattern. It was possible the crash had taken too much out of the iron dragon.

What choice did he have but to try?

Jason clutched the pearl and focused.

In this case, he focused on his anger at what Therin

promised to do to the dragons. He focused on the way that Therin intended to use them, and he focused on the power he knew was within himself.

There was an anger within him.

It had always been there, and yet he never let it out. He kept it confined. Living in the village, powerless as he often was, there was no way to unleash that rage. And having been around the iron dragon, having known what it had experienced, Jason recognized it.

It wasn't the same as the ice dragon. That was a sense of home. This was a sense of rage at what he'd gone through, anger at what others had done to him. And because of that anger, Jason knew that he could pull upon it.

The iron dragon started to glow softly.

It diverted enough of Therin's attention that Jason pulled on power, summoning it through the iron dragon.

As he did, he forced that power from him. It exploded through the dragon pearl and slammed into Therin.

It sent Therin flying. He crashed on the far side of the clearing.

Jason watched, but he didn't get up.

He breathed out heavily. "Thank you."

The dragon rumbled softly.

He tried to move his leg, but he couldn't.

"Is there any way for me to heal myself?"

A surprising voice answered.

"You would have to draw power through the pearl and into yourself. You can use it that way."

"David?"

David stood several yards away. His hands were clasped in front of him and he swayed as if unsteady. A gash on his face that Jason hadn't noticed before had started to heal.

"Try to draw that power through you. I would offer, but I don't know that you would trust me."

At this point, Jason wasn't sure who to trust, and David was as good as anyone. David had been a part of this.

Jason focused on the energy of the cold. He thought of the experience he had with the ice dragon. He thought of his home.

He drew that power through him.

He gasped.

The cold was overwhelming, almost more than he could handle.

It forced him to spasm, and his entire body straightened as he struggled against the power passing through him.

Jason cried out. The only thing that he could think of was to try to hold on. Pain surged through him. It was cold and hot at the same time.

And then it retreated. As it did, the pain within him began to draw away.

He let out a shaky breath, and he looked up to see David watching him.

David nodded. "How do you feel?"

"I've been better."

"I'm sure you have. It's surprisingly painful for something with such healing power."

"I didn't realize it hurt like that."

Jason tested his leg. It didn't hurt as it had before.

He leaned forward, getting to his knees, and took a deep breath. Could it be that he would actually survive this?

With the thought, there was a burst of energy near him.

Jason looked up.

Therin stood.

David turned toward Therin, raising his hand, but with a burst of power, Therin sent David flying away.

Therin smiled at Jason. "One of the advantages of dragonskin is that it absorbs most impacts. I must admit I am surprised that you were able to summon so much power. What was that? The ice dragon? I can only imagine how useful he will be once we tame him."

"Not the ice dragon."

He pulled on the anger flowing through him at the way that Therin had attacked David. The way that Therin attacked him. There had to be something within the power he could summon, some way to use it to overwhelm Therin.

"It doesn't matter what it is. All that matters is that you will—"

Jason didn't give him a chance to finish. He pushed all that anger, letting it flow through him, and drew through the iron dragon. There came a blast of orange heat, and it exploded through Jason and into the pearl, slamming into Therin.

Therin braced himself, and he managed to hold out, letting the power part around him. Jason pushed more and more through him, letting all that power flow, and yet there was nothing he could do to injure Therin.

Therin was far too powerful for him.

"I need your help," he said to the iron dragon.

The iron dragon stirred, but he hadn't fully recovered. He tried to move but all that happened was that his body writhed, heat rolling down his torso.

Therin started forward. "You don't understand yet, do you? You think you would work with the dragons, and that is your mistake. The dragons are to be trained. Used. They are not to be your friends. And yet, you still don't understand. I will ensure that you do. In time, you will understand plenty about the power of the dragons." He reached Jason, pressing heat out. It wrapped around him, circling, a spiral of it. It wasn't painful, not the way it once would have been, and he suspected that had to do with the dragonskin. There was still the energy of it, and he could feel it washing over him, and regardless of what he wanted to do, he tried to resist, but there was nothing that he could do.

The heat began to compress, squeezing in upon him.

Therin took a step toward him, watching as he did. He smiled. It was a dark and angry expression, and Jason trembled.

"You have made a mistake in thinking you could take on the Dragon Souls. Pride will be your downfall."

There had to be some way to overwhelm this power.

He had other dragon pearls. He thought about mixing fire and ice, exploding it. It had worked on the wall between the cells. It had to work on Therin, and all Jason had to do was bring that power together.

He couldn't reach into his pockets. His hands were squeezed by the heat.

Therin neared him.

He dipped his hand through the heat barrier, grabbing for the dragon pearls. He took everything Jason had. The ones he'd taken from the fallen Dragon Souls, the ice dragon pearl. The only one he didn't take was the one clutched in his hand.

Heat rolled through Jason, and he squeezed the dragon pearl.

He tried to summon anger, but fear was the only emotion he knew right now. He wanted to run. He wanted to be anywhere but here, and yet he couldn't do anything. He could barely even breathe.

Therin smiled at him.

"You thought to claim from the Dragon Souls. That was another mistake. With these, I can track the dragons you twisted."

Jason strained, trying to take a deep breath, but his breath didn't fill him as it had before.

He let out a cry of frustration.

The iron dragon stirred.

"Help me," he cried out.

The iron dragon rolled and sent a hint of power, but it came slowly.

Therin reached for Jason's hand. Jason cried again, trying to fight.

When Therin pulled his hand up, he started to peel back his fingers.

He wasn't going to get the iron dragon pearl. Of all of them, Jason feared what might happen to the iron dragon most. The ice dragon had some resistance, and with the chill he possessed, he suspected he could use it to overwhelm the influence of the Dragon Souls. And there was something within the ice dragon himself that seemed to have an innate resistance. The iron dragon was different. He'd been tormented. Held captive. And anything the Dragon Souls might do to him would only make that worse.

Somehow, he had to fight.

He squeezed on the dragon pearl, pushing power through it, letting his anger fill him. Something within the dragon pearl began to change.

Heat flared in his hand, and the metal, if that was what it was, began to roll over his hand. When Therin pried his fingers open, it seemed as if he had dipped his hand into molten metal.

Therin stared at it. "What is that?"

Strangely, the molten metal seemed to connect Jason to the iron dragon's power more effectively. He called upon it, letting anger fill him, but even that wasn't necessary. He was able to connect to the iron dragon, and he used that power and pushed it outward, exploding it into Therin's chest.

He went tumbling away.

The heat that wrapped around him and constricted him dissipated.

Jason glanced over at the iron dragon before running toward Therin. He held out his metal hand, forcing it toward Therin, and when he got to him, he pushed power out once again. He let the power of the iron dragon flow through him, and it slammed into Therin.

Therin staggered back.

Jason called upon it again, using more power, but this time Therin was ready. He wrapped some sort of protection around himself so that when Jason's power struck, nothing happened.

"Interesting trick," Therin said.

Therin twisted the dragon pearls that he'd claimed.

One of them was the ice dragon pearl, and it flashed, glimmering, and Jason lunged for it. He wasn't about to let Therin take that dragon pearl with him.

Therin darted back, dancing away.

Jason staggered forward, trying to reach him, and he managed to swat Therin's hand, knocking down the dragon pearls he was holding.

Therin laughed.

"Do you think I need those?"

He raised his hands and then brought them down. He slammed into Jason, knocking him to the ground. He crouched on hands and knees, trying to crawl forward, and yet there was nothing that he could do. Whatever Therin had done to him prevented him from moving. He tried again, attempting to crawl toward him, trying to find some way to knock him down, but he was unsuccessful.

More and more power began to press down upon him. He was crushed. His arms and legs slipped out from under him. He lay on the hard-packed ground, his face pushed into the earth.

Therin stood near him. "You will suffer."

And then a strange sound occurred.

It sounded almost as if it were raining, but the sky was still blue. More and more of the things that sounded like raindrops began to shoot down, and Jason was able to twist his head off to the side just enough to see that spikes of ice were raining down around them. Therin shifted the focus of his heat upward, trying to melt the ice, but the ice dragon continued his attack, raining shards of ice, shooting them toward the ground. The heat managed to liquefy most of them, but not all. Therin was struck in the chest by one, and he dropped to his knee.

At that moment, the iron dragon swung his tail.

Jason thought that he might carve through Therin, but Therin shifted some hint of power, and it managed to catch the tail, preventing the Dragon Soul from being cut in half.

Jason sat up. The pressure on him had released, and he looked around.

The ice dragon hovered, shooting icicles at Therin.

The iron dragon was on his legs, unsteady but swinging his sharp tail, the entire length of his body glowing with orange light. And other shapes appeared in the sky. Shadowed forms of dragons. A dozen of them. Maybe more. All of them attacking Therin, using their energy as they did.

Therin shot Jason a look, and then he twisted his hands in a strange pattern. A burst of flame shot from the ground, and then he was gone.

Jason sagged back, leaning on his hands and knees, and stared up at the sky.

The dragons had saved him.

21

He rested with his back against the iron dragon, who radiated a comfortable warmth. He glowed softly, though not with the same intensity as he did when he was attacking. The ice dragon had departed, though he was nearby. Jason could feel his energy, and every so often, the ice dragon sent a wave of healing washing through him. It helped to restore him, to strengthen him, and he couldn't help but feel thankful for it.

David sat cross-legged not far from him. He stared into the distance. He muttered under his breath, and Jason wondered who he was talking to, though it might just be himself.

"He escaped," Henry said. His arms were crossed in front of him and he had an angry tilt to his jaw. Blood had crusted on the side of his cheek, but whatever injury he'd sustained had been healed.

"He did," Jason said.

"And now he knows about these two dragons."

"He does."

He looked up, trying to comprehend the dragons perched all around them. They were arranged in a formation, the five dragons that had come from Dragon Haven toward the center, and the others that Jason had freed with them. Surprisingly, the red dragon was alive, despite what Therin had claimed.

"What will you do?" Jason asked.

"We need to protect this land," Sarah said, marching forward. "The rebellion had abandoned any attempt at trying to claim additional land, but if you can protect the dragons, pushing our influence might not be necessary."

Jason took a deep breath, letting it out slowly. The pain in his body began to retreat, leaving him with an ache, but it wasn't nearly as bad as it had been. "I don't know that you need me for that."

"You're the one who knows how to do it."

Jason looked over at David. "He can help."

"He's an Auran," Sarah said.

"An Auran who's been helpful. An Auran who worked with me to fend off this attack."

Jason didn't know what motivated David, but he did believe David wasn't going to harm them. And there was something David was not sharing with them, though he thought he needed to know what that something was.

"Will you help?"

David looked up. "I cannot."

"Even after everything you've seen."

"And what have I seen? I've seen rebels who continue to attack, who celebrate the dragons in that unhealthy way. I've seen a man my people would call a slave who has more power than he should. And I have seen Therin bring to bear a dangerous sort of weapon for Lorach." David got to his feet, clasping his hands behind his back. "These dragons are impressive, but they shouldn't exist."

"Without them, we wouldn't have survived."

"On the contrary, without them, none of this would have occurred. There would've been no need for a fight. There would have been no need for you to get involved."

"I'm sorry I got involved."

David turned and watched him, saying nothing for a long moment. "You should not be."

Heat exploded around him and he twisted his hands in the same movement Therin had made, and flames circled him. He disappeared on a blast of fire.

Jason stared at where he had been.

"What now?" Sarah asked.

"Now I return home."

"Even after what you know?"

"I know the dragons will need my help," he said. The more he thought about it, the more certain he was that was true. He would do whatever it took to offer that protection to the dragons. The ice dragon would be a part of it, and if they could free more of the dragons, then he would. It wasn't for him to decide what would happen then. The dragons would choose. Regardless of what

Dragon Haven thought, they would make up their own mind.

The forest in the distance caught his attention. The dragon there would need help and protection. There were other hatch mates that would need the same. The ice dragon would be a part of that. The iron dragon, too.

Jason glanced down at his hand. The dragon pearl had molded onto his flesh, forming a second sort of skin. It had encircled the entirety of his hand, all the way down to his wrist. It was a deep gray, and strangely, he was able to flex his hand. Every so often, he thought the metal shifted across the surface of his skin, but then that sensation disappeared.

"You aren't going to abandon the dragons," Sarah said.

He took a deep breath. He didn't have an ice dragon pearl anymore. The one he had was broken, shattered when Therin had dropped it.

At least Therin didn't have it, either. He didn't have any of the dragon pearls he'd claimed from Jason. Which meant Jason didn't have them, either. For his part, he didn't care. None of that mattered to him, not anymore.

"I'm not going to abandon them. I do need to visit home, but I will return."

She turned to him, taking his hands. "Do you promise?"

He looked into her eyes. There was warmth, and there was something else. He felt a twinge, and a different kind of warmth flashed through him, one he never felt in his village.

Family first...

"If I return, will you put me in a cell again?"

"You understand why I had to."

"I don't understand. I'm not sure that I ever can, but I'm not returning for you." He looked at Henry. "Or for you." He didn't know what had become of William, but William was a friend, regardless of how short a time they'd known each other. But he wouldn't even do it for William.

And yet, he would for the dragons. They needed his help.

Jason looked up, staring up into the clouds. Somewhere up there was the ice dragon. He let out a heavy sigh, wondering whether he would even be able to contact the dragon.

Without the dragon pearl, it might not be possible for them to have that same connection, and he felt a bit of regret at that. He had enjoyed the fact that they shared that bond. It was something that reminded him of where he had grown up.

A cloud parted and a shadow streaked toward them. Jason smiled to himself as the ice dragon crashed down near him. He leaned his head forward and Jason climbed onto the ice dragon's back.

"Just like that?" Henry asked.

"I'll return. But my family needs me right now."

"What about them?" Henry asked, looking around at the dragons.

"They need me, too. And I will be back."

With that, the ice dragon took to the air.

Surprisingly, the iron dragon followed, jumping into the air, his body fluctuating with heat. He circled behind them and then disappeared.

"Stay safe," Jason whispered.

He had no idea if the iron dragon could even hear, but that probably didn't matter.

The ice dragon flew, heading north. As they traveled, the air became colder. The wind whipped around him. Eventually, snow started to swirl, making it difficult for him to see, even with his dragon sight.

He was warm, almost hot, and he realized he was still dressed in the dragonskin. And he couldn't even change back into the bearskin. David had his clothing, which meant that he was going to be stuck wearing the dragonskin.

"You don't care for it?"

"It's not so much that I don't care for it, it's more that I know how others will react to it."

"Others in your village wear it."

"They do."

Knowing what he did about the Dragon Souls, he now had to wonder where others in the village had acquired their dragonskin. As far as he knew, it had been handed down over the years, and yet, why would that be?

It was a question for another time.

He watched over the dragon's neck, hugging it tightly as they circled ever closer to the icy northern cold. In the distance, the mountain peak pierced the sky, and he stared at it.

"Why don't we return near the cave?"

"If you choose," he said.

They swept down and the dragon glided to a stop, landing within the stream.

Jason leapt off the dragon's back and looked over at the ice dragon. "You need a name."

"So you've told me."

"So does the iron dragon."

"If it's important to you."

"I think you should have a name for yourself, not because it's important to me."

"Would it be easier for you to call me?"

Jason grunted. "Without a dragon pearl, I don't know that I'll be able to call you." That wasn't entirely true. Somehow, when he had wanted the dragon to help him return home, the ice dragon had known and had come down for him.

Maybe they were connected.

"The pearl was nothing more than a medium," the ice dragon said.

"What do you mean by that?"

"The pearl allows those who don't have a natural ability to draw upon it. It would make our bond stronger for you, but even without it, you don't need it."

Jason shook his head. "I don't have enough connection to draw power without it."

"And yet you have."

The dragon glided off, sliding through the stream before disappearing into the cave.

From there, Jason had no idea where the dragon would go. And perhaps it didn't matter.

He looked up the slope of the mountain, staring into the growing clouds. It was afternoon, which meant the storm was coming. Wind whistled, and in the dragonskin, he was far warmer than he ever had been before. It fit him well, molding to him, and he started forward.

As he walked, he plunged through the snow. If the ice dragon was right and he was able to use power without the dragon, then he should be able to employ it to walk above the snow.

How had Henry and Therin done it?

They had imagined it. At least, that was what they claimed. In doing so, they'd allowed power to flow through them, and they were able to summon enough to walk above the snow.

Jason focused on power, letting it fill him. As he did, he found himself floating.

He laughed to himself. Maybe he *could* do that.

As he walked, the wind no longer bothered him quite as it had. He lost track of time as he headed up the face of the mountain, and he tried to count off how many days he had been gone.

Several days. In that time, what had changed here? His sister should have had enough meat, and yet, he wondered if she did.

When he reached the edge of the village, he saw a figure behind his home.

They were digging through the snow.

The thief.

Jason darted forward and grabbed them, throwing them down. He used more force than he had intended, drawing upon power he didn't know he had.

The person rolled over and Reltash looked up at him.

"Dreshen?"

"*You've* been stealing from us?" Jason said. He stood over Reltash. "You would deprive my family?"

Reltash stared at him. "Who did you steal the dragon-skin from?"

"No one from our village." He leaned close. As he grabbed Reltash, he lifted, drawing power through the ice dragon. He threw Reltash back. "You will leave my family alone. You will not steal from us."

"And why not? You have to be stealing from someone. There's no way you would have caught that much on your own."

"What makes you think I was on my own?" Jason loomed toward him. "If I find you stealing again, I will make sure it's the last thing you do."

He glared at Reltash until the thief scrambled away, disappearing into the growing darkness.

Letting out a heavy sigh, Jason turned back to the home and headed inside. There was no one within, and he paused, looking around, checking the back room. His mother was there, resting quietly, breathing comfortably.

Where was his sister?

It was late enough that she should be here.

Unless...

Jason stepped back outside, looking down the slope of the mountain.

He ran, sliding every so often, but mostly running, and he reached the cave.

When he darted inside, he held his breath. He could feel the ice dragon somewhere in here, drawing upon his energy, but there was something else, and he wasn't sure what it was.

As he approached, he did so slowly, carefully, holding on to the power of the ice dragon. It was a time like this that he wished he had the dragon pearls, but maybe he truly didn't need them. He still had the strange connection to the iron dragon, the glove that had formed over his hand, and with that, he had a link to a different sort of power.

He reached the inside of the cave. A figure stared down into the water. A pair of crystal blue eyes looked back up, but the dragon didn't move.

Was that a Dragon Soul? They were clad in a heavy black cloak, a thick fur that reminded him of Henry, but he didn't think so. None of the Dragon Souls would wear that kind of clothing—other than Therin.

The build wasn't right for Therin. He thought Therin was still gone, and he doubted the man would've returned to the cave, not without reinforcements. He would've known better, and would've realized that he wouldn't have much of a chance at trying to capture and control the dragon without having other Dragon Souls with him.

There was only one other person he could think of.

"Kayla?"

She spun toward him, her eyes wide. Her gaze swept over him, pausing at his dragonskin cloak, then moving to his hand, and finally to his waist. Jason looked down before realizing he had a sword strapped there, a weapon he had never used and had no idea how to wield.

"Jason. There's a... There is a..."

He stepped forward, grabbing her, wrapping his arms around her. He took a deep breath, nodding. "I know."

"There's a dragon in the stream."

"I know." He led her away, motioning for her to sit, and she did so slowly.

"How long have you known?" she asked him.

"Since the last time I was gone."

"You didn't tell anyone?"

"I couldn't. They would've tried to hunt him."

"This is a *dragon*."

"I know. And there's something you should know." Jason glanced to the dragon, who poked his head slightly out of the water before retreating. His eyes blinked before they disappeared altogether. Jason frowned. The dragon had wanted her to see him. "It's about our father and how he died."

"A dragon killed him."

"That's what we believed, but that's not how he died." He took a deep breath. It was long past time that his sister knew. It would make it easier if she did. Perhaps he could convince her to head down the base of the mountain, to safety, where he didn't have to worry about her finding enough to eat. "Let me tell you what I've been doing."

"I want to know about the dragon."

"What I've been doing has been all about the dragon."

Kayla turned toward him. Jason took a deep breath and then began to tell her everything.

The Dragon Misfits continue with book 3: Forest Dragon!

Looking for more in this world? Check out the Dragonwalker series, staring with: Dragon Bones.

ALSO BY D.K. HOLMBERG

The Dragonwalkers

The Dragonwalker

Dragon Bones

Dragon Blessed

Dragon Rise

Dragon Bond

Dragon Storm

Dragon Rider

Dragon Sight

The Dragon Misfits

Ice Dragon

Iron Dragon

Forest Dragon

Elemental Warrior Series:

Elemental Academy

The Fire Within

The Earth Awakens

The Water Ruptures

The Wind Rages

The Spirit Binds

The Chaos Rises

The Elements Bond

Elemental Academy: Spirit Master

The Shape of Fire

The Cloud Warrior Saga

Chased by Fire

Bound by Fire

Changed by Fire

Fortress of Fire

Forged in Fire

Serpent of Fire

Servant of Fire

Born of Fire

Broken of Fire

Light of Fire

Cycle of Fire

The Endless War

Journey of Fire and Night

Darkness Rising

Endless Night

Summoner's Bond

Seal of Light

The Dark Ability Series

The Shadow Accords

Shadow Blessed

Shadow Cursed

Shadow Born

Shadow Lost

Shadow Cross

Shadow Found

The Collector Chronicles

Shadow Hunted

Shadow Games

Shadow Trapped

The Dark Ability

The Dark Ability

The Heartstone Blade

The Tower of Venass

Blood of the Watcher

The Shadowsteel Forge

The Guild Secret

Rise of the Elder

The Sighted Assassin

The Binders Game

The Forgotten

Assassin's End

The Elder Stones Saga

The Darkest Revenge

Shadows Within the Flame

Remnants of the Lost

The Coming Chaos

The Depth of Deceit

A Forging of Power

A Threat Revealed

The Council of Elders

The Lost Prophecy Series

The Teralin Sword

Soldier Son

Soldier Sword

Soldier Sworn

Soldier Saved

Soldier Scarred

The Lost Prophecy

The Threat of Madness

The Warrior Mage